Selected
Short Stories

Selected
Short Stories
Gwyn Thomas

Foreword by
Michael Parnell

seren

Seren is the book imprint of
Poetry Wales Press Ltd
Wyndham Street, Bridgend, Wales

A CIP record for this puiblication is available
from the British Library

1-85411-001-2

*Seren works with the financial support of the
Arts Council of Wales*

Printed in Plantin by
CPD (Wales) Ltd

CONTENTS

Acknowledgements

These stories have previously appeared in the following publications:

'And a Spoonful of Grief to Taste', 'The Couch, My Friend, is Cold', and 'Myself My Desert' in *Where Did I Put My Pity? Folk Tales from the Modern Welsh* (Progress Publishing, 1946);

'The Hands of Chris' in *Saturday Saga and Other Stories* (Progress Publishing, 1946);

'My Fist Upon the Stone' in *Welsh Short Stories*, (Oxford University Press, 1956);

'Where My Dark Lover Lies', 'The Pot of Gold at Fear's End', 'The Teacher', 'O Brother Man' and 'The Leaf that Hurts the Hand' in *Gazooka* (Gollancz, 1957);

'Arrayed Like One of These', 'That Vanished Canaan', 'Land! Land!' and 'Hugo My Friend' in *Ring Delirium 123* (Gollancz, 1960);

'The Joyful', 'Blue Ribbons for a Black Epoch', 'Off the Beam', 'A Horse Called Meadow Prospect' and 'An Ample Wish' in *The Lust Lobby* (Hutchinson, 1971);

'Violence and the Big Male Voice' in *The Montrealer*, 27.12.64;

'The Cavers' in *The Reporter* (USA), 5.2.66;

'Hastings — A Vagrant Talk at Night' was a BBC Radio 2 play in 1966.

Foreword

When Gwyn Thomas died at the unhappily early age of sixty-seven in 1981, his name was probably known to many as a journalist and television personality who were unaware that just two decades earlier he had been widely considered one of the most gifted and exciting writers to be produced by Wales. His chubby, articulate, often smiling, often lugubriously frowning face had regularly shone forth from the television screen or from the pages of the *Western Mail*, and his name in a broadcast programme was for many sufficient promise of a feast of verbal fireworks and comic anecdotes as he pontificated on one of his favourite topics, so that it was with a sense of personal loss that many who had never met him heard the announcement of his death.

But this vividly memorable and eccentric Gwyn Thomas, dutifully performing his hilarious, touching and sometimes absurd word-dances in public places, was only one of several personae inhabiting the body of a much more mysterious, in some ways deeply sad man, whose true joy in life came from writing and whose real memorial subsists in the novels and short stories he published in the twenty years between 1946 and 1966.

It was ironically the adoption by the media of Gwyn Thomas's wonderful comic gift and his flair for instant linguistic response which weaned him slowly and inevitably away from developing it to its fullest potential. Born the youngest of twelve children of a penniless Rhondda miner into a world frequently harsh and lacking in material satisfactions, and later married to a wife to whom in his devotion he wished to give all that a woman could want, he could not resist an opportunity to earn comparatively rich payment when it presented itself. No request to provide a script for even the most ephemeral television or radio programme, no invitation to contribute to newspapers and journals, no call to perform as after-dinner speaker or media pundit could ever be rejected after a youth and early manhood where there was so little for the taking. The consequence was that after he was 'discovered' he found increasingly little time to write the large-scale books which he had in mind and which the critics looked for.

This may not have been altogether a disaster, though most of those who know his work well will mourn the death of the novelist in Gwyn Thomas as early as 1958 when publication of *The Love Man* turned out to be his last work in the genre. The relative lack of time for extended and comprehensively worked out stories however did have the effect of forcing upon him a discipline and economy which were not marked features of those long, leisurely novels of his which appeared between 1950 and 1955. It was as early as 1953, when Malcolm Muggeridge recruited him to the pages of *Punch*, that Gwyn Thomas really had to begin practising the economies required for shorter pieces. He took to the 1500–2000 word length required for *Punch* with delight, and rarely afterwards reverted to the virtual novella length which had been natural to him at the beginning of his career and which is exemplified so well in his first book, *Where Did I Put My Pity?* (1946). By 1975 he had published about two hundred short stories, and it may be felt that this is some compensation for the novels that were never written.

The world of Gwyn Thomas's short stories is the same as that of the novels, as indeed it is that of the radio plays for which he was celebrated in the 1950s and the six full-length theatre plays which he wrote between 1960 and 1978; it is the world he knew intimately from his childhood and from which he never really moved away: the world of the South Wales Valleys with Rhondda at its heart. In all his life there was never anything he liked doing better than sitting in pub or club or barber's shop, listening to, observing and talking with the inhabitants of those valleys, and committing to memory their tales and yarns, their turns of phrase, their opinions expressed with such individual verve and all the comments that summed up their responses to the grittily earnest and bizarrely baffling world they all experienced together.

If he loved these people for their own sake, he also cherished their doings and sayings as stimuli for his writing. His family, especially his father, provides the inspiration for many stories; the friends and local characters whose lives illuminated his boyhood and youth figure in many more. Almost any scrap of gossip about the local community might turn itself into a story as he modified events and characters to fit them to his view of things. As a young man he lived unemployed among the vast army of jobless in the Rhondda; later, for twenty-two years, he was a teacher of Spanish and French largely at the Grammar School for Boys in Barry; while still a teacher and thereafter he became a media personality, known as much for his appearances on *The Brains Trust* or *Tonight* or for his television, films and newspaper journalism as for the literary writing which had first brought him to public attention. Throughout all, his home was in South Wales, for the last fifteen years of his life at Peterston-super-Ely in the Vale of Glamorgan; never, for more than a few days at most, would he allow circumstances to detach him from that part of the world where his roots held him fast. Equally, throughout all his fiction, his material rose from life as he had lived it and seen it lived in the community about him.

Always a prolific writer, who seemed to write almost as much for therapeutic reasons as from any serious idea of communication with some imagined public, Gwyn Thomas, emulating the Shakespeare of whom it was reported that 'he never blotted out a line', poured his stories onto paper at a tremendous speed, rarely making any corrections of any kind. Where his manuscripts are emended, it is usually a matter of his having had to print a word which his wife had been unable to read; rarely are there second thoughts, re-made sentences, alternative epithets or any such evidence of a refining, editing process to be detected. In 1965 he told two schoolboys who came to interview him for their school magazine, *The Avonian*, that this was because he first worked out every detail of his stories in his head; then, after suitable time for reflection and consolidation, "by five o'clock he could simply sit down and commit it to paper without a moment's hesitation".

The same lads were told that he had never needed to make copious notes "to retain words, phrases and ideas" for his mind was "like a honeycomb, highly suitable for storing information". While this had certainly been true for most of Gwyn Thomas's life, it was in fact at just about this time (he was fifty-two) that he began to worry that his memory was no longer quite as keen and willing an instrument as it had been. For the next fifteen years or so he was almost never without a small pocket notebook into which he would jot down, at the first opportunity, all sorts of material which might conceivably be of use to him as a writer. He filled forty-five notebooks before deciding not to bother any more and was so secretive about the habit that it came as a surprise to his widow when they were discovered after his death. They give a rare insight into the mind of a man whom it is difficult to know. Here, to show something of how a story grew in his imagination, is a transcript of several pages from notebook number 16, undoubtedly written down soon after a conversation in a pub where the first stirrings of the idea had been witnessed:

Story: Lecturer in political science living in Home Counties. He has living with him his father, ex-miner. (Son's name is Piers Pringle — father, Powys Pringle, now a security officer in a New Town factory.) Piers' professor is a man who has become very reactionary and wants to prove that if one probes into the existing roots of the Labour movement one will find unique examples of inertia and putrescence. "It is only a traditional and carefully laboured snobbishness, based on a distinctive ability, that provides a preservative dignity. To recognise one's privileges and to guard them against the trampling trespassing swing. The present arbiters of political power cannot even preserve the amenities of their municipally provided toilets."

Piers tells his father about this. "That professor," says Powys, "is a liar. In the town we came from, Holly Vale, there is a Workmen's Hall. It was founded by Walter Clegg, the greatest miners' leader that ever was. Walter is dead. But his spirit will be alive in that Hall. You will find its rooms thronged by the same dedicated dreamers, saying the good word for mankind, the alphabet of their hearts an assertion that one day all broken lives will be made whole, the idiocies of grief appeased, the walls of spite laid low, our ancient terrors overcome."

Piers goes to Holly Vale. He finds the Workmen's Hall a mindless cavern of bingo and drunken buffoons. The library has been sold, the lecture-rooms knocked together to make an entertainment room. The chairman, Vic Wilde, shows Piers around. He introduces him to the 'gurner', the man who wraps his lower lip over the top of his head. Also to the man who trains dogs and sings ten bars of a duet, 'Homing', with a mynah bird. And to the male voice choir who appear on stage wearing miners' helmets and sing patriotic songs: 'There'll always be an England', 'Fishermen of England', 'England, Of Thee', the climax coming with 'Land of Hope and Glory' and the simultaneous unfurling of the English and Welsh flags. All these turns are going to be submitted as possible entries for the Hughie Greene show. The night ends on a note of orgy.

End of story: Piers writing his report: "In the town my father came from, Holly Vale, the Workmen's Hall was founded by the miners' leader, Walter Clegg, in 1920. The mine-owners' papers called him 'King' Clegg, deliriously, yet with a taint of fear in their contempt. Clegg is dead. But his spirit is alive in the rooms of that hall, thronged by the same dedicated dreamers . . ." Piers throws down his pen and rubs away his tears.

That bitter story was never written, and the same fate awaited the germ of many other tales sketched out in the notebooks; it was almost as if the energy to return to polish them up and get them into print was lacking once he had written down some version, even an unfinished one.

Perhaps therefore it is fortunate that there was no initial sketch of the many stories from which we here make our selection. In many of the published stories occur the same groups of characters, some of whom also turn up in the novels either with the same names or something very similar. There is, for instance, the family group, where father is just 'Father' but the brothers become Dan, Emrys, Milo and so on, and father's friends are Waldo Treharne, Naboth Kinsey and others; memorable local inhabitants include cinema proprietor Luther Cann (Cann the Col, the *Coliseum* being his pride and joy) and his assistant, Charlie Lush (Lush the Ush); another group includes Edwin Pugh (Pugh the Pang, who suffers greatly for humanity), his nephew, Tudno, Milton Nicholas the social philosopher, Teilo Dew the Doom, Gomer Gough the Gavel and Theo Morgan the Monologue, who also turn up in the novel,

The Shadow at My Side; and there is the group which inhabits the Bannerman Club, Jason Grace, Pomfray, Waldo Falkman and the others, not to mention the criminal elements, Wynzie Phipps and Ludo Brisk. It would be a huge task to take a census of all Gwyn Thomas's people; I have counted well over a thousand named characters in his fiction and that's just a preliminary trawl. Neither would it be a straightforward job, for though many of the central characters are stable, the peripheral ones come and go, sometimes changing their names — Luther Cann for instance turns up in one story as Mr Mooney, and Mr Rawlins in two different stories ('That Vanished Canaan' and 'A Season for Wizards') tells of the disasters attending the attempts of one of his former pupils to earn pocket money; the stories are the same, but the boy in one is named Merlin Pugh, in the other, Jethro Sugden.

The townships in which he placed his characters are variously named, chief among them being Meadow Prospect, Belmont, Mynydd Coch, Ferncleft and Birchtown. Anyone who tries to assign to these a precise geographical location is in for a frustrating time. Birchtown seems usually to approximate to Pontypridd and Meadow Prospect is undeniably Porth, but are not Belmont and Mynydd Coch also remarkably like Porth? And Ferncleft seems to be in the coastal strip between the Rhondda and the Bristol Channel, sometimes three and sometimes more miles from the sea: Tonyrefail, perhaps, or even Cowbridge; it is not Barry, for that seaside town seems to be disguised as Fernlea on the few occasions when it figures at all. Unless, of course, Belmont, with its Bannerman Club, its grammar school and its parent-teacher association, is Barry — topographical clues are few and far between, and anyway Gwyn Thomas would not mind conflating two places if it suited his purposes.

Gwyn Thomas began writing stories soon after leaving Oxford in 1933 but did not achieve publication until 1946 when he was nearing his mid-thirties. At that time he published some of the best of what he had been writing in the previous half dozen years; all the rest of his juvenile output he abandoned. Thereafter he wrote increasingly in the short story medium, selling his work regularly to *Coal* and *Punch* and later *The Teacher* and finding occasional markets in other magazines, some on the far side of the Atlantic. Selections from his work were published in six volumes during his lifetime: *Where Did I Put My Pity?* (subtitled 'Folk Tales from the Modern Welsh'), 1946; *Gazooka*, 1957; *Ring Delirium 123*, 1960; *A Welsh Eye*, 1964; *A Hatful of Humours*, 1965; and *The Lust Lobby*, 1971. *A Welsh Eye* was a collection of essays but included two stories, 'Revivalism and the Falling Larks', the affecting story of Jennie Bell from Meadow Prospect and her love for a visiting revivalist preacher, and 'Dusk and the Dialectic', the story of Charlie Barlow's lecture at the Birchtown Institute. *A Hatful of Humours* contained twenty-six pieces reprinted from *The Teacher*; they were essays with a strong anecdotal flavour, but only three or four would qualify as short stories. There was also a volume entitled *The Sky of Our Lives*, 1973, which was put out rather naughtily by Hutchinson as a collection of new stories but which was in fact a reprint of the stories 'Oscar' and 'Simeon' from *Where Did I Put My Pity?* together with the novella *The Dark Philosophers*, previously published in *Triad One* in 1946.

These publications contained a total of about eighty stories (if my arithmetic is right). When Poetry Wales Press decided to publish a *Selected Short Stories* in 1984, the editor naturally made his choice from the material in them, taking only one, 'My Fist upon the Stone', from another source (*Welsh Short Stories*, OUP, 1956). This meant that there were still over a hundred uncollected stories at large in various publications, if one were lucky enough to come across them. When invited to help with the production of this new edition of the *Selected Short Stories*, with the opportunity to add six further titles to those in the earlier edition, I thought it would be a good idea to look again at the uncollected tales rather than to revisit the standard volumes. It proved a pleasurable though daunting task, for selection from such bounties was extremely difficult. In the end I chose just one story from those former collections ('The Leaf that Hurts the Hand' from *Gazooka*) and five from among those many stories that have never been reprinted.

The other five have been chosen not only because they are good stories but also because they represent some of the different periods and modes in Gwyn Thomas's story-telling. 'The Hands of Chris' is very early, written in the late 1930s though not published until 1946 when it appeared in a volume called *Saturday Saga*. Like the novel *Sorrow for Thy Sons*, written in 1936–7 and posthumously published in 1985, it shows the writer at his most serious, offering a documentary piece strong in anti-fascist feeling; it is the most untypical story in this selection, being simply and straightforwardly written and having none of the special Gwyn Thomas linguistic characteristics that later made his prose so instantly recognisable, but it is worth reprinting for the force of its content and as an indicator of the kind of development that happened in his fiction as he came into his maturity in the 1940s.

'The Leafless Land' does not appear to have been published before, though it may have been read on radio; again it is an early story, selected now because it typifies a certain style and attitude in Gwyn Thomas's writing. In this comical first-person story of the sexual frustrations of an un-named youth attempting self-consciously to conduct his courtship with Caroline Pugh under the unfriendly eyes of her father and the too-interested citizenry of Meadow Prospect, we have a document that may suggest quite a little about the personality of the writer as well as give pleasure for its wry view of man as a sexual animal in an unsympathetic universe.

From the time of his first recruitment to radio by Glyn Jones and Elwyn Evans in 1949, Gwyn Thomas wrote frequently for the medium; his play 'Gazooka' was a tremendous success and was followed by a long string of very pleasing but now forgotten pieces which the BBC would do well to look at again in these days when so much mere dross finds its way onto the air. 'Hastings' is a play for a single voice, written as part of the celebrations of the nine hundredth anniversary of the Norman Conquest. Ideally it would appear in a volume devoted wholly to printing a selection from Gwyn Thomas's radio work, but since no such enterprise is under way I think it merits a place here to exemplify that work and to provide an opportunity to savour the writer in another mood, poetic and romantic though still with one foot firmly rooted in earth. In a small compass this story offers a compact and moving account of a great moment in Britain's history and presents us in the person of its narrator, Alcwyn, with a character as memorable in his way as any other drawn by his creator.

'The Cavers' was first published in magazines in America and Canada before being taken up by the BBC and broadcast as a 'Morning Story' in 1973; most recently it was read again as a Morning Story by Ray Smith in 1984. It is included here as an example of the autobiographical stories in which Gwyn Thomas delighted to recall his father and brothers and their usually ill-fated activities in the days of his youth, of which perhaps 'The Limp in My Longing' and 'The Pot of Gold at Fear's End' (which appear together in this selection under the second title) are among the best known.

'Violence and the Big Male Voice', published in *The Montrealer* in 1964, is an early story in the Gwyn Thomas mainstream: set in Windy Way, high above Meadow Prospect, and featuring the gang who meet to talk at Tasso's Coffee Tavern, it treats of music and singing, of love and betrayal, of law and justice, and allows Willie Silcox the Psyche to demonstrate in the case of the vengeance-bent Marty Moore how music hath charms to soothe the savage breast. Touching as well as amusing, it has an undercurrent of that almost ferocious irony which manifests itself in Gwyn Thomas's writing through wit and highly individual metaphor.

While no anthology can possibly satisfy everybody into whose hands it falls, I think this book goes a long way towards being an ideal introduction to and reflection of the work of Gwyn Thomas. In as far as it is inadequate, I hope that it will in due course be replaced by a Collected Stories, a vast and splendid volume which will have a better chance of doing justice to a writer so prolific. In the meantime, I hope it may bring to its readers as much joy as the work of preparation has brought to its compilers.

And a Spoonful of Grief to Taste

Y ou know how it is in our part of the valley. They are mad for singing in choirs. If you can sing a bit, you get roped into a choir and if you can keep your voice somewhere near the note and your morals facing due north where the cold is, someone with pull is bound to notice you and before you know it you are doing a nice steady job between the choir pieces. If you sound like a raven and cause the hair of the choir leader to drop out like hail when you go for a hearing, you mope about in the outer darkness acting as foot-warmer for the boys in the Exchange.

I couldn't sing at all. As a kid I was handy enough and did very well as one of a party at school that did a lot of songs about war and storms at sea, with plenty of actions showing how wind and death are when they are on the job. I must have sung and acted myself out with that group. I was good. I sounded like an agent for doom. I put the fear of hell up my father who was a sensitive man, often in touch with terror. He shook like a leaf and supplied most of the draughts he shook in. When I sang that very horrible part-song 'There'll be blood on the capstan tonight', he averaged two faints a verse, and his head went up and down so often with the faints I could almost keep the time by him. That didn't last long. When I was about fourteen I went bathing in that deep, smooth part of the river they call the Neck or the Nack. I dived in. When I came out my voice was broken, broken as if somebody had been after the thing with a hammer. At first I thought my father had dived in after me and arranged some submarine antic that would keep me away from part-songs for a couple of years. Then I was told nature works in this fashion, although some people get more warning. I could hardly talk till I was eighteen, let alone sing. I tried to get into a few of the local

17

choirs as a background noise. I got nowhere near except when the conductor was giving a talk on why his choristers should keep away from rivers when an eisteddfod was coming up. It was only my father who had any use for me. He put me to stand behind the front door to frighten off the bum bailiffs. We had plenty of them coming to our place. It was like a training centre for them. There were new brands of debt that were named after my father. My job was to watch out for them and say in this funny croak I had that there was death in the house, much death, and didn't they know that there was some respect due even to the poor. It always worked. I sounded just like death, gone rusty with the boredom of always pushing people in the same direction and hearing no more of them. Between my long experience with those church-yard chants I had learned in the part-song group and the ten-foot drop my voice had done, I bet those bailiff boys could almost see my scythe as I stood there mooing at them through the door. They would flee, wondering, no doubt, how much my old man still owed on the scythe.

But here I am now, busily engaged in the building trade, driving towards the New Jerusalem at so many bricks a day, putting fresh heart into people in this town of Meadow Prospect who have been living in furnished rooms or sharing a belfry with the bats since the Rebecca Riots. I am the only man in our part of the valley who has found a place in such a tidy and dignified traffic without once having sung the 'Messiah' or recited the whole body of Psalms backwards and forwards with an apple in my mouth or done a salaam before the wealthy.

I didn't want to be a builder. At the time I'd have been anything. I'd have gone around the roads collecting fertilizer for the Allotment Union if my father had managed to get me a permanent bucket. But I wanted to get away from behind that door. I was sick of being posted there as a scarecrow for the bum bailiffs. I croaked that statement about death being in the house so often and with such passion it wouldn't have surprised me to see death sitting down with us at meals, chatting cosily and complaining about the quality of the grub, which it would have had every right to do, for the grub we had was rough.

When I was about nineteen, my Uncle Cadwallader came to stay with us. He was great on doing jerks to get strong. It was a treat just to sit down and watch Cadwallader on these jerks, wondering what part of him you were likely to see next. He had the biggest chest ever seen in or around Meadow Prospect. At rest, the kitchen walls just about fitted it. But when he had the thing filled to the brim with air, and that was a favourite caper with him, someone or something had to be moved, fast. He was always jerking and practising to get bigger and stronger, and sometimes he looked so much like life's final answer to death I thought he would keep it up until his muscles began to glow like lamp-posts with a sense of perfection and eternity, and then Cadwallader would float off the earth and look for larger stamping grounds among the planets. Sometimes, when he came in from a night's drinking at the pub, The Crossed Harps, he'd lift my old man clean off the ground and jerk him up and down. First of all, my father didn't like this, and thought of laying the poker on Cadwallader. But after a while he said that he had grown to like this motion and that it made quite a nice change from just standing still doing nothing much at all except keep from falling. But I think he laid aside the poker idea because at the speed he went up and down in Cadwallader's grasp, Cadwallader made too blurred a target for any good work with a short weapon. On top of that, Cadwallader was working and paid well for his place. He never lost his job. This was a rare thing in Meadow Prospect, and he was often regarded as a miracle or a mirage by those free-thinking boys who gather in the draughts room at the Library and Institute and talk about life and do a good job between them of burying all hope. Cadwallader was dull as a bat and with his strength he could have picked up a colliery and shaken the thing hard to see if there was any coal left inside. He was a great comfort to all the wealthy and to the coal-owning wealthy in particular. We often had the womenfolk of the mighty come along to see Cadwallader, offer him sugar from their hands or a soft vegetable, coo names at him, stroke him, and generally treat him as a horse. If he could have got in the way of talking in sentences and praising the state of things as they were, he would have been taken up by the Government and made into a prince or a mayor or a rent-bloke or something. But all he was was strong and daft, and that, they say, is not enough. He didn't talk much at all, and he had a way of moving the muscles of his chest to show when he wanted something. We had to tell him to open the front of his shirt wider whenever we didn't get the full gist of what he was saying. And Cadwallader got tired of having my father peering in to get the exact intonation,

Anyway, he stopped lodging with us. He went up to the Terraces to live in what they call sin with a very big woman called Agnes who had thick red hair and a fine record in sin. This Agnes had worn out about forty blokes without getting any paler herself and she cottoned on to my Uncle Cadwallader when she saw him throwing a cart at a horse that had nearly run him over. She said here was a man who would see her through to old age without going on the Lloyd George every whipstitch. The old chopping and changing had started to get on her nerves and give her religious thoughts.

This was a big blow to my old man. He had actually begun to pay back some debts that had been going about for a long time past in short shrouds, with the money he got from Cadwallader. His manner with the bum bailiffs had become quite cheerful, opening the door to them four inches instead of three and calling them bastards once and with a smile instead of twice with a meaning frown. The only thing he could think of doing to keep hope alive was to take out a threepenny insurance policy on Cadwallader, with an eye on Agnes's past record, and to keep away from that group in the Library and Institute whose forebodings filled him as full of shadow as a mountain of dirt. I told him openly that from what I had seen of Cadwallader, I would say that if there was to be any passing out, both parties would reach the door together.

After a spell my father got the idea that if I went up to the Terraces where Cadwallader was living and pleaded with him, he might come back to us. I could talk in short simple phrases that Cadwallader could follow without going mad with nervous worry. That is why I was picked to do this pleading. I had also made up a short poem about his tremendous chest expansion that filled him with pleasure. But I could not shift him an inch from the side of Agnes. There was something like the hot middle of the earth in the thick redness of that woman's hair, and I could get the feel of the grip she had on Cadwallader. I made no headway with him, and one Tuesday afternoon I made my way up the Terraces for my very last bout of supplication with Cadwallader. By that time I was sick of the sight and sound of my uncle. He was a friendly enough man when he was not twirling you over his head like a club and praising toil, but it wore me down trying to argue him out of his desire for this Agnes, and to move him to pity with stories of my father worrying himself thinner than the poker that he had once thought of crowning Cadwallader with. The only thing that lit a light in his eyes when I talked, was my poem about his chest. He liked that, especially an easy couplet in the middle that got best rhymed off with chest. That notion was near enough to the ground for Cadwallader to see in plain without having to stand on tip-toe. But once off the poem and he dropped into a coma as fast as a stone. He rested in these comas. He got part of his strength from them.

When I reached the Terraces I saw great crowds of people. This was not common. Usually the people in the Terraces were asleep, working, sitting in a stupor on the doorsteps, or stroking their rabbits, pigeons or despair in the backyards. The crowd was thickest in Cadwallader's street, and at first I thought his passion and his strength had carried his lust for exercise to a peak where he had thrust Agnes through the roof without thought for her or the tiles. The people were excited. One voter told me that the colliery company which owned the streets around, and most of the people in them, had put up the rent of twelve of the houses, and the tenants in these houses had refused to pay any more rent until the company saw sense. I found that Agnes's house was one of the twelve. I saw Agnes standing on the pavement talking loudly, swinging her arms and flouncing her hair in great crimson waves upon her neck, and giving an outline of the sort of sense she was waiting for the company to see. I felt sorry for all these tenants who were being put on the wheel, but I could not see the company seeing anything but the company even with someone like Agnes dragging their eyes towards the target. Agnes had persuaded the tenants and their friends to resist. I could see a small group of listless and pallid men standing near her and taking in her commands. The man who was giving me the news of these developments told me that these boys were those lovers of Agnes who had blazed the trail before Cadwallader, the few who could still stand at all. People were building a barricade in the street made out of furniture that nobody wanted any more. Most of the furniture in the Terraces looks as if no one wants it any more, so there was a very poor quality about this barricade altogether. The idea of it was to keep out the band of policemen and bailiffs and so on who were shortly to come in the name of the company and drag out these people who had buried their rent books ahead of themselves, which is not legal. I thought this made my job with Cadwallader all the easier. If he was going to be evicted it would be better all round if he just came down to the bed of the valley with me and took his old lodgings with us straightaway. But I found him in a harsh and brutal frame of mind, his mind all stoked up to a high flame by the speeches and antics of Agnes, his heart full of impatient hatred for the evictors and their assistants. Agnes must have been talking to him in signs to make him understand so much. He seemed really to have grasped the issue neatly, and was now waiting for the action to start which would allow him to lay down the issue and transfer his fingers to some unfriendly neck. I began my pleading, orating hard about the condition of my father, his gloom and hunger, lacing the whole with some selections from that poem. But he would not listen. I got down on my knees, conjuring him to have done with this tomfoolery of conflict and let himself be evicted like a decent citizen. I didn't even give up when Agnes, hearing the drift of my talk, began kicking at me from the rear and Cadwallader, to follow suit and to pander to this Agnes, who was the moontug upon the broad yearning waters of him, started to push my head off my shoulders with his thumb which was about the size of your leg. He kept the effort to this thumb to show me this was only a caution, given without malice even though it might end up with me walking about the Terraces wondering why I stopped so short at my shoulders. Then Agnes said I was probably a spy, sent up there after a lot of coaching by the bailiffs to do this pleading and get just one party to evict himself and set the ball rolling in favour of the law and the coal-owners. She quickened her kicks and said she could now see through my game, and if it was that she was kicking I was not suprised. She suggested to Cadwallader that I should be reduced to eight parts and served up raw to the bums when they should start peering over the barricade. She opened her mouth so wide when she said this that she got it full of red hair, and that gave her words an old, flaming, dangerous look. Cadallader started after me, holding up one finger as if measuring me up roughly for the rending. I gave up and began pelting down the Terraces with him after me. I could hear Agnes tallyhoing after him like a mistress of the wolf-hounds. I got to the barricade. I climbed up it like a monkey. As soon as I got to the top a policeman spotted me. He did not look very bright. He had probably come fresh from a long talk by the Chief Constable on the disasters, ranging from a terrible crumbling of the nation's brick-work to the organized ravishing of his women folk, if these Terraces were allowed to get away with this defiance. I could see his mouth drooping with concern, ripening into panic as he saw me. He yelled, "Here they come, boys," and reached up and gave me a hard clip with his baton that stretched me out cold on some sort of sofa, more numb than the millpuff that came staggering out in armfuls from the torn upholstery. This did not please Cadwallader who remembered, Agnes notwithstanding, that I was his nephew. So he went over the barricade and dealt that policeman a lot harder clip than the one the policeman had given me. The policeman joined me across the sofa and we were both full of nothingness, tickled by millpuff. Then a lot of other people followed Cadwallader on his wild way and the policemen and bailiffs were driven to the bottom of the valley. But not for long.

When I came properly to myself, I found myself being marched by an army of policemen down to the police station. With me were about eighteen other men, Cadwallader among them, looking as dazed as I was but walking significantly in the centre of the group, like a king-pin. At the station we were charged with rioting, and I was still so boss-eyed with the fetcher I had from the baton that I could not even ask them what the hell they were talking about.

Everybody made a great fuss of me as we were waiting for the trial. I came right out from behind the front door when the bailiffs called about my father's debts and there was no need to make a single statement about death or calling next week. They were off. Some of the wisest voters in our part of the valley, boys suckled on grief and unrest, told me that I had struck a fine blow for tenants all over the world. I started to go to those classes at the Library and Institute that my friend, Milton Nicholas, used to run on the 'History of Our Times', giving the light to such subjects as the workers' struggle for lower rents, longer lives, higher ceilings, sweeter kids, and kinder days. Milton, though young and on the frail side, shone like a little sun on the gloom and wilderness of these topics. I started, with a thawed and astonished brain, to understand that it is a very bad thing, a very wrong thing, for colliery companies to go slapping extra rent on voters who don't get enough to eat most of the time, and to send bodies of policemen and bailiffs to evict these voters whenever the landlord is in a mood to disagree. And Milton showed me how I personally fitted into all this. He likened me to that Wat the Tyler who had put a hammer to the head of some tax collector or nark who was eyeing Wat's daughter and taking Wat's mind off the tiles. The boys in Milton Nicholas's class clubbed in and bought me a strong hammer, and Milton, when it was handed over, made a short speech in which he said that sooner or later the world, in its endless devising of discomfort and evil, would yield me some nark or collector who would give just the right kind of lip and have just the right kind of head to send me racing for the hammer. This gave me a proud feeling and I began to hope that when the trial came along the judge would order me to be kept in jail for ever like that poor bloke who was all beard and fish bones in that picture 'Monte Cristo', so that Milton could say something about me from week to week as an example of those who were giving their lives for freedom. My father was very worried when I told him about this hope, especially the part about the beard, because he hates hair on the face in any shape or form and thinks a man should be neat even in the County Jail.

The trial came and I could see that the judge, who was dressed in a way I had never seen before except in carnivals, believed in rent and was stern towards all people who rioted and played hell with bailiffs. Every time he opened his mouth I got to feel more and more like Monte Cristo. But the man who was defending us made out that I should never have been in the street at all, and mentioned that Cadwallader had been clearly seen chasing me, with a promise of murder right across his face, towards the barricade, and the fetcher I got from the policeman which put me across the sofa as cold as one of the legs, was simply a practice swing let off by the policeman by way of getting his muscles loose and ready to help the landlords lose their chains. It had nothing to do with my head at all. It had come along at the wrong moment. The judge was impressed by this and peered at me and muttered something a few times about me being young, as if I was Cadwallader's father and keeping very fresh for my age. He said, "Let us separate the chaff from the grain." The chaff was such personalities as Cadwallader, at whom the judge didn't bother to peer. "This boy," went on the judge, "has no doubt been seduced by the rash bolshevik elements who mar this valley. He has been corrupted by idleness. The thing here is to nurse this bent sapling back to mental health. We will have him taught a trade. What trade would you like to be taught, my boy?" At first I was too busy playing up to the judge by looking bent and corrupted and explaining this programme in mutters to my puzzled comrades to make an answer. He asked me again. I remembered that Milton Nicholas had told me that money-lending was a very secure line of business where you didn't have to change and bath every time you came home. It sounded to me just the thing for people who were not in it. I mumbled something about having a strong fancy for money-lending if I could find something to lend. "Excellent," said the judge, laughing with pleasure. "An excellent choice. A bricklayer. A wise choice. I judged rightly. This boy has the right stuff. Let him be taught to lay bricks." I hadn't said a word about bricks but that is how it happened. They sent me on a six-months' course to a Government Training Centre, and the night I went away Hicks the Bricks, the contractor I've worked with ever since, had a piece in the paper giving his views about the problem of the young, to which Hicks seemed to give even more thought than he gave to bricks, and saying that when I returned he would provide me with a job. Cadwallader and the other boys went to jail for a few weeks, and when he came out he found two other voters going in and out of Agnes's house. He noticed that, put together, these two were just about his weight, and Agnes pleaded that she was only keeping them about the place as mementoes of fuller times and to keep the mats in place until

Cadwallader's return. But he had read passages from the large printed Bible he had found in his cell, and he told Agnes she was the sort of woman they had set dogs on in the days when print was larger. And he came back to the house of my father trying his best not to bark, and to pour the rain of his new resolution on the hot ache of his longing body.

That is how I came into the building trade. I was too sorrowful at having fallen so far below the golden hills of striving martyrdom on which I had been sent briefly to walk by the words of Milton Nicholas to feel gratitude or gladness. The only thing I learned to the depths at the centre was to stay right away from all fish that looked like whale, because I had a poisoned stomach from eating fish that looked like that. Our foreman says I am so bad a hand with bricks I ought to sign articles with the Eskimos and specialize in igloos where the walls are supposed to be curved in just the way I curve them and not meant to outlast a good warm spring. So that is the way to do it. When a man of power, like that judge, asks you to choose your path out of hell, mumble your reply and let him put the pattern out of his own wisdom upon your blur of sound, for in the end it is his choice it will be and the hell of your beginning will face you at the end and the heat of hell grows no less hot; only you and your fibres, with weariness and understanding and the laughter that will ooze from the dampest blankest wall of knowing and feeling, will grow less swift to smart at the pain of its burning. That, and helping a boy like Hicks the Bricks to get his name in the paper. That sets you up and eases the cold, whatever the great distance one's eyes must cross before they light once more upon the golden hills.

Arrayed Like One of These

I have known little of elegance. South Wales in the twenties was a forest of blue serge and, among the older men, suits of black material hard as teak and meant to outlast the earth. After twenty years or so under a steady fall of rain and sermons the stuff went a deep green, and I have seen many a seatful of deacons that made the preacher look like Robin Hood, a Hood who has chopped down the trees of his paradisal wood to make chapel furniture and plagued by a Marian eternally old and forbidding. It was a material that creaked like armour, and one of my darkest recollections is being shepherded to punishment by a group of elders after some witless antic on the chapel gallery and hearing the distinct deathly rustle of their suits. In that rig people of forty really looked cut off from life.

There was a good deal of amateur dressmaking. Someone would get a very rough pattern from a newspaper and work on it in a kitchen lit for groping only. I recall at the age of about five being in need of a shirt. I had set my mind on something fancy from the shops. There was a girl in the Sunday School on whom I wanted to flash a clear impression. But it was not to be so. Partly to teach me that sex and Sunday School, even at the tentative age of five, do not mix; partly to help a struggling widow, a close neighbour, who had taken up work with the needle, it was decided to place the order for the shirt with the widow.

The material chosen for the shirt was the most earnestly brown stuff I have ever seen. It would have looked well in a tent. It had been bought cheap from a packman who had almost lost his reason lugging this great lump of sad-looking fabric about. My father was so impressed by the melancholy on the packman's face that he bought a thick wad of the cloth, and he was delighted to see what a load he had taken off the packman's mind, even though he was now going to lift it on to mine. When I saw the colour of it I wrote a message on a wall for that girl in the Sunday School telling her that I had gone to India.

My father told me that this was the widow's first job and that we should not be fussy or demanding.

"He's only a kid, Mrs Supple. All a boy of that age needs is a rough covering. Don't bother about finesse or exact measurements. He's a shy boy. He doesn't like to be fiddled with, and I can see by your eye, Mrs Supple, that it can register a clear impression of size. Trust your eye, Mrs Supple. A shirt is a friendly sort of garment. Don't bother about an inch here, an inch there."

Mrs Supple didn't. The finished shirt was brought to us on a Saturday night as I was standing in the bath in front of the kitchen fire. My father brought the garment in to me, looking very pleased and saying that Mrs Supple had more of a gift than even he had imagined. My father slipped the shirt on to me. My brothers stood around staring and I could taste their astonishment. The front of the garment was about the size of a shirt front, a dickie. The back fell right down into the water of the bath and was a good inch longer than I was. I was like some new gruesome type of bird. Mrs Supple had also used all two feet of the neckband she had ordered. My father could have come in with me and we would still have been breathing better than normal.

"It's a fine shirt," said my father. "You couldn't expect anything stodgy, anything the same." He tried to keep his eyes on the enormous drape at the back. "I told her a kid your age grows like magic. She's given you coolness where a man needs it most and warmth where you'll appreciate it best."

I stepped out of the bath. The effect of the shirt was even more striking when one had a full view. My father sat in the corner smiling, praising Mrs Supple and saying that as a boy he had hated always having to wear shirts that were the same distance off the ground all round. As I walked around the kitchen trying to work this new fact into my existence my brothers followed me around as if I were a potentate, and my father said he had never seen any bit of raiment that so brought out the dignity in me.

28

I wore the shirt for several months. I still haven't quite recovered my sense of balance. And the mound of cloth that accumulated around my middle like a lumpy sash still has people convinced that I was once a cripple healed in the revival of 1921, a splendid year for miracles and early greens.

It was many years later that my father went into action on the clothing front again. We had been discussing a chronically shy neighbour of ours, Aaron Phipps, and his sympathy for this voter had caused an axiom to ripen in his mind. "If you see a man who is failing to look life in the eye," he said, "lay a helping hand on his neck muscles."

He had a tic of compassion that made him find people on every hand who seemed to be dodging life's eye but they usually turned out to be men who were chronically wary and were dodging everything about life, not just the eye. But we went to work on the neck muscles all the same and at the end of each experiment it was our necks that were in need of the sun-lamp.

At that time I was due to take my Final Schools at Oxford. I needed a suit of 'sub-fusc'. I had avoided dark suitings from the age of thirteen when I was thrown down the stairs of the Sunday School by a teacher who had been made distraught by our Darwinian banter and driven by jagged doubts first to quoits and corkwork, then to the cheaper drugs. Also in that year, in dark blue serge, I had had the experience, at the funeral of an uncle, of being thrown into an open grave by an elderly cousin demented by grief and ale. So, in 1934, after a fair spell dressed in tweeds, I had to find a suit in the lower chromatic register. The last suit I had bought had been one of bold checks. My father had wanted at least one of the family to look like a bookie although no group of people could have been more remote from horses seen in a sporting light. But the check suit had given my father a lot of pleasure, and often when I had come into the kitchen when my father was exchanging perplexities and roast cheese sandwiches with the lost bewildered preacher, Mr Cornelius, he would add a mile to Mr Cornelius's maze by forsaking theology and asking me if there had been any scratchings and what the future was for the turf.

I could have managed the business of the suit in a few days if left to myself and was making my way to the newly opened branch of a nationally known outfitter when my father stopped me and said:

"You want a new suit?"

"That's it. Dark. Got to be dark. A feudal regulation."

"How would you like to strike a blow for Aaron Phipps?"

I thought at first that my father wanted me to give the money I had set aside for the suit to Phipps and I said no. First the exams, I said, then succour Phipps, if need be.

"Oh no," said my father. "I just want you to let Aaron make your suit. He's just made a start with that very sad tailor, Horatio Clemett the Cloth, and it would stiffen Aaron's confidence if you asked him to make you a suit for such an important event as an exam."

My father, true to his basic rhythm of complexity, did not take me at once to the shop of Clemett and let Phipps measure me. He introduced me to Aaron Phipps that night in the coffee tavern of Aldo Nitti. Aaron had thick glasses and the most pointed set of nerves. He had been through a thorough mill of mishaps. He was jumpy and was not improved by my father's way of suddenly bending over him and saying that his day had come. He now looked like a lion tamer who has thrown away his whip and is urging the lions to leap to their last black climax.

"Aaron" said my father, "has got a natural gift of style and he'll be a first-class asset to Clemett the Cloth if he can be nursed back into a belief that things can really fit. His last job was with Tiller's fairground. In charge of various contraptions that go up and around. Swings and roundabouts and articles like that. Aaron gets vertigo. He gets giddy just watching people wheeling around on those painted horses and cockerels that are such a feature of Tiller's merry-go-rounds. And Aaron would have the idea that they were going to fall off. He would leap on to the back of a horse or cockerel and hang on to the customer. Sometimes it was a woman and Aaron got a thrust with hand or shoe for his trouble. This made him giddier and he would rush to the lever or brake and bring the whole contraption to a halt with a jerk that sent voters flying about the fairground like chaff."

Aaron smiled at me and made a gesture of pulling something towards him.

"Too abrupt," he said. "I'd warn them to hang on but there

was such a racket of music from the panatrope."

He began to sing 'Let a smile be your umbrella', a popular fairground tune of the day, but Aldo Nitti told him to stop because Aaron's voice was penetrating and caused a pervasive buzz among the taller toffee bottles.

"Well," said my father, "the fairground owner told me that Aaron came within an inch of bringing organised jollity in the zone to a full stop. But now Aaron is going to have a fresh start. It seems that his mother, who died a short while back, was a lover of Clemett the Cloth."

"Very close, let's say," said Aaron, "very close." He blinked. "The gas meter was in the front room."

My father cautioned Aaron with his eyes that he had made another nervous leap ahead of his narrative. "To get on in tailoring, Aaron," said my father, "you'll have to learn to talk smoothly to the clients. It won't do to make them wonder why your stories sound as if they've been blown up in the middle. If necessary, check the facts of each story on your fingers."

Aaron went back a page.

"I had a penny in my hand to put in the meter. The front room was dark. I fell over Clemett. I lost the penny. Clemett told me not to bother and I could hear my mother, very muffled, seconding him. He has a very harsh voice in the dark, Clemett." By his tone I could sense that Aaron did not take much to Clemett.

"And he's not much better in the light."

"So Aaron's mother made Clemett promise to give Aaron a start in the tailoring trade. But it seems as if Clemett shot his bolt as far as love was concerned with the passing of Mrs Phipps and he's trying to bully Aaron into some other trade. But we'll show Clemett. Aaron's the boy to make your sub-fusc suit for you. Give him a chance."

Aaron fished a book of styles from his pocket. It looked ravelled and years out of date. On its cover was a group of men who had borne off the palm of neatness in the year of the book's publication. I put my finger on one of these and told Aaron I would like to look like Jimmy Walker, the Mayor of New York, a noted dandy, and Aaron said that if he ever set eyes on Walker he would bear this in mind.

My father took me to the shop of Clemett on the afternoon of the next day. It was one of the darkest shops in Meadow Prospect. Some years before Clemett had turned against his own trade and had stated in the Discussion Group of the Christian Men's Guild that, without going all the way with those elements who sat naked around lagoons and one or two local voters he had spotted through gaps in the ferns, humanity would be a lot better off for being less well covered. He had been told off by the Christian Men and advised to go and think it over.

Aaron was in the back of the shop, hardly visible and pushing a large, hard bristled brush along the floor.

"A terror for keeping the floors clean, is Clemett," whispered my father. "Dreads the plague and keeps on having his brushes stolen. So he keeps Aaron at it. That way he always knows where the brush is and keeps Aaron frustrated."

Clemett shook us by the hand and apologised for the gloomy atmosphere.

"Many of my clients come to see me in a state of grief for funeral suits and they wouldn't want too garish a light."

"I can see that," said my father. "Death leaves the voters in mixed states." And he went on to explain to Clemett about sub-fusc, Oxford and the examination and I could see that he had left Clemett as much in the dark as the shop. Behind me in the shadows the rub of Aaron's brush was like the rustle of doom, putting me on edge and I was wishing myself out in the light and my father through the floor-boards.

Clemett produced one of the thickest books of patterns ever assembled. Sub-fusc was no problem here because among these hundred heavy slabs of cloth, any one of which could have gone straight on to a grave, there was not one tint that rose above a blackish grey. It was clear that Clemett had long been seeing humanity as a kind of cortège. I picked one out at random. I could not go wrong in that clamp of shadows. But my father told me not to take it. He had been fingering his way through the samples and he had come up with one which, on first touch, felt like two-ply sail cloth. My father was most impressed and I could see that Clemett too was keen on this particular fabric.

"That," said my father, "strikes me as a pretty durable weave."

"The average cloth in that book of samples," said Clemett, "would last fifteen years. But that cloth there would see you right for twenty-five."

My father said this was just the thing. He had, he said, seen many people like deacons and merchants wear suit of this material and the fact of having themselves encased in such impenetrable, deathless stuff had given these voters a stern unsensual look which had improved their work with morals and merchandise. For myself I was thinking that when they saw me in this raiment at Oxford they would declare that Roger Bacon the alchemist was back.

Mr Clemett now got a pencil, a book and a tape and told me to take off my jacket.

"If you don't mind, Mr Clemett," said my father, "we've heard a lot about Aaron Phipps' very gifted way with the tape and my boy would like Aaron to handle the order."

Clemett's first impulse was to carry on with his measuring and wait until he had the cash in his hand before telling my father that he was off the hinge. But my father had rushed to the back of the shop, snatched the broom from Aaron's hand and was pushing him towards us. He took the tape off Clemett, not without what looked like a bit of a scuffle, and gave it to Aaron.

"Now then, Aaron," he said. "Here's your chance to become the best loved tailor and stylist in the gulch."

"Do your best, Aaron," I said in the softest voice I will ever employ outside dreams. "You know the main points; chest, legs and that."

"Don't you worry," said my father. "Aaron and I have spent hours talking about men's styles in the café of Aldo Nitti and by the time he's finished he's going to launch a new race of dandies."

Then began one of the most strenuous ten minutes I shall ever know. Possibly, left alone and helped by drink, Aaron Phipps might have arrived at a series of figures on his pad that would have furnished me with a jacket, a waistcoat and a pair of trousers roughly in touch with my shape.

But he had no chance. First there was the whole phalanx of insecurities that kept the base of him in a fearful throb. Then there was Clemett who was leaning against a shelf, glaring at

Phipps and humming a hymn in one of the lowest and most threatening voices west of Chepstow. But the top turn was my father. Every whipstitch he would startle the wits out of Phipps by stepping between us and saying in a voice of real command:

"Plenty of slack there now, Aaron. A tight suit will be no good to my boy when he's working hard and bulging his brain out in that examination." And instantly Aaron would let out so much tape he'd lose the end of it. My father would follow this with a warning to Aaron not to overdo the bagginess and then the tape would come back around me, constrictive as a python. Once my father challenged a measurement and found that Aaron had the tape around himself and me and finding some kind of happiness in the thought of being roped in and safe from Clemett. I told me father to come in and keep us company but he told me that this kind of callow irony might be all right in a place like Oxford but it was not going to do Aaron Phipps a lot of good when he caught the full flavour of it.

Then we came to the trousers.

"Now don't forget, Aaron," said my father. "You'll need some of your most delicate measuring when you come to what they call the fork. They say the whole soul of a suit resides in the way it hangs from the fork."

Aaron was not at all sure about the fork and applied the tape to a point between the shoulder blades. Covertly, not wishing to embarrass Clemett, my father showed Aaron where the fork was. "And don't forget, Aaron, you'll need a firm precise measurement at the fork. No guesswork there."

Aaron nodded and made a grab at that quarter that left a dark psychotic scar on me for years.

The suit was delivered on the evening before my departure for Oxford. My father watched me put it on. As he saw the monstrous inaccuracies of Aaron Phipps twist my body into the likeness of Quasimodo he did not show any depression. When I pointed out that one sleeve seemed to go out of business at the elbow and the other was waiting for the delivery of another arm before it would show any fingers, all he did was praise the quality of the cloth and he also said cryptically:

"What the artist sees is not always what we see."

I tried on the trousers. At the sight of them even my father fell silent. I could feel my rump aching through the space for the feel of cloth. I felt like Grock. The trousers had a length of fly that would have inhibited Messalina. By the time my father had helped adjust the endless rows of buttons I felt like a bond in a safe-deposit box. My father stood back and gave judgment. "It was probably Aaron's first traffic with the fork. And he was flurried. But I see the hand of Clemett in the design of that codpiece. Years ago he swore to make the libido feel like a war-memorial. He's done it."

For the first three days of my Final Schools the ushers let me into the Examination Hall well ahead of the other candidates because I looked so abnormal. During the first four papers everything was sloped at an angle I had never seen before because Aaron's right sleeve forced my fist eastward. On the fourth day I half unpicked the seams and that helped a little.

It worked out not so badly. I wrote an essay on French writers in the modern period whose work was like a howl of pain from a trap of outrage and I could never have got the authenticity into the analysis if it had not been for the tailoring of Aaron Phipps. Those trousers had me right there in the trap and I howled with the best of them.

Aaron went on to a fair success. Now and then his primal terrors would come to fresh bloom and his skill with the tape would go to tatters and for a few months after we would see some voter walking about like Lon Chaney.

But my father remained complacent about it to the very end. He claimed it was my revulsion from the chapel tradition that made my limbs contract or twist at the touch of that heavy sombre material. He saw that I was not accepting this and he went on: "That suit was Aaron's map of his own inner self. And one day he will make you a free new suit, one with matching arms to show that he now feels all his nerves and desires to be right down on the flat sane earth." He became very thoughtful.

"All the same," he said, "he could have brought the seat of those trousers a few feet off the ground. Walking behind you was like following a procession."

The Hands of Chris

Remember the old slump days, before the war?

In those days we lived in a street that stood on its own on the eastern slope of the valley. The eastern slope had fewer houses on it than the other. It was steeper. The houses of our street were not worth living in. We complained a lot: the ceilings were too low; the roofs were too ragged; the rent was too high; but we didn't have the money to move with and we had no place to move to. The owner of the street knew that, so we lay in his hand and squealed. We had good voices. We squealed in different keys and that made pretty music.

Sometimes we even got to like living there. The people were as warm and good as the coal in their fireplaces. The street, being on its own, was like a little village, separate from the rest of the valley folk whose homes lay beneath us or across the valley from us. We all knew each other in that street. We even got to like the smells of the place and they were so many they took some knowing.

Right at the end of the street was a flat green patch that served as a meeting place for all us men during the summer days. It was good to have the fresh grass under our bodies and even the valley beneath, with its twisting half-slums and endless pits, bitter and sad as we always thought it to be in our minds, seemed pleasant and without conflict as you stared down at it between its barriers of green mountain.

When the days were fine we did most of our eating on the grass of our open air meeting place. We got used to the rhythm of one another's talk and when the rain drove us indoors we were angered by the swish of cleaning cloth on dish or floor and we kept our back doors open and shouted, knowing that there would always be one of our friends sitting at another door waiting to shout a reply.

Big Chris Magg was one of our company. When he first came to live in our mountain street, he was muscle and grin and muffler and not much else. He drifted in from one of the Midlands coalfields. When he first came he spent his time wolfing all the food he could lay his hands on and his lust for women was built in storeys that no number of women seemed to fill. He'd work around the clock and think less of it than the clock. In those days he didn't know the difference between a red union and a yellow union. He was everything the coal-owners wanted and Chris stayed like that until the coal-owners showed they could get on even without him by closing down all the pits in the district. Then Chris began sitting with us on the green patch at the end of our street.

We started a Penny Fund for buying books. We all gave a penny a week and when there was enough money in the kitty to buy some book we wanted, one of us would go down to the bookshop in the valley and get it. Then the book would travel around us like a coin until we had all read it, and by that time it was dirty but better read than most books all the same. We took turns at starting discussions on books we knew most of us had read. That way we got ideas on what was happening in Europe and outside Europe. There wasn't much of what well-off people would call moderation or open-mindedness in our ideas. We hadn't been raised in public schools, any of us, so we couldn't afford to be open-minded. We got the rough edge of living, in work, out of work, and in the houses we paid too much rent for. Fascism was a real thing to us. We didn't have to be out in Spain to know why miners and peasants should want to fight until they dropped against the dolled-up thieves and bullies who masqueraded as their owners and task-masters. We knew a lot ourselves about being cuffed, badgered and cheated and our fathers had known their share too. So there was a lot of passion and temper in the way we looked at the world and talked of it.

We couldn't get Chris to read much. He said he'd never had much chance to read and, from what he told us of that Midlands coal-field he had drifted from, there seemed to be a very widespread and successful plan to keep the voters in a state of great backwardness. But Chris would listen to the talking as violently as he had ever swung a pick. His eyes were always glued to the person who was speaking and his mouth would gape with the effort to understand every word that was spoken. Every time we talked of the people's armies the world over that had been formed to fight oppression, his eyes would glow, and every time we mentioned those who had butchered and deceived the common people and acted worse than beasts in defence of their own privilege, Chris would wriggle about in the grass, rub his large, hard hands together vindictively and mutter: "B'stards 's they are!"

He was always nervous about asking a question when we were all there together. But as soon as he could get just three or four of us together, he'd ask us more than we knew about the war that was going on in Spain. He wanted to go out there, he said.

Then, one summer evening, we got visitors in the valley. The first we knew of this was the sight of a lorry with wire netting around the sides drawing up in the square of the valley's biggest town. That was the town nearest our street. Inside the lorry was a gang of about thirty young fellows in black shirts. They gave the upraised arm salute before alighting from the lorry. I got a good look at them. Some of them were weedy enough, pasty-faced lads with a taste for military moustaches who looked as if this little adventure was giving them a sense of glory they'd never get from licking stamps in the offices where they worked. It made my stomach itch to see the way in which these bright little fellows hitched their buckled belts and cast what they most likely thought were masterful glances at the miners and their wives who passed on either side of the lorry. The rest of the band were rougher specimens. The looked like boxing-booth toughs, flat-nosed, thick-eared, stupider and heavier than the hefty, nailed boots they wore on their feet. I wondered at what rate they hired their fists out and what stance they'd adopt if they were ever struck by a thought. I saw them fix up a loudspeaker apparatus. I hastened up the mountainside to tell the boys in our street how we were being favoured.

I made my way along the street and let my friends know. I found Chris staring up at a white cloud formation outside the house in which he lodged. He was lying on the stone-flagged paving with his back against a short wall.

"The Fascists are here," I said.

"Who?"

"The Fascists."

"The b'stards, you mean?"

"That's it, Chris. Franco's pals."

"Well, I'll be damned. Just let me see them."

And down the mountainside hared Chris faster than I thought a man of his size could hare.

When I got back to the square, the fighting was well started. I couldn't get very close. Occasionally, through an opening in the crowd, I could see Chris battering his way through the well-disciplined little cohort of blackshirts and being whacked very hard on the skull and the back of his neck by two pursuing policemen who seemed to have as little effect on Chris as if they were stroking him.

It was soon finished. The cohort was surrounded by a stout cordon of policemen. The police-inspector was there, bawling so loud we thought he'd burst under pressure of his own voice, which seemed to be going right up into the air like a thick column. The defended Fascists were grinning as if they had achieved some kind of victory. They were marched to the lorry. The police re-formed between us and the lorry. I had never seen such a thickness of flesh. The policeman standing in front of me had shoulders like a castle wall and the red flesh of his jowl poured over his stiff blue collar like molten metal.

The Fascist lorry moved off. The tougher of them cocked a snook and yowled loud derisory yowls. The pasty-faced lads in the centre of the band looked a bit sick and scared. A fusillade of stones, thrown from the back part of the crowd, bounced off the lorry's wire netting. The lorry moved off out of the valley as quickly as it had come. The police, their batons still drawn, jostled us back home, some of them laughing and joking with the people, others looking as solemn and strained as if they had just stopped a split in the Constitution.

We found Chris in a corner of the square, his face against a wall and looking so dazed and bloody he might have been dead-drunk. The back of his neck was a flower-bed of deep-coloured bruises, his hands were a pulpy mess of torn flesh and blood. He had been hitting people until his hands gave up the ghost. We got him to a doctor who bandaged him; then home, where Chris sat in a corner, his hands stretched out close to the fire, his eyes looking just like the fire, big, proud, triumphant.

Then, the summonses were issued. Chris kept an impressed silence when we told him he was sure to get one. But he didn't. There were eight people summoned. These were men and women who had been prominent in the organisation of all popular movements for a long time past. As far as we could make out, four of these citizens had been nowhere near the scene of the fighting. But it was pointed out that even if they could prove that they had been in heaven or hell at the time of the fighting, their speeches, thoughts and writings during the previous ten or twenty years of struggle against the more wanton stupidities of the way in which we lived could be used as evidence of incitement. This kind of reasoning baffled us, but most of us had taken up being baffled as a kind of hobby. Of the remaining defendants, two had been seen exchanging blows with the blackshirts, two had stayed on the outskirts of the crowd doing much more in the way of restraint than incitement. But of the bloody-fisted Chris there was no mention at all in the law's reprisals.

Chris was boiled when he heard. He took his bandaged hands to the police station. I went along with him to help him out if he became speechless, which is just what he was as he marched along to the police station.

"Where do you think I got these?" he asked the police-sergeant as he held out his hands.

"Don't know," said the sergeant.

"Where the hell d'you think I could have got them?"

"Punching something as likely as not. Get out of here. We don't want you. Get out of here while you're safe."

Chris's mouth tightened and his hands twitched. I dragged him away while he was still inactive under the burden of all the thinking he was trying to do. I had a notion that Chris might end up in the Tower of London if he got any more violent and challenging with the law, the air all round being so full of summonses and law and order.

Chris walked up the mountainside beside me, sad, huge, still aching. "What the bloody hell . . .?" he flared out once. I shrugged my shoulders and he fell silent.

When we reached our street, he had become calm. He turned gravely to me and nodded his head several times. I nodded back, agreeing to the full with whatever thought it was he was trying to express. "The world," he said at last, "is full of them."

"Of what, Chris?"

"B'stards."

"You're right, boy. You've hit the nail on the head, boy."

The next day, Chris went along as usual to sign the register at the Employment Exchange. The clerk at whose box he signed was a prim, small man who always kept a tiny reservoir of liberal ideas at the back of his two-by-three brain that he could betray every time he wanted a better job. The job was no better because there were so many men of his own stamp using the same tactic. He glared at Chris with all the malevolence of the small bureaucrat who sees a chance of being mean coming up over the skyline.

"What's the matter with your hands?"

"Smashed 'em up," said Chris with pride.

"How did you do that?" The clerk pulled a long pencil from his breast-pocket and wetted the point on his lips.

"I smashed 'em up fightin'."

"Fighting. A rioter, eh?"

"That's right," said Chris satisfiedly.

"You'll be dealt with, my good fellow. That's your freedom of speech, eh? Beating up clean-limbed young chaps who'd put you all to some useful work. We won't be seeing you for a couple of months after the cases are heard."

"What you mean?"

"You'll be in gaol."

"Not me."

"Not you? Haven't the police seen you, seen your hands?"

"They seen 'em. They don't want me." There was a terrific, heartfelt disgust in the voice of Chris.

"Small fry," said the clerk with contempt. "Beneath notice even as a rioter. No doubt the police put you down as a dupe who's had his punishment already. But that isn't to say that we shall be as clement as our good friends in blue. Oh, good gracious, no. There's something we can do for you."

"What's that?"

"Stop your dole. You're not fit for work. Hands smashed up. Not fit. You're going to be thrown off benefit for a couple of weeks, my brave lad. You don't get it all your own way, do you?"

"You mean," said Chris, picking his way slowly from word to word, "you mean, my dole'll be cut for a bit. I'll be getting less?"

"You'll be off benefit. That's what I mean, see?"

And the clerk began to laugh delightedly. He laughed for about three seconds. There was a roar from Chris that made the waiting queue behind him think the slump they had been suffering from was now getting to closer quarters by way of the roof. Chris's hands shot over the counter and landed with a bandage-padded thud on each side of the clerk's head. The clerk went down to the floor more from fright than concussion. Chris stared for a moment at his hands as if beholding the bodily substance of the fresh pain he had made to burn in them. Then he dropped himself, went down like a tree, passed out clean as a candle to get beyond the agony of his broken fingers.

So Chris got his summons after all and he was put away for about the same time as the others. That made Chris feel a lot easier in his own conscience and it gave much pride to all those who lived in our street for we felt that, at that moment, history was close to us, as close as the rent collector, which was very close indeed.

My Fist Upon the Stone

L ife did not change much for Rhianedd Hicks and her son Abel after the death of her husband John. They lived, as they had always done, by and for themselves. Abel increased in meagreness and the fierce urge to possess as he crawled, with tiny impulses, towards middle age. Through all strikes at the pit, crises, holidays and temptations, Abel advanced with the quiet, sliding stride of an earthworm towards his ultimate goal of peace and security, the goal he knew he would never recognise even when he had reached it.

The inside of the cottage near the brook where they lived changed not at all with the passing of the years. They made a patient replacement of their furniture as, unit by unit, worn to death and gone even beyond the passionately repairing hands of Abel, it collapsed and sent them crashing to the floor.

Abel returned from work in the evening of a day in early summer. It was a day that followed the exact pattern of all the days in Abel's life. He was weary and stiff for the masters had no more devoted worker than he. He pushed the cap back from his forehead because there was an ache between his eyes. He watched groups of children playing in the back lanes of the streets through which he passed. Their antics baffled him and he preferred not to watch them but his eyes rarely left them as he passed. His mouth dropped with wonder as he stared at them making themselves filthy by rolling in the dirt, making grotesque cameos as they mimicked their elders, piercing their ears with shrieks that sickened Abel with their violence. And when they sat, solitary and solemn, there was a hint of intense irreverence in their thoughts that frightened Abel more than the racket they made as a pack.

He found his mother waiting for him. She was wearing a black overall. Her face was keen and strong as it had always been. She watched every move that Abel made and in odd corners of his person detected things that made him a shadow of the dead John, and there was in her eyes as she stared at Abel a hunger that frightened him sometimes, like those kids.

He washed his hands and sat down at the table. He drank many cups of thin tea, unsugared, flavoured by a sickly brand of tinned milk. He ate thick bread plastered with jam that heard of fresh fruit and let the acquaintance drop there. Mrs Hicks stood near Abel as he ate. As his teeth crushed the jam from between the bread slices and caused it to trickle out she caught the falling pieces with her fingers and Abel licked them from her finger, smiling. They came close to each other and were happy when they did things like that. Abel's only hint of passion was in the love he bore his mother.

While Abel had his tea, a bucketful of water boiled on the fire for his bath.

When he finished his eating and drinking, he brought in the tin bath that hung from a nail on the outside wall of the cottage. He placed the bath near the fireplace and poured the water into it. His mother helped him to remove his boots and his trousers, heavy with pit-dirt, pit-water and sweat.

Abel lay with his legs doubled up in the bath, enjoying the warmth of the waters on his body. His mother watched him, studying the leanness of his body, enjoying the spectacle of mighty unremitting thrift that sang from every protruding bone in the body of her son. Sometimes she would crane her neck and stare down into the bath, watching with a kind of fright for any sign of awakening passion in Abel. But Abel was cold, colder than ice. Rhianedd was reassured, proud.

When Abel got the dirt from his face, trunk and legs, he stood up in the bath and handed a square of soaped flannel to his mother. Lovingly she ran the flannel through all the complicated hollows of his back. From the gentle, careful, loving swish of the flannel Abel derived the only deep joy there was in his life outside the joy of accumulating the strength through possessing that would make him proof against the life torment that twisted the weak and the unprepared . . .

Then Rhianedd towelled him from tip to toe. Dry, he sat in his shirt in the corner chair. She occupied the chair she had always sat on, near the table, looking out upon a square of brilliant green mountain. Every evening they did those things, sat like that when they had been done. No day different from the day that had gone before. The monotony preserved them as if they were pickled in spirit.

"Your father would love the sun on the mountain," said Rhianedd.

"Yes."

"He was a good man, Abel."

"Yes."

"But no better a man than you, Abel. No better."

"I have done my best," said Abel with thin lipped complacency.

"Your father was a fine, saving man."

"Yes."

"But no more saving than you, Abel."

"I have tried to walk in his path."

"You have walked further."

"I have done my best."

"You will never know the things he knew, Abel. You will never know the hunger to dig earth that made him sad. Your life will be yours. No one will ever be able to tell you you have no right to live where you want to live. You will be free, Abel, and there will be no want in your life, Abel, anywhere, anytime. You have lived a clean and careful life, my son. I am proud of the way you have lived."

She stroked his bare knee to show her pride.

"You will always care for me, Abel?"

"Always."

"You want no other woman but your mother?"

"No other woman."

All this sounded like part of a catechism, repeated until the words had worn fibre thin on their lips.

"What do you think of other women, Abel?"

"They are sluts."

"That's right, Abel. And what kind of sluts are they?"

"They are sluts who deceive and who would steal from me that which I have laid by to make us free from care and worry."

"That's right. And what do you do, Abel, when you see these other women who are sluts when they look at you to make the passion rise in your heart?"

"I do not look at them. I turn my eyes the other way. I do not see them. But when I close my eyes, I see their thieving fingers close upon my heart to take it away from you. I see their hands upon my savings to waste them in bad living, to leave me without covering against want and wind. I never look at them."

Abel was forty when the manager told him he was to be made an overman. The manager broke the news cunningly and with an eye to theatrical effect. It happened on a Sunday evening.

The chapel that Abel, as well as the manager, attended was full to capacity. It was a special occasion. The chapel was being visited by a preacher famous for his mane of white hair and the howling vigour of his rhapsodies that had been known to drive the peccant so fast into the arms of conversion they bounced back and returned to their normal quota of dirt all on the same night. The chapel was full of bodies and warm with the blood and breath of them. The chapel windows were heavy with mist. The children in the window recesses played subtle and endless games with the lazy trickles that flowed down the windows' leaded panes, laying moneyless bets on the speed at which this trickle or that would reach the base of the window. Occasionally one of the children would pause in his play and press his water-cooled tips against his temples to relieve the clogging congestion of the head that oppressed most people in the overheated, overcrowded building.

Abel sat in the front row. Immediately in front of him and occupying a central part in the deacons' seat and smiling with a benevolence almost savage in its fixedness at all whose eye he caught was the manager. He had large white hands. He kept one of them outstretched on the shining ledge of the deacons' seat. He did the same with his face with the difference that his face was not divided into fingers and could not be outstretched for the public view without causing a stir. But his face, like his hands, was white, large, well kept and was shown off to good and full effect as he kept it half-turned towards the people in the congregation who had much too much sense socially to make too often the comparison between the manager and a bleached, decorated ham.

The white-haired preacher sat in the pulpit glancing at some notes, casually, as if they bore no reference to the sermon he was about to make. He was evidently conscious of having many eyes upon him. He avoided looking directly at the congregation. When he raised his head, he stared with green brilliant eyes at the chandeliers, shaking his hair upon his neck, passionately voiceless castanets, like a lion wondering how to fit the machinery of his vast, unearthly lusts into the limited background of religious nonconformity. Every time he looked upward in that way, he heard murmurs of admiration rising like marshmist from the scores of upturned mouths as this spectator or that commented on the preacher's almost incredible likeness to Elijah. There was not one member of the congregation old enough to have known Elijah but the admirers were working on the picture of Elijah that hung in the Sunday School annexe and with that picture as a guide one could well say that the preacher and the prophet were either brothers, the same man, or a professional model living in two ages at once to make himself insurable. Abel from his front row stared at the preacher and told himself that in that man, his courage, his fire, his beauty was the moving embodiment of a million things that crawled about in Abel, still vague, afraid, unintegrated. The manager, when he glanced up at the preacher, considered that had the latter not got a call he would have thrived as a coal broker. A pair of eyes like that could be relied upon to paralyse even the amoral antics of the Coal Exchange.

One of the deacons stood up and droned out a list of announcements relevant to the chapel's life. The offertory for last Sunday. The identity of the notable who was to address them. A money gift to the chapel's fabric fund from the collected officials of the manager's colliery. The death of some child-ridden woman to whose fabric no officials' fund had been devoted. When the announcements were finished, Abel and six others rose from their seats to take up the collection. As they collected, a local tenor stood in the middle of the pulpit steps and began to render the ballad, 'Nirvanah'. He was not too sure of the words. He was fumbling, redly nervous. His voice was sucked up into his nerves from time to time and got lost there.

Every time a coin dropped with more than usual noise into the collection box his singing would flag into a dim rattle that was neither here nor there. The occasion being special, the people seemed to be throwing their coins into the boxes at no distance less than six feet. The tenor was only three quarters of the way through his song on the road to Nirvanah when the collection was finished with. The precentor beckoned the tenor to a stop. He came down from the pulpit steps and returned to a more Christian atmosphere. Abel walked down the aisle with his collection box wonderfully heavy in his hand. It was a record collection. The manager smiled at him more broadly than ever as he laid the collection box on the table beneath the pulpit. When he returned to his seat, the manager turned around to him.

"You are a good member, Abel, and a good workman," he said.

"Thank you, sir. Thank you so much."

"You'll be having your reward, Abel. Never you worry about that." The manager waved his right index finger with extreme archness in front of Abel's eyes and Abel, whose imagination got hot and twisted every time he was excited, thought he saw in front of his eyes, a fat waxen moth.

"You're going up in the world, my boy," continued the manager. "From the end of next week, you'll be an overman. We've approved you. You've passed all your tests. What do you say to that, eh?"

"Oh, thank you . . . Oh thank . . . Oh dear . . . . Oh . . ." Abel was overcome. His tongue was tied to his shoulder blades and he felt as if his tongue were reins and he a horse and the manager a proud confident rider sending him in a prancing cloud of speed around the chapel. The manager hushed him to silence. The preacher was due to begin. Abel swivelled about excitedly in his seat. He opened his mouth to speak, thinking his mother was sitting in her usual place at his side. But Rhianedd had been ailing for some weeks past and had absented herself from the Sunday night service for the first time in many years. The woman at his side into whose face he found himself mouthing was a strange woman whose frown was a clear warning that if Abel wanted to play shady games of the character he was obviously trying to play he should choose a victim less old and less wise. The absence of his mother hurt Abel. He would have given a lot, short of actual cash, to have had her with him at that moment to tell her the news there and then without delay, to see her face, that small deep smile on her face when the sorrow left it completely and made her look almost like a stranger to Abel . . . He missed the first quarter of the sermon, wondering and worrying about how his mother was feeling, hoping she would be better on his return, knowing she would be better when she heard that the manager had made him an official at last, like his father had always wanted him to be.

The preacher fulfilled all the hopes of the congregation. He spat fire, was fire. Some of the deacons glanced queasily at each other in the fear that the torrent of rolling heat that came from the man's mouth might start melting the silver and copper coins in the offertory boxes. Even those who had given most to the collection felt that the cost of living was going down as they felt the flood of word-passion rush through their bodies to warm them as food and drink would warm them. The preacher's text was the Word made Flesh. His words had a musicshot fleshiness that thrilled the brains of all who had ears to hear. When he spoke of flesh it was his own flesh he pointed at and pinched to hammer the text home even into the furthest window recesses where the children sat still, stunned by a torrent of words prettier, more rapid, less comprehensible than trickles of water down leaded window panes. Into the preacher's ecstasy, adding its thin flames to the central pillar of flame, entered the ecstacy of Abel. As the word had been made flesh, so had Abel been made an overman. The one act was no less miraculous, no less bewitching, no less evocative of worshipping, wondering hymns than the other. When the preacher talked of God, Abel looked at the manager. When the preacher began, in the passionate, rocking singing monotone of the Welsh possessed, a mighty canticle of praise to God, "O Great, Sweet, Blessed Father . . .", Abel sobbed in his throat, raised his right arm in an involuntary twitch towards the manager's well-tailored back and felt big, adoring tears on his cheek that made the strange woman at his side who was looking at him from the corner of her eye think that Abel had whatever he had badly. Abel wiped away his tears . . . Ecstasy made water. Abel was in a daze till the service ended.

49

While the congregation dispersed, he waited for a chance to shake the manager's hand in thanks. The manager was busy shaking the preacher's hand, diffidently, cautiously, as if intent on not spilling any more of the precious rhetoric from the grey-haired master.

Abel went home, smiling with his thin lips at the far stars.

He found Rhianedd sitting motionless before a blazing, stacked-up fire. She did not move as he opened the door. She did not move as he walked across the kitchen towards her. There was a faint smell of scorched cloth in the room. Abel saw how close Rhianedd was sitting to the fire. He thought it must be her pinafore that had scorched. He pulled her chair away from the fire, gently. She smiled up at him, reassured.

"I was cold," she said, "I came close to the fire. I was very cold, Abel." She laid the side of her face against his arm. From the slight trembling of her body, Abel knew that she was in pain. Her face had grown deep yellow, sunken as if the caressing hands of sorrowful ghosts had worn deep hollows in its surface. A bucket full of water was coming to the boil on the fire. The quiet trembling set him on edge, made him afraid. He felt a sense of ending, dissolution, dumb and senseless agony in the air. Never before had he had a thought, an impression, so dramatically complete. His mind was not yet free from the emotions that had played upon it in the chapel. He wanted to cry but he had cried once that evening and he thought that to cry twice would be overdoing it. He remembered what the doctor had said a few weeks ago. The doctor had shrugged his shoulders and said "Let her rest. Feed her up. Get her things and let her rest, for God's sake. Or she'll go." But Rhianedd had set her face against that course: "I have not cost you so much so far, my boy. I won't start now. We have saved well, us two." Abel had felt that there was folly of some sort in those words but the words had been so much of a piece with all that he and Rhianedd had ever said, done, thought, that he could not put his finger exactly on where the folly lay. And the folly lay vicious and content upon the sad, still living tissue of Rhianedd, consuming her, killing her at so much the hour, and liking it because death found in Rhianedd a kinship with itself. She was of the sacred circle of things that move without seeming to be touched by life, to whom the stretching out of days in living is but the widening and twisting of a silly detour to the grave. At the back of Abel's mind was the insistent twang of a conviction that if his mother wanted to die, she knew best about that. As far as he could remember she had never been wrong about anything.

"They've made me an overman, mam," he said, talking right into her ear. "The manager's made me an overman. He told me in the chapel. Didn't you always say he'd make me an overman, mam?"

As he spoke he watched her move her head slowly upwards, smiling at him with a smile that was an indecisive shadow around her indecisive lips. He told her again what he had said before. He said it more clearly, slowly, loudly and laughed as he spoke thinking his laughter would be something big enough for her to use to grab hold of and come closer to him. But her smile grew no deeper nor did it show one atom more of understanding. He felt he was speaking into a distance that was cold, endless and stupid. He said God several times to see if that would help. It just made him feel more scared, bewildered. It made him feel he was sharing his secrets more than was necessary.

"We'll move, mam," he said. "From now on we can save as much as we always saved yet have enough left over to live in a nicer place. Somewhere not so damp, can't we, mam?" His eyes were close to her eyes. Distance, cold, endless, stupid. His words came back to him with icicles on them seeming to cut his lips as they came back to rest. He felt her struggle to bring her body nearer to his, her mind nearer to the words he was saying.

"We will stay here," she said and he knew that she meant it.

"Of course, mam. Of course we'll stay. Haven't we always been happy here?" He sought desperately for things to say that would keep her listening, talking. Things slipped through his head too nimble and too swift to be caught on his tongue. He looked at the bucket on the fire.

"What is the bucket on the fire for, mam? What is the water boiling for, mam?"

"For you Abel."

"For me, mam? I am clean. I have been to the chapel, not to work, mam. I am clean."

"To the chapel?" she asked. "Not to work?" She smiled again, this time more purposefully than before. Her smile seemed to say he was being silly and saying things to mislead her.

"Bath now, Abel. I have always helped you to bath, haven't I, Abel? I like to see you bath, Abel. Get the bath now, my son."

Abel left the room. He came back with the bath. He laid it in its usual place on the hearth mat. He poured into it the water from the bucket. He stripped, his eyes fixed on Rhianedd as if from his eyes, as long as they stared at her, would come the little warmth she needed to keep the flicker of feeling inside her. He sat in the bath going through the motions of cleaning himself. She sat on her chair watching him as she had always done, admiring the spindly leanness of his frame, the hard defiant protrusion of his bones. He stood up in the bath. She held out her hand for the soaped flannel. He gave it to her. He felt the minutest flick of the flannel on the top of the shoulder blade. He heard a harsh protracted coughing sound from Rhianedd, heard her fall back on her chair. He spun around violently in the narrow bath, slipped, hurt his thigh, made a mighty splash of water. He saw Rhianedd sit still, unmoving in her chair, a straggling track of soap-suds spangled from her lap to her neck. He pulled his trousers on, twisting himself double as the trousers caught around his legs, calling the name of his mother repeatedly, frantically. He carried her upstairs and as he paused on the sixth stair to ease the weight of her on his arms and to bend his head to wipe his eyes on the sleeve of her dress, he felt her die as definitely as ever he had heard her or seen her walk, sing, talk, weep. It was a clean vivid sensation like tripping over something in the dark. The sensation enveloped his mind completely, was assimilated quickly into its every cell and by the time he laid her on the bed, he felt as though he had never known her alive. He lit a candle. In his body he had a curious mounting feeling, the feeling he had had when climbing in a cart to the top of the hill from which he, his father and mother had looked back for the last time upon the fields in which he had been born, in the rocky, passionless North, the fields that had defied their desire and their love, fields where he had known hunger and grown to hate it as he would never have the force to hate anything again.

He snipped the long untidy wick of the candle to make it burn less quickly and went slowly for a neighbour.

The Leafless Land

I t is no wonder that I turn pale at just the mention of love. When passion comes my way no luck ever comes with it. I understand that this caper goes smoothly with some boys and that they slip blandly into full knowledge and a satisfied middle age. But not I.

Just consider what happened to me in the matter of Caroline Pugh. Caroline is the daughter of Octavius Pugh. He's the element who cleans the Infants' School in Meadow Prospect. He is a very clean-looking man himself. He has very little hair and his head shines like a beacon after a bath, and he walks about mostly in a boiler-suit because he is a cleaner and never rests in keeping the school spotless. Until he came into my life by way of Caroline I didn't know that anyone could be called Octavius. It's a name that would make anybody bald and no doubt this Pugh has been troubled with his hair for that reason. Normally I'd be for anyone who works hard keeping down the dirt on this earth, but here I am formally hoping that Octavius Pugh has only seen the beginning of his worries. I even hope his head will fall out to keep his hair company.

I'd been courting Caroline for about a fortnight. She is the fat girl who stands in the back row of the altos in Saul Hopkins's choir. Her voice has always had the tone and volume of a good trumpet, but alongside Octavius she's a whisper. She's pretty short and ought really to be put to stand in the middle of the choir if Saul wanted the audience to have a decent view of her, but she's in the back so that the public will have her voice in smaller quantities.

I was meeting her twice a week. I met her by the Memorial Stone. Caroline is poor on slopes and is against mountain walks for that reason, so we walked along that lane which runs alongside the river. We could never walk very far even along that route because Caroline kept glancing over her shoulder as if she was being pursued, and she'd tell me what a brutal, ferocious nature her old man has even though he gets his living in a quiet place like a school. He's as down on carnality, it seems, as he is on dirt, and doesn't even wait to get into his boiler-suit to show his hatred of it. He's told her he'll brand her if he ever catches her with a boy or if she stays out later than eight. I don't know what this branding amounts to because my own line of trade is assistant carter in the Great Western Railway, but he also told her that he would probably be driven to kill the element he caught her with and I understood that part of it very well. I don't want to be killed, even for a very friendly girl like Caroline. I'm not for living eternally but I would like to get something back on my weekly contributions to the Social Insurance.

I found that eight o'clock rule a nuisance and a handicap. I'm no ram like most of the young voters who investigate the flesh around Meadow Prospect, but I'm all for being given a fair chance. I'm not bold with the girls. If I meet them at six I'm still awkward and in need of a lot of stoking up at eight. Besides, that lane by the river is very public. It's always full of elements who want it to be private, like courting couples and Thaddeus Nixon the Bazaar who owns it. I've never known a short stretch of earth better off for people who look at you as if they wish you were elsewhere on this planet. That didn't improve my method or my style of talk with Caroline because I'm sensitive of the eyes of voters to whom I am unwelcome. But Caroline, doing some of her best glancing over the shoulder to give the remark force, said that this lane was the one place in Meadow Prospect where her old man was never likely to be because he can't stand the smell of the river which isn't clean, not by his standard. I saw the point of that and thanked the river for having that effect on Octavius.

All the same, I found that I could make no headway in the lane. So I forgot what Caroline had told me about her old man being a monster out to brand and kill and I said to hell with the lane, what about somewhere private where we can examine love's great climaxes without feeling in your ear every whipstitch the elbow of some voter who is out on the same programme as yourself in the crowded bushes of that riverside path. Caroline got frightened and repeated, half singing her words in her heavy alto to deepen the effect, what she had told me earlier about the leanings of Octavius. She added that he now had rheumatism as well as a soured psyche and was feeling so much more savage as a result that he had got hold of one or two elements from the static section of the Ministry of Labour, who would never have any steady work to do again, to walk in front of him for small payments and let themselves be beaten senseless with a thick broom he carried with him.

It seems that Octavius, as cleaner of the Infants' School, has got even more brooms than inhibitions, and has one in particular which is as thick in the body as you or I and is very handy with it.

But I told Caroline, with a seam of despair in my voice that not even a daughter of Octavius Pugh could mistake, that I was sick and tired of that lane, of being stared at by everybody in Meadow Prospect who can still walk and take an interest in passion. There were voters with eyes that had been weakened by long years in the pit, and they had a way of coming very close to you to observe your every move, and in fairness to these boys who would have wasted a lot of fine curiosity on us I had to tell them that Caroline and I were just beginners and that the diploma-holders were further up the mountain.

And I found something about the smell of that river that cut the heart out of my desires, filled me with wry laments. It is surely one of the darkest rivers this side of that stream of Lethe of which I've heard in lectures at the Library and Institute, but if the voters of Lethe had put into their stream articles one half as strange as those I've seen floating in the Moody there would have been trouble in hell: cats, dogs, pigs, chickens, even, occasionally, a voter to improve the tone. Looking at the surface of that river, the imagination cannot be placid, cannot achieve the optimism without which you cannot feel that passion is worth all the gonads you are going to burn black for its sake.

I told Caroline that if I couldn't find a place where we could get closer I would shortly be throwing myself in with the other articles in the river, and floating down to the sea and glad to go. I suggested the covered playground of the Infants' School. You can't get wet there and it's near her house. She went pale, fingering her beads. She said that her old man actually lurks there with the express intention of surprising courting couples. He catches quite a few during the rainy season, which is endless in Meadow Prospect, she said, and he keeps himself almost fit laying about them with his broom, the thick one.

I grew tired of the tremor in her voice, thinking that she might have contracted some of her old man's distaste for adventures in affection. I told her that she must be wrong about Octavius, that nobody could be such an ogre as she had painted him unless he is being especially paid by the government to find new ways of putting human charity out for the count. She asked whose old man was he, anyway. But I kept arguing, and my best argument was that if Octavius was suffering with the rheums as she had said then he would be in no fit state for lurking and beating lovers numb. I added, seeing her look doubtful, that if she did not see things my way I would soon get so sick of being marched up and down that riverside path and driven into fits of the shakes by a twisted libido and that river's mocking smell I would probably up and join the Singing Apostles, a new and noisy sect that had just set up among us.

So, very sadly, as if she were telling me goodbye, she said all right, we would go to the covered playground. She said on the way there that she hoped I would still recognise her and still love her after her old man had given her the brand and I, eager not to have her change her mind, said I certainly would, if I were still alive to do the loving. On our way to the playground I took Caroline so fast along the river path that a lot of voters thought there must be a flood and followed us.

We found it very dark and cosy in the playground. It's well covered. It's covered with the whole Infants' School. This playground is really a sort of cellar with great red-brick pillars at the entrance which would give thoughts of the tomb to any element who was not approaching it with his mind full of love lyrics and a mania to know what things life keeps hidden. It must be a fine place for love for those boys who know how to go about it, and when the flag goes up over the Infants' School which will announce that Octavius is well over Jordan I'm going to advise my friends to try it. It's as cosy as most kitchens and has fewer beetles and voters interested in the rent walking in and out.

In the darkness Caroline and I made good headway. She was

in fine trim after all those weeks of walking about. Saul
Hopkins's choir was also in dock until the next autumn and she
did not have that to work off her strength on. Naturally, being
cautious, I left off kissing Caroline every so often to cock my ear
and listen for signs of Pugh. Caroline said that in that dark blue
boiler-suit of his, which is big enough for Pugh to let himself
down into it completely and hide his face, he might be any one of
the many shadows around us. This gave me a creepy feeling at
first, thinking it would be a pity to be struck down now that I was
getting to know Caroline so well. And on the whole I don't get
much fun as an assistant carter with the Great Western Railway,
sitting behind horses most of the day and talking with my mate
Theodore Clapp, who has been on the cart longer than I and has
come to see the whole of life as the back of a horse.

But for all my caution and vigilance I heard nothing. I told
Caroline it would not surprise me to find that her old man had
gone along to listen to those boys who talk very persuasively in
the Discussion Group at the Library and Institute, and been
made to see the folly of all violence and the rightness of love, even
the clumsy brand for which we were now holding up the flag in
the covered playground. I returned to the work, full of bliss and
vigour. Tonight, I said to myself, I am going to know all, all the
mystery I will know for sure, as sure as I know my name and the
pattern of the great hills around Meadow Prospect.

I was aching all over to know the whole truth and I groaned
every so often to show Caroline how I felt, for I was still too shy
to utter the words that echo the groans in the heart of a man.
Every time I groaned, Caroline jumped, thinking that it was
Octavius starting to roar and tensing himself for a spring. So I
gave up the groaning and followed a quieter policy, because
Caroline is not a small girl and her jumps, even the coy ones,
were never dainty. And all the time I was muttering into my
mind like a prayer that between now and eight o'clock I was
going to know all, that all the vagrant, tantalising hints were
going to be embodied into a solid, single revelation.

After a while I gave up holding Caroline around the waist.
That struck me as being a very simple manoueuvre and, in action
with a major frame like Caroline's, tiring. I dropped my arms to
my side, partly to relax the muscles, partly in a spirit of rough

experiment. I let my hand swing about. Suddenly I found my hand full of some object that was damp and full of strands. The lips of my brain formed around a loud hosannah and I broke out into an awful sweat. I said, "Jesus, Caroline, Jesus." I was speaking in an awesome whisper. I felt the thing tenderly again and it felt like the head of a mop. I whispered "Jesus" again and asked in an even quieter voice, "What is this, my love?"

"What is what?"

"This, Caroline, this," I said, and worked my fingers around the strands at greater speed. Bombshells of excitement were going off every second within me. I couldn't talk. Caroline could feel me wriggling about and asked what the hell was the matter with me.

Then I found a kind of pole attached to the article in my hand. I was just going to blurt out that this was stranger than anything I had ever anticipated, even after those amazing talks I had had about the secrets of nature with Theodore Clapp on the cart. But on the instant I felt very puzzled and remained silent. I thought that if this thing I was fingering felt like a mop-head and it is attached to a pole, then it is a good bet that the article will turn out to be a mop.

These simple bits of thinking can have a terrible quality at moments like those. Your mind spring-cleans. I sweated some more and then I asked myself, and I asked Caroline too, to ease my solitude, where the hell this mop could be coming from. I looked hard into the dark.

Then I heard a loud shout, and it sounded more like thunder than a human voice ever will again, on account of the covered playground being like a cellar and I like a well-stretched eardrum from tip to toe. A match was struck and there, crouching six feet away from me, holding this mop in front of him like a fishing rod, with a crazed look on his face or as much as I can see of his face over the collar of his boiler-suit which comes up to the base of his nose, was Octavius Pugh.

At first I thought I was paralysed, because I couldn't move. Then I knew I was paralysed because Octavius had caught me a homer with the head of the mop and it landed on some nerve in the back of my neck which took all the feeling away from me. Later I was glad of that because Octavius fetched me about five

more whacks, and he would have kept it up for the rest of the
evening if the head of the mop had not sprung off and gone
rolling away into the gloom of the playground. Although half-
paralysed and desperate, I bent down and helped Octavius look
for it, even enquiring about his rheumatism and inhibitions
when our heads came close in the course of groping. I did that
because boys like Milton Nicholas who try to improve our social
thinking down at the Institute tell me that however black the
immediate outlook the conciliatory approach is the only thing
that promises an improved species.

Octavius went off without finding the head of the mop and I
wondered for a moment whether it might not be lodged in some
part of me where it didn't show. I tried to steady Caroline who
was shaking like a jelly and assured her that my arguments must
have made a deep impression on Octavius to send him shooting
off like that. I said it wouldn't surprise me if he came back not
merely with apologies but with sandwiches and a cup of beef-
extract which is good to sustain the careless fervour of youth.

Caroline peered into the dark and her jaw dropped. The light
in her eyes and the breath from her mouth poached my whole
head like an egg. For a moment I was glad to have the hot,
yearning, terrified thing harden into an insensible detachment
there in that pitch-black corner. Then she gave me a push that
nearly finished off the job that her father had begun of making
me senseless. I got to the main gate only a few yards ahead of the
thick broom which Octavius had gone back to the house to fetch.
The mop, I learned later, had been a mere whimsy, the gesture of
a man whose fingers have become delicate at the job of
tormenting the life-urge.

Caroline says that I might as well join the Singing Apostles
who get to look blither every week. But no. For every voter, even
Octavius Pugh, there is a road back to enchantment and serenity.
To despair of helping him find it, that is death.

Myself My Desert

I am a surprised man. I am nearly old and I find the world full of work, worry, cloud. It seems only the briefest time ago I was putting up defences, barricades high as hope can sing, against these very things, but here they are, in possession, moving among my ruins with horrible quietness, picking up the scraps, glinting, gold-veined scraps of what used to be me and they laugh as they look. I am no new joke to them. But I am to me and I wish I could laugh, too, but I cannot. I know now that to live is only gradually to become, in ways and looks, part of the earth that only lets you go for a little canter and is waiting like a lusting thing to be on top of you again, stopping up your laugh, your groan and all your foolery of seeking food and sureness in a slipping, fruitless wilderness; of clutching fear's hand in the dark you share and bawling lullabies to make it sleep that sound so loud they keep the world awake and finding, when you take the trouble to glance, that your hand has gone and the hand you clutched is now your own. It looks alien and feels dead because it is yours and yet not yours. Even as you stretch it out to caress the heart of one you wish to love it edges back with crook-fingered irony at your throat to teach you that love and even simple quietude quickly wither from a life made solitary, sour and spoiled by the kind of anxious, servile groping in which I have long served an apprenticeship and have now gained my master's ticket. I am the most mature groper in Meadow Prospect and children are told by their parents to stand back when I pass and give my worries a nice long swing. I also run a sick club and benefit society for dead serfs who whisper questions to me every Friday night about how things have been since Wat Tyler's day and to thank me for all the good welfare work I am doing on their behalf, for they tell me that after lives like theirs, their ache is

60

everlasting and they are never healed, not even by centuries of apology from death. My dreads are now so broad in the bottom and swift in the wheel I am allowed to wear a badge like a busman and take on passengers at agreed stops along the roads of Meadow Prospect.

We grow, as we live, to be more and more like the earth in ways and looks. I see, in me and the mass of men around me who have been pulled miles out of shape and plumb by work, rent, kids, pain and the whole battery of antics that have been thought up to make the world unpopular and dangerous in its dirtiness to all the space and stars that envelop it; I can see the greyness of dust and hear in the words they speak, to make a spit of protest against the grip they writhe in, the hugely daft and meaningless motion of the wind itself. We are the wind in our self-made Autumn that strips us of its last leaves of wanting the tree of our hurt, expectant essence which stands out, sharply and darkly desolate, against the momentarily gleaming nadir of some not forgettable longing. We slip eagerly into an unchanging mood of dusk from which certainty is banished with a curse, where the man who comes round with pencil and book to collect something on the back-payments and the official who calls in, in times of distress, to see if we are still poor enough to be receiving the Social Insurance will not be too unlike the brother who might one day find his way to our cavern to put his fingers on our sores and dip us into the gold of a singing freedom and a wantless peace.

Milton Nicholas, a young rebel of Meadow Prospect and a wise boy who seems to be kept as busy and worried by hope as I am by a kitchenful of kids and an intolerant wife, tells me he is astonished to find so mature a voter as I, a man who has been kicked so often in the teeth he now holds a spare set at the side of his head to fool the boot, who has spent so much time in and out of the mill he has had three lots of thanks and a bonus bag of old husks from the miller, believing in any notion so childish as this of a brother who will come around knocking, dipping and curing thirteen to the dozen. I admit this brother will need eyes like a lynx, lungs like that gigantic tenor Teilo Watts, who only needs to breathe when he wants to put out the lights, and plenty of help from the Ministry of Labour to find his way in so dark, hilly and redundant a place as Meadow Prospect. But I am tired. I want to be childish for a change. If this notion will make a fool of me, well, I will go the whole hog and be made a fool of. I do not mind being deceived, it is better than being earnest, toilsome, fertile, bothered, leaked on by age-sick roofs. In a world so full of men who hurt the truth and get paid at so much for every groan we hear coming from it, it is a pleasant and dignified thing to spend some time at home making your very own lies for your very own bemusement.

We are ourselves, says Milton, our ill and healer, and he paints a picture of us cutting and bandaging the self same limb like that of Ambrose Josephs the Ambulance who did himself great damage to have things to practice on when he was preparing for a first-aid competition and nearly went mad with worry when he found he had worked himself into a fit and could not call upon himself to apply the cure and the special grip he had rehearsed for just this occasion. To be ill and healer makes the whole business much too crowded. And I've already got to jump on to the window ledge of the kitchen and stay there when my kids are all in at the same time if I want to get out of the place unbruised. The brother will come, will have to come for I have spent too much time and talent in the wasting of my little wealth to play any part in its redemption. When he comes, he will be me, of course. Me, with nicer hair, a cleaner shirt, a body straighter and nearer beauty, not as stupid or dirigible as I, shorn of my fear, weakness and shabby littleness, I in my tiny and exultant moods of effective love. I as I would be in a world whose ears were open to my voice, whose heart was open to my pity. And I feel this brother when he sat down over a plate of chips would tell me what an understanding face I had, what troubles he had had with rent and work and kids in the days before he got his green card from the Ministry that led him to this steady work as a brother. So there's hope for me. I keep the light of this odd and nearly comical belief flickering in a corner less to keep me warm than to give my fine team of shadows a sense of competition and responsibility. When they see the flicker, the jealous doubling of their blackness is a beautiful thing to see.

I should, by right, have done something dramatic and ringing to show my anger at the forces that have led me, quietly and cleverly, to stand like a breathless buffoon gutted of his little bardry, in a patch of scrub sandy with issue and my powdered rock. Had there been the slightest sign of love or even zealous hate in the fingers that have pinched me to my mean and meagre shape, mine would have been a less acrid aloneness, but they have gone about their work with the bored, unhurried malice of the rain that comes slipping in mist form from the hills. I have been kippered without fuss and that is as little good for the mind as for the entrails. But that notion of a dramatic and ringing protest has haunted me. The materials of agreeable drama, however, are few in Meadow Prospect, few and small, to be sought only in darkling corners and on all-fours, a position that gets you locked up on an indecent hints charge in less than no time at all. And to work up a passionate chime in any key means slapping your head against a strong wall and that means you are both audience and performer for there is no way of making public the twanging agony of your skull bone. Then there is religion which many boys in the Meadow wear like a low bowler of pure flame around their heads. I tried it once, but whenever I talk to the world about me or my soul or the darkness, dressed, astounding, itchy, that is pressed between my scalp and toes, I begin to smile and laugh, then shriek with a sense of tininess and fragility — and that has made me unpopular with all sects, who have now put me down as a pagan maniac not to be trusted with the mysteries. Then there is drink. I know many in Meadow Prospect who have worn a good inch from the sill of each and every ale house in the district without getting any shorter or wiser themselves (and the lack of wisdom is a golden and blessed thing), whose lives are a dun, soft, unangry marsh. Tread on them, and in moods of desperate questing after fun I have trod on them, and there is only a squeal, simply a squelching squeal that goes clean back to the first stir of life, when things must have been rarer and easier. They have been shorn of all the symphonic, artfully articulated anguish that makes such resounding jests of you and me. Still, I have been tempted, on this night of revel and that, to meditate over the beer upon the roundness of my peg, the squareness of my hole, and the swiftly wasted brevity of me, to stand, at the full, pulling the tide of passionate wishing to rattle in the pebbles. That at times would have been good, but beer costs much money and had I done so, my many kids would have looked at me even more closely than they do now and I am afraid of other people's eyes, especially when they are trying to burrow their way to the very core of my strangeness.

Instead, I have chosen a cheap and easy goal for all my dreams. I have stuck my head far into a comfortable cavern of crook books, books, for choice, where the thieves and murderers are not caught. I like to think of this mad, brutal margin where the laws of my own subservience and helplessness are kicked into the bin. It makes less tormenting the itch of precariousness set up in me by the threat of men's regulations and the space of emptiness and death that stands guard with sightless diligence over those regulations. It is good for me to read of the antics of these boys who burgle and butcher with more confidence and profit than I labour and receive my wages. On days of little cheer when the wind of thought is cold and I am bare I hold these outlaws and myself up to a strong light and wonder which of us is dream and which nightmare. In the flurry of doubt which follows, I feel less menaced, less doomed to be forever a target for anyone who has the impudence to knock upon my door or upon my head. So, I am never without one of the books. My eyes are off their pages only when I sleep or am actually engaged on the work of digging and hauling for which I am paid. If by chance or through weariness I sit down and am content to sit, unreading, and if then I feel on my neck the wheezing cough of some fear about food, furniture, kids or death, I whip out my thriller like a gun, put it to my brain and blow it out. In a second I am as dead to reality as I might have been if my father had been a monk or not interested.

These days I get a lot of chance to read. I am one of a gang of road-menders who are at work on a mountain road which links Meadow Prospect with a town in the next valley westward. Up on the mountain we seem to be in a place where the rain trains for all the falling and driving it does elsewhere. When it rains we have a rough shelter of tin sheeting and sacking where we sit and wait for the rain or us to pass. We drink tea, sleep or talk; only I read. My friend, Milton Nicholas, who is also a member of this platoon of roadworkers, looks with disgust at the covers of these books I read. I cannot make Milton understand my feelings about life and he is always trying to draw me into arguments about the meaning of living and the mission of humanity. These arguments fill me with the same choking sadness that I feel after a session of dodging and quibbling with Redvers Rees the Rent, the boy who acts as agent for the property owners of Meadow Prospect. Milton, Redvers and I are on different stars, bawling at each other and giving an ache to space.

Milton says these books I read are a blow to the mind of the working masses. Milton has a long catalogue of things which he makes out to be blows to the mind of the working masses and when I told him one day as far as I could see the working masses must be one solid bruise from ear to ear he said of course and warned me to watch out for the deep shades of black and blue on the average thought. There is only one way to trip up Milton Nicholas. Two trees, a length of wire, a dark night, Milton half-blind, and a good push. His mind has sure, bitter feet.

Take this morning. The rain was not actually falling but plastering the miles of mountain top with a mist to have something soft and quiet to fall on. We could not work. There was no sound in the shelter except the sound that is always coming from Theo Gummer the Hummer who is always humming to himself slow Welsh folk songs as if he is applying the cool moss of their sadness to his heart to keep the heat from withering the savage anger that blazes in his eyes. Theo is like Milton in many ways and would like to see humanity stooped double under a pack of progressive purposes, but he talks about it less than Milton. His tactic is humming. I was in a corner reading a new fourpenny I had just bought about a crook called the Cobra who is just like a snake, only upright. I was enjoying this book and in the little space of mind behind the belt where I was sorting out the details of the plot, I was imagining to myself with what a nice swing things would go if I could be a bit like this Cobra myself, watch in the bedroom window for the approach of Redvers Rees the Rent, nip down at his knock and amaze him on opening with my full suit of stripes and a length of fang that would soon have him swollen, black and beyond the need to worry on behalf of the property owners. From another corner Milton Nicholas was giving me the full beam of his earnest, searching eyes. Theo poked his head through the shelter to make a report on the weather. He told us that the mist was thickening to a whiteness that would soon have us outside the shelter guiding the rain to earth and sending rockets up to ask Meadow Prospect for a good reason to explain why we should be fooling about on the mountain at all. Then Theo began to hum much louder than usual, a sign that he had just thought of another way in which the world could be touched up. The hum sounded too loud between the sheets of tin.

"Shut up, Theo," I said. "You're putting me off reading, boyo, and this story's got me gripped." Theo stopped. He could see from the sombre look on my face, and the way in which I tapped my finger on the page that I was in earnest. "He's going to strike again."

"Who's going to strike?" asked Milton. "What is the issue of this strike? Who's striking against whom? Are the union officials in favour of this strike?"

"You've got unions on the brain, Milton," I said. "I mean the Cobra's going to strike."

"Who the hell is the Cobra?"

"He's the bloke in this book, a crook. He's fitted up with a forked tongue and he hisses every time he kills anybody. That's why they call him the Cobra."

"That's as good a reason as any. And is all that in the book you're reading?"

"All here. He's just going out on a job now on this page. He's in his bedroom practising his hiss."

"His what?"

"His hiss. That's his kind of trade mark."

"Such books, Adam," said Milton, "are the greatest blow of all to the mind of the working masses." Milton fell silent, thinking out a new list of appeals with echoes of a pitch that would shatter my stillness. While he was silent, I thought of my name, Adam. In a place like Meadow Prospect where there is still a lot of talk about Eden and its advantages, such a name makes a man feel older than hell, and that does not help. Then Milton started again: "No doubt, the boy who makes up these stories about the Cobra has now been made a lord or something for converting his millionth wage earner to being an idiot full time. It used to be revivals that made people start to drivel, go blank in the brain and turn their back on thought and conflict.

Now it's these dreadfuls, these thriller books. Seems to me a great waste of time for anybody with any sense keeping alive in the face of such opposition. When such books as this Cobra article go out of date they'll have thought up some new kind of religion to revive people with. You read any more of those books with a few characters only a bit richer than the bloke you're reading now and you'll be turning up to work with short trousers and an application to the Council for a rubber comforter of a size to fit a man's mouth and a child's mind. There are revolutions and wars, not to mention some old-established capers as hunger going on around you like a wonderful bloody circus and you go roasting your wits away with the antics of this coot who stands hissing in a bedroom. I bet he was a revivalist in the old days, that Cobra. He probably found it was healthier to go out and kill people outright than to delude them at so much an hour in mission tents which is long and drafty work. I can see the Chamber of Trade lining up to present this Cobra with the forked tongue they rushed to buy cost-price as soon as they heard he was giving up preaching, giving it to him with full fuss and ceremony wrapped in a hand-bill which tells him of the poisons he can get cut-rate through them once he gets launched on the job."

I did not say anything. I am always crouched on the slender butt-end of silence, hanging on. I can never find anything to say to Milton. He is in no phase near to me. The very notion of farness must have arisen from a mind that was looking at another mind. The stars themselves might be the minds of over-bright men still twinkling away at the old and ashen game of self-communication and being edged further into endlessness and damned with a deeper sense of distance for all their efforts. When Milton and I try to talk, the long-dead and the unborn mouth at each other through glass. Before beginning to read again, I was tempted with a virgin impulse that brought me pain to argue the toss with him. For all his gab, I meant to say, I did not see him earning anything near as much as the Cobra, who made about a million pounds from the three voters he left writhing in the first five pages. Before I had finished the sentence, Milton would have replied that with conditions as they are in the road-mending trade he would never earn anything near as much as the average grass-snake provided it had the right outlook, the right accent, and a way of getting in and out of people's pockets.

So I said nothing and placed my eyes squarely on my book. I want to be left alone to read as much as I want to. Two years ago last April I scratched out my last hair with worry. I have a chalk mark on the bedroom floor to show the very spot where it landed and a chalk mark on my head to show the very spot where it took off. Since then my head has provided Milton Nicholas with his one and only joke: that when he sees me with my cap off he does not know whether he's talking to Adam or the apple. This is not much of a joke, but for a grim lad like Milton, laughterless and top heavy with ideals, it is a start and with watering of a patient sympathy might turn out to be the first shoot of a creeper. And after my own hair went I took to scratching my wife's and that drove her to wearing a thick hat, her thickest with a double lining of felt, asleep and awake. There is nothing like wearing a thick hat, especially when lying down, to make a person take a harsh and joyless view of life. So to hell with worry, I say. What good is it to live if you are crying your eyes out all the time over people hungry, people dying, people in debt, people caught and spun to a sickened dumbness in a back-cracking wave of unfathomable woe? When your crying is done and your eyes are out they are pecked at, stuffed without avail into the thousandth part of one man's hunger and forgotten. Leave me on my shadowed edge with my grinning comrades who help themselves to the wealth and life of others. They restore part of the balance of dignity I betray. I dream that one day I will have their gift of daftly simple and unbruisable assertion, a fugitive from all pity and feeling. I dream that, and feel my hand tremble and my chest contract as I hear outside the footsteps of some policeman who might be coming to tell me of some fresh and fineable little trespass committed by one of my kids, the rap upon the door of Redvers Rees come to tell me the latest dodge whereby the rent has been hoisted up a peg or two. I am a wingless and sitting target. No praise or knighthood should be given to a man who settles for me in the end.

And I dream, too, of the brother who is I, who will never come because he is, as I am, lost and terribly afraid to be found.

The Couch, My Friend, is Cold

I am not bothered any more by the business of passion. Once I was like a dog lost in great spaces seeking an end of this caper. I aimed to serve all the women in the world as combined minstrel and mat, taking in the whole body of maidens in Meadow Prospect, the town I live in, as a practice canter. That is a silly mood, a silly wish. It is neither healthy, allowed or possible to cover so much ground.

I've got over that longing now. If a man has a sense of proportion and direction he can deck his life out with some nice shades with just one maiden. I'm engaged now, I'm courting steadily. I'm sparking that lean, white-skinned girl, Vera Fisher, who won the crooning contest down at the Coliseum Cinema two years ago.

The Col is the biggest cinema in Meadow Prospect but it is rough. There's so little air there the people take turns at breathing. A man stands at the end of your row and lifts his arm up high when it's your turn to stop choking and breathe in. It isn't clean either. When you get tired of scratching yourself, the boy at the end of the row, who acts like a kind of captain, gives another sign and all start scratching the voters in front and this makes a nice change and creates hundreds of fresh friendships because you can't really be surly or standoffish with somebody who's struggling to get his hand down your collar and do you a good turn.

Another thing about the voters and their kids who go to the Col is that they are always hungry and bringing out stuff to eat; whole loaves and swedes and things like that. They are friendly about this, too. You can eat three to a loaf but no more than two to a swede, because they say this makes too much noise, and when such a racket is being made you cannot hear the dialogue of

69

the people on the screen unless you've got your ear in the loudspeaker or somebody at your side, who's seen the picture before, can tell you what's going on.

That's the place where Vera won the crooning contest. She hasn't got a very strong voice and doesn't sound as good in public as she does in her own front room, where she and I do most of our sparking. And the night of the contest, especially when Vera who was the last competitor came on, the hunger of the people reached a top note. Between the munching of bread, the crunching of the swedes, and the remarks of the people who were lending these articles or stealing a bite, the noise was so great I had to put my ear on the floor-boards of the stage, and even Vera had to clap her hand over her own ear to get the drift of her song.

What swung the prize her way was her father, Horace Fisher. Horace is the man who stands in front of the Col and shouts the name of the picture that is on. He also acts as a thrower-out, and if anyone down in the threepennies where the going is hard, gets killed, Horace goes down and cautions the guilty party and threatens him that if this kind of antic goes on the party will be put out and refused admittance in future. Horace is a short man but he has a fierce, fighting way with him that has cut down crime in the threepennies to such simple acts as climbing in through the roof without a ticket, and taking the plush seat with them when they leave the hall.

When Vera was singing, Horace stood in the wings of the stage working up a glare in his eyes and fixing it straight on Mathew Russell Upper Register, who is called that because he is the best sotto voce or head voice in Meadow Prospect. Mathew was the judge that night. He is a weak, nervous man and dreads people like Horace Fisher, whose hatred and arms flash out like lightning around them.

Mathew could not hear a note of Vera's song. He was in the second row and every time he leaned forward to hear better his curls tickled the neck of the woman in front of him who went into a laughing shriek, then gave Mathew a fetcher with her hand and told him she was on to his games. At the end of Vera's song, Horace ran down to where Mathew was sitting and shouted at him in a menacing undeniable way, "She's a lark, Russell. She sang like a bloody lark, boy.'' Mathew, half stunned by the racket and the woman in front, smiled and gave Vera the prize without a struggle.

She's very soothing to me. When I'm worn out by my work for Hicks the Bricks, the contractor I work for, I lie back and she sings right into my ear such soft-sounding lyrics as 'Sleepy Time Down South', the very number she won the contest with and it always has a restoring effect on me.

So to all my friends and comrades I give this advice. Get engaged, boys, as soon as you get enough money together, and you find a girl who can do something more than giggle and give you an empty, used-up feeling between the ears. Somebody like Vera, a girl low-skulled and slow to think, who will understand nothing unless it is lowered with care and patience into her mind, but who will act as a lull, a pause of peace in the high winds we live among.

That's the recipe. No use lunging about with passion tall and multiple as the stars, looking in odd corners for the light of love in places where you know you won't find anything more than darkness in its darkest, bitterest forms and stuff for the ashman, especially in Meadow Prospect which is a well known place for ash.

Only rarely now, in moments made uneasy by the itch of weariness or wonder, do those broader longings of yesteryear, reaching out to the smallest further bits of beauty and fulfilment on the other side of the earth, blow along to make me feel tiny and a fool. Just a dipping touch of hand or voice from Vera and I lie still, in a tomb-like contentment. Sometimes when I talk in this way of maidens to boys I know in Meadow Prospect, I can see some of them edge away and look on me as jingles, a man of animal notions, for the preachers have wrapped a thick mantle of furtive shadows around the subject of maidens and the mantle is tight and bereft of buttons.

The average boy in search of passion in Meadow Prospect feels as if he's been forced to put on three full suits of winter woollens. Many of these boys are singers of religious songs in vestry choirs, and they have kept so far away from all soiled thoughts they have a waterproof certificate of purity from the Board of Trade wrapped around their heads. But they haven't developed yet. Wait until the old sap starts to rise and they find themselves in some dark corner with the feeling that nothing they'll ever say will ever be understood by anybody, just aching for somebody with a soft voice and a softer body to come along and reduce their talk to half, and tense them up to feeling that they are the only thing that counts this side of the Government.

They can put up as tall a barricade as they like of hymns and fears and dogs and pigeons, between themselves and the longing to find a stable for their passion, but soon or late they'll know that it is only in a maiden they will find anything silly, deep and utter enough for them to slap the face of death with, and make it feel mean and chastised like we do. They'll hate it in the nights when they get the notion that they're on their own in the world, that all the other people have just heard the sun and moon talking grimly of the last great blow-out to come, and crawled off somewhere to get their Insurance cards stamped up to date and be on the safe side.

It's terrible that, that waiting in solitude for the stars to come banging down from the sky and catch you in the soft part of your neck, especially for a wild, sensitive chap like me made raw by much thought and trouble. I feel things too clearly, like a blackboard that is being written on. That solitude again would kill me off like a fly.

I'm not saying that you should go about with a club or a regiment of maidens trailing at your heels. Just one will do. Find her, then do a day's work for a man like Hicks the Bricks, come back aching and wondering where you put your spine, then lie down in front of the parlour fire and have that maiden, in a voice like the thinnest silk, floating, twisting, crooning some number like 'Sleepy Time Down South' right in your ear. Time and sleep and silk, all done to a turn before the parlour fire, that's something worth getting up early and doing regular work for.

And then there are other boys who don't go much to chapel or sing in the vestry choir, who have no fears to speak of, who grow up full of pity for everybody, which is another kind of love again. It's a kind that does not take you so often to the same address as the kind I've been standing up for. The boy who's got the biggest load of this sort of love is my friend, Milton Nicholas, who gives more passion to any single thought than I do the whole being of

Vera Fisher.

Milton is not bothered by girls at all. Perhaps that is because the girls don't take to Milton. He goes about as often as not like a bit of the revolution that's been left out on the sill to cool and washed off by the rain, and looking as if he's just managing to hang on to his clothes in a wind, his features all grimaced up as if he's one of those blokes who drink Epsom for the fun of it.

If Milton was walking home with a maiden, and that could only be if they lived in the same direction and walked at the same pace, he would, no doubt, talk to her about the origin of evil. This would probably tire the maiden and put her right off Milton, even though Milt had spruced himself up to look handy for the occasion, because all this maiden would want is a good, long look at this origin and not to hear a lecture about it. A sample, then a talk about the history of the thing. That's the time table.

Milton is very stern about boys who give up most of their time to the passion of bodies, like me. He asks me every time he sees me, how does this Miss Vera Fisher compare with the good of man. Put like that, of course, Milton is right. I think a lot but I'm nowhere near as full of thought as he is. I'm not as stern. He has a big, dark head, broad enough to be an estuary for all the streams of grief that come flowing out of man. It's all right for him to say that songs like 'Sleepy Time Down South' are a bruising blow at the brains of the working masses. He's got his zeal and his knowledge to keep him warm.

I've got zeal, too, but I can't keep it up like Milton. The trade union sent Milton to college and ever since then he's been spreading more light than the gasworks with much less smell and cost. He's the tenderest man we'll ever see in this place. All the time he seems to be feeling all the pain of all the people around him. His insides must be bruised blue as if people were marching over them. His feelings are heavy shod and never rest.

That's the way he wants to be and that's the way he'll keep on being. And there are many men with hard and dirty minds who make his life a misery, who would subscribe out of their own tight pockets money enough to build a thick gaol for all such boys as Milton Nicholas, men like that bowler-hatted son of a bard, Mr Macwhirt, my foreman, hand-carved from the finest

73

teak and a prophet of class-divisions and longer working days. He's deaf as a post to all projects like the good of man. If he's heard of it at all, either he would wonder how much it would cost to build or he would consider it a threat to him and his bowler. If ever he saw the good of men he'd put it under his bed and take pleasure in lifting it from time to time so that it would have no chance of taking firm root. The more I think of Mr Macwhirt the more I feel like telling Milton to find himself a streetful of maidens, put his zeal and dreams in mothballs for about fifty years and give his passions the airing of the century. If he did that there'd be a lot more warmth for Milton and a lot less hope for me who lie down of an evening with Vera Fisher and watch the parlour fire as we weave our croonful fancies.

Yes, a lot less hope for me and all men like me.

Where My Dark Lover Lies

To be struck dumb, all of a sudden and in one's tracks, by a sense of this earth's sadness, that has always been my failing. "Rest and pay the thing the tribute it deserves." That is what my mind seemed to say. But since Morlais Moore is no longer with me to water with his words the deepest of my pensive roots I am less touchy and my feet have learned the trick of shuffling forward through the plush air of stupefaction, of giving an assurance to those around me that I am no less daftly and numbly enduring than they.

A grey little column of thoughtfulness was Morlais Moore, the tenderest thinker we had in all Windy Way where we lived. He moved serenely among us, pale and wonderfully comprehending, a brilliantly lit-up question mark which annoyed all such men as my father who watched life in a more cautious and recessive mood than Morlais. Upon his strict humanism and aloofness from the acts of prostrate worship which they loved they blamed nearly all our troubles, including the heavy rain which tormented our hills. My father was never slow to stand up prophetically and revile me when I came in late from a session of talk with Morlais and his friends at the Institute. He told me that the fluid of Morlais's soul was dark and mordant and I would find myself hollowed and unfit to prosper if I did not find myself a sweeter and simpler companion. But it was Morlais alone who redeemed those early days from a shapeless squalor, Morlais alone who made me dream of a time when the wind of some great dignity and purpose would fill the sails of all our being and make the planet seem less sullen and alien than it usually did from where we stood in Windy Way. I would have sworn that the soil of that loyalty could never be made barren. But it was; and the rapturous unity of days and senses, time and essence, that had grown from it was known to me no more.

There was a girl. As she walked through my life only to bear a wound her name and face are not to be recalled. It was on a fine June evening I found that she had vanished to London with a seducer of the first class from the next valley. That evening Morlais had asked me to come along to the Institute to hear him give a talk on the upward spiral of man's conflicts. But I was in no way to listen to anything as sane and reviving as Morlais's calm assertions of perfectibility. I went home.

My father was a noisy, distracted man with a fine edge to his manias that would bite into my distress and make it less. He was one of that numerous sect in Windy Way which claimed that a terrible rusting silence of contempt and uncharity creeps into life in proportion as man thickens his seam of bumptious aptitude. They fight against that silence by talking and thinking only in the most roaring tones. My father had also, to cut down still further any margin of mute unease in the life around him, obtained a gramophone that kept the house full of good sound. It was an instrument with a gigantic horn, bought out of the compensation for a leg smashed in the steelworks. All the records he had were of tenors. He had so many of them and played them so constantly I was alarmed when my own voice in due season dropped down into a splendid baritone fullness. I thought I was a freak and my friends had to assure me that my tone was as common as the upper register on which my father doted. That night of the love-betrayal, I found him sitting tearful beside his gramophone. The mechanism had snapped with age. In his grief he had broken several of his records and they were around him on the floor in a circle of brilliant blackness like the fragments of his own exploded mind. "Tell me if there is anything I can do to help you," I said with a tenderness towards him in my voice I had not used before. "And I'll do it."

He asked me to accompany him to a meeting held by that famous revivalist, Aaron Reed. I walked hesitantly along with him, for Morlais had told me often that Aaron Reed was a false one, a pain to life with the scalding urges of his soul-terror. But I was in a mood to be perverse. "Aaron will do us both the world of good," I said.

Aaron had planned a master stroke for that evening. Instead of addressing the people inside the chapel he asked them to congregate within the very precincts of the chapel graveyard. A small temporary platform had been erected for Aaron in a corner that caught the final downswill of evening light. Aaron was a man of flame. We may dispute about what fed his fire, but the flame was there, and the mark and the smell of charring stayed in the minds of all who heard him. His subject that night was the living and the dead. Aaron was against the living and, to show how full of hooded and sinister reservations he was towards those at present on earth, he addressed his remarks directly to the dead, on or near whom we were standing. He called upon them, whatever their state, to come and visit their loathsomeness upon the vile quick. A lot of people fled, thinking that Aaron was going too far. Others, alarmed by the intimate urgent note in Aaron's voice as he called upon the horde of disinterred avengers to split the corrupt earth and set to their task, pressed with agonized bodies upon the tombstones to keep the earth intact and the dead placid. But Aaron's words were just the wild apocalyptic meat my spirit asked, and I pushed these cravens away from their work of oppressing the helpless dead. I called upon Aaron's allies not to dawdle and shouted out my supporting plea that life with its short shirt of frayed acceptances be shamed and overthrown.

When they came back to their senses people crowded around me to compliment me on my trumpet of a voice, my spout of scalding prophecy. Aaron Reed himself was interested. He promoted a collection which was to pay my first year's expenses at a theological seminary with which he had a link. A month later I entered that place and was instantly oppressed by the narrow solemnity of its aim and method. My whole self split with thirst for the uproarious libertarianism I had known in Windy Way, at the side of Morlais Moore. Part of my thirst I slaked with ale, part with tears, I wrung the hand of the college's principal when he told me I was too fond of lying in simple rapture in the hedgerows of the Lord's highway to travel very far on the road itself. He asked me to go.

I returned to Windy Way after a spell of vagrant and manuring privations. I thought that I would rush at once to the dwelling of Morlais, enter into the cool chamber of his merciful wisdom and remain within it for ever. But I did not. Perhaps it was the look of lonely madness in my father's eyes asking me for companionship, some hint of stability in his crumbling dusk. Perhaps the seminary, idle and planless as my progress through it had seemed, had given my mind a crafty and opportunist slant, a vulgar hint of some inward power to be developed. I did not seek out Morlais. Once in a while I saw his eyes, already bright with the promise of that death which made brief work of him, search my face and heart as we passed in the street or in the portal of the Institute, but I made him no sign. There was something I wanted, some bit of crass immediate fulfilment which I knew I would never find in the shadow of Morlais.

I throve in the company of the pious, sustained by the colour and drama of their nimble propositions and massive yearnings. I kept company with Millicent, the daughter of Uriah Bagley, an undertaker of the place. Uriah foresaw a fine future for me in his trade, with the quick ripples of compassionate melancholy on my face and the cello-throb of sorrow in my voice. I needed only to learn the practical details of the craft and court Millicent without any trace of the goatish levity which Uriah claimed to have seen in my earlier phases. I agreed. This seemed the kind of harbourage I wanted and I entered into it with delight. The very night that Uriah told me that within a year he would admit me to full partnership I heard that Morlais was near to dying. I grinned into Uriah's face and gave Morlais not even the peel of a used thought.

Millicent and I did most of our earnest courting in a shed alongside Uriah's workshop. He was one of the most diligent providers the dead will ever have and he worked to all hours. Between the beat of my passion and Uriah's loving hammer-strokes I was hung on a rack of painful and complicated rhythms.

It was a soft day in autumn when I put on a black suit, a bowler and a winged collar to assist Uriah publicly for the first time. He said that since my initiation was to be gradual and easily digested, I was to see none of the preliminaries on this occasion but would meet the procession at the bottom of Windy Way, a short distance from the Black Meadow, our burying place. Also, he said he was choosing an inexpensive turn-out, of little moment, at which I would be able to question him at will about this detail of procedure and that.

The funeral was indeed meagre and there was as bleak a look on Uriah's face as I fell in at his side as there was on the black, rain-filled sky. The body was being borne along on a clumsy old-fashioned bier. I recognized two of the bearers. There was Edwin Pugh the Pang, called that for his way of wincing at any mention of the bruises sustained by our species in the cause of being so special. There was Teilo Dew the Doom, called that in tribute of the atrabilious visions of disaster and collapse that had eaten his mind hollow through the years of an underfed life. The whole procession struck me as eloquently quaint.

"Who is this?" I asked.

"That philosopher bloke from up Windy Way. Morlais Moore. Dies without a penny. A roomful of books but not a penny, not a decent death policy. Couldn't even afford the hearse. They made a collection."

And Uriah tapped his top hat in disgust. An oppression like black serge buttoned itself around my mind. I had always known that between myself and Morlais there would come another meeting, and I felt a great sap of significance rise in that moment. The pain must have overflowed in me and I was not surprised when I saw Uriah make a violent grimace, put his hands to his stomach and mutter something about the chronic gripe that always came down upon him when he saw death treated shabbily and without proper forethought. He asked me if I could see this business through to its end.

"Oh yes," I said. "To its end." And I could hear the words twist themselves into a frightening laughter down the endless corridors of my regret.

Uriah rushed off home. We reached the tall gates of the Black Meadow. They were locked. I beat upon them and called on whoever was within to open in the name of fate to which I now felt myself to be professionally affiliated. A man came excitedly along and told us there could be no burial. The chief caretaker, Wonno Slee, that very morning, after twenty years on the job, had been driven to hysteria and flight by the sight of so much quiet negation filing in through the main gate. An hour before he had been reported climactically drunk two valleys away, in a high pagan mood, waving the graveyard's keys in front of him and defying death to get into the Windy Way Black Meadow except over his dead body. As we were being told this, the clouds broke and the rain came solidly on us. We saw the point of Wonno Slee's despair and wished it a happy issue, but we were getting soaked.

Over the road was a tavern called The Rising Lark, kept by a prim performer called Mathew Studley. As we approached the doors Mathew stood there, his arms upraised and his mouth gaping, shocked that men who were supposed to be halfway through a solemnity should be jostling into an inn. He told us to go away. But my thoughts about Morlais were so tender and mad to kiss, coated with a fine fundamental flavour, that made my senses sing a dark alto lament, that I pushed Mathew to one side and told him not to be a discord. We left the bier and coffin in the shadow of the high walls of the Black Meadow entrance. We could see them, forlorn and dripping, through the window of the snug in which we took our seats.

We drank deep, more amused in a bitter and hurtful way with the passing of each pint by the clucks of dismay that came from Mathew Studley, and we warned him to be less of a trade-mark for man's wasteful fussiness. I stood up by the window and gazed through the curtain across the road. The rain was becoming more masterly and strong. I thought of the long winter days when the wicked misery of kindred storms had depressed me, yet exalted Morlais, for he would not allow even the antic twist of a private mood to debase the promise and value of life. As I stood there, Edwin Pugh told me, in a voice like a night-wind, of how much Morlais had missed me at the last going-off, of how I, with my special brand of big-eyed, sardonic wonder at the whole of being, had been the one thing able to move Morlais to a forgetting laughter. And all together, our reflections on how cheerless had been the life of Morlais Moore, crushed between the rock-faces of his and the world's distress, how without warmth, solace or crown, made us feel we would willingly have drunk on with no return to the bane of total awareness. And now he was there, abandoned, soaked, stared at through the streaming window of a hot inn parlour, denied admission even to the Black Meadow which is one place that should always be ready to find a spot for the badgered. The big fire in the snug thickened the gold of Studley's ale and wrought in us passionate liberality, a great raw material of love.

"Restitution," I said quietly into the plush curtains of the window. "What would the face of a full restitution in such lives as ours be like to look at?"

We grew reckless as we took the shroud off our regrets and timidities and told the things to dance and be at ease. I felt smoothly potent and effective. I sent Mathew Studley off on a false errand. Mathew had been conditioned to believe anybody in a winged collar and he swallowed whole my story of his brother in Windy Way who wanted urgently to see him. We slipped over the road and brought Morlais into the snug to share our exultant comradeship and comfort. We placed him out of sight beneath a bench and we were glad he was beyond consciousness, for he had always regarded drunkenness as a crude and pitiable manoeuvre. As the afternoon drew to a close, the boys invited me to deliver a final statement on life and death and the way they have of sliding up and down the torn hillsides, happy in their muck.

Then in rushed Studley, alight with rage, scorching our soft thoughtfulness. He bundled us out, threatening us with a spell in the County Keep, our gaol, if we did not instantly leave him in peace. He and his wife got us outside and bolted the door.

We argued to decide which of us should go back and tell Studley about Morlais. We all trembled as we talked because Studley is an austerely unprogressive man who had always regarded Morlais and his discontent as a pest, even when Morlais was alive and walking about Windy Way. What Studley would think now was enough to make us faint. Teilo Dew said that I, as Uriah Bagley's assistant and dressed up in such dark clothes, was the proper person to go. I took my collar off to show my neutrality as far as Bagley and ritual were concerned at that moment, and I told them it would drive me mad to have Studley's tidy little spear of rage tear into me after all the hymnal thoughts about Morlais that our minds and mouths had been singing. Edwin Pugh the Pang, who was still in tears, agreed with what I said and we decided to give the matter time. In whatever context, you could always rely on Edwin Pugh the Pang for this kindly, Fabian approach.

We picked up the bier and returned it cautiously to Uriah's warehouse. I went home and had a short nap, resolved on picking up the thread of my respectability, sitting upright in my chair and keeping my bowler on during the whole sleep so that my mind would not be too undisciplined even in dreams. Then I went to Bagley's house. I got Millicent by the fire and using a face and voice that had all the reds and browns of autumn in them I induced in her a mood of extra affection. When I was on the point of explaining to her about Wonno Slee, the rain, and what had happened in The Rising Lark, in came a small army of people led by Mathew Studley who was in a whiter heat of spite than before. He was followed by our largest policeman, known for his Prussian bearing and unfriendly helmet as Sewell the Spike. Studley spoke, stuffing so many vindictive words into a minute, the minute ached and sickened. He told how their domestic help, a woman of frail nerves and melancholy bent, had gone into the snug to do a little cleaning before the evening session and had moved the bench to get her feather duster to work. She had seen Morlais and had needed two shillings' worth of brandy to get her in motion again. I tried to explain about the cold and the rain, the empty draughty chamber of living in which Morlais had spent his days, of how we had been trapped by the wild rapture of a moment to make him that last foolish brotherly gesture. But my voice was a faint indistinguishable stand in all that hubbub. Spite was on a rich pasture and in no hurry. A fence of small, pitiless men were closing in on me. Through the slipping shadows of my panic and disgust I could see the wise face of Morlais with all its death-proof mercy and hopefulness, and I was about to bawl at all these people to be silent, be silent, silent.

But Uriah Bagley, whose face had now lost its first sheen of anger and gone over altogether to cunning, said he could explain the whole matter. Studley, winking at Sewell in his excitement and warning him to keep his manacles handy, dared him to do so and added a guess that it was I who had persuaded both Slee and Bagley to promote this phase of frenzy and irreverence into the graveyard trade.

Uriah brushed Studley aside and asked them to recall how full of contempt Morlais had always been towards those who make their peace with the harmless flaws of our social living, who look out for themselves and get on. They all said yes. Even I said yes, plucking at the festering splinters of things unsaid that pained between my heart and throat. "Remember the frown he gave my prospective son-in-law, Waldo Phelps, when Waldo here showed signs of settling down with my daughter Millicent in a responsible trade. But even in death Morlais was out to push his malicious destructive fist through the lives of others. No doubt he gave testamentary instructions to those two other querulous social moles, Pugh and Dew, to set this afternoon's events in motion. Slee was snared into dereliction. The body was misdirected into The Rising Lark and the stage was set for Waldo Phelps to be denounced as no fit man to be an undertaker's assistant. But we see through his design. We are not going to be ruffled." Uriah grasped Studley by his collar and was shouting desperately into his ear as if telling him to move up on the last raft. "We will not play into the hands of Morlais Moore. We are not going to be ruffled. Tomorrow, Waldo will again supervise the interment of this cantankerous misfit and there will be no mishap, will there, Waldo? The earth with dignity and peace will claim its own, won't it, Waldo?"

I shifted my eyes from the peremptory blaze of Uriah's eyes, I tried to close my ears to the pleading suggestive moaning of Millicent. Then the underpinnings of my grief and wrath collapsed. I smiled and said yes, yes, yes, wanting to build my rickety bridge of affirmations into an utterly thoughtless, hurtless land.

And ever since then, the soil of me has been at peace, its furrows tidy, its crops regular and far. But I have not been able to hear, see or feel the beating rain without having my secret core contract in a wince of disquietude, knowing myself for hours on end to be shrunken and betrayed.

Violence and the Big Male Voice

Life is, among other things, a sculptor, and a pretty one-eyed performer at the craft. It is astonishing the number of people, responsive to the thrust of suggestion, who walk about fingered and squeezed into shapes they never intended to have. When we were discussing, in Tasso's Coffee Tavern, at the bottom of Windy Way, who was the most savagely and untidily sculpted human being we knew, we decided the vote went to Marty Moore.

Marty was a good fourteen stone, soft as an old pear to the touch of other people's wishes. He was gentle, dangerously so in a world so full of assertive nuisances. We met him for the first time when he was about seventeen. Already he was broad as a fireplace, large-headed, curly-haired and always smiling.

His voice had just come back to wholeness after a rough passage into manhood and he was eager to try it out on somebody. His parents were an old, weary duo who had had Marty too late in life, and who had no time for music; they told Marty to air his strong baritone voice well out of earshot. So he joined our glee-group, the Aeolians, and his voice stood out even against that bed of bass-velvet. Our conductor, Lucknow Lewis, a close man who never gave much away except the beat, became very fond of Marty and was known to offer him some of his very best cough-drops.

All might have gone well with Marty if he had stuck with us in the Aeolians, draping his wits with the loose-fitting garments of such simple, sedative numbers as 'In the Sweet By and By'. But one Saturday night, returning from Birchtown where he had been giving a concert, Marty got into an argument about the technique of bass-singing with a member of the Meadow Prospect Orpheans, a dogmatic lot of voters. Before we could persuade Marty to let it drop, there he was in the middle of Meadow Prospect station, looking like Samson, scattering the boys from the Orpheans like chaff.

It so happened that our policeman, Lavernock Leyshon the Law, was nosing about there at the time. This was strange because we had an agreement with the station-master that if these Saturday night celebrations took place on his premises they would be staged after the last train had gone and that we would never throw each other onto the line where we might be a hindrance to the early morning milk-traffic. There was a further article in the pact, that we could carry our own wounded home without calling on the station's First Aid resources which were skimpy. But Lavernock Leyshon, holding his head well forward to give the silver spike on his helmet all the prominence he could, went up to Marty and put some special grip on him that had Marty looking up at us from between his legs and asking Leyshon for his spine back.

Leyshon put him into a corner and said that by right he should have Marty sent to the County Keep for rioting, but the Meadow Prospect Rugby Team, of which Leyshon was a member, was very short of good forwards that season. The very next Saturday Marty was wearing the jersey of the Meadow Prospect Vandals. He knew little of the rules and just waited for Leyshon to single out an opponent with a nod of his head; then Marty went in and drove the opponent nine or ten inches into the ground. If you have seen a Sultan and his personal strangler, but in striped jerseys and in the Celtic fringe, you would have an idea of how Marty and Leyshon looked in that setting.

As a popular Rugby player, Marty bloomed. We saw very little of him at the Aeolians. He became well-known at the flashier taverns and at that dance-hall, the Damascus, called that by its owner, Darwin Drew, to encourage a slinky Eastern type of movement among his clients. There Marty met Ursula Thowley, a girl of great beauty, a mistress of the tango and every other kind of rhythm that turns its back firmly on the Sunday School.

In her private moral habits she was, we were told, as loose and comfortable as an old shoe. We heard that Marty intended to marry her. We met him at Tasso's and advised him against this, trying to tell him as tactfully as we could that some years ago this Ursula, then in her very early teens, and her mother had got into trouble for using their house to run some branch of home-industry that was not allowed.

Marty, as innocent on these topics as a spaniel and just as merry, laughed, thinking that Mrs Thowley had probably been making mint toffee out of season. "I know what I want," he said, and about ten minutes later, being as slow a thinker as he was a talker, he added, "and if you elements don't mind your own business, I'll be clipping you with Tasso's tea urn."

As soon as Marty inherited the home in which his parents had lived, he got married. We wished him well but it would have taken a vow of pure steel applied sharply to the back of the neck to keep Ursula constant. We saw next to nothing of Marty. We heard that Ursula had quickly blunted the edge of her new discipline and was tormenting Marty for extra money, which she spent in a gay, eager rush.

Marty at this time was working in the Meadow Prospect saw-mills, a place that buzzed with saws and blinded with dust. There was not much chance of overtime there because the owner, Prospero Wilce, held cautious views about timber and man's lust to be killing and mutilating trees. We noticed Marty's movements becoming slow and clumsy. He no longer went with Ursula to dances. She said his steps had taken on a lurching quality which gave no joy to her or credit to the Damascus. One evening Marty came into Tasso's and said: "I'm getting my headaches again."

"What do you mean, again?"

"Didn't I tell you that as a kid I fell over that quarry up on Merlin's Brow?"

"No. You didn't tell us."

"Well, I did. I got headaches. They went. Now they're back. Sometimes in the day a red curtain comes down. Pure red. Terrible."

"You're worrying about something, boy. Don't worry." Even as we said that we realised that it was about the daftest advice you can give to any section of humanity which has a backbone of petrified anxieties.

Even so, things might have worked out for Marty if he had not decided to leave the saw-mills, to get away from the buzzing and the dust, and start work with a diligent but mean man called Tudwal Doodey, a carpenter and handyman, who had established a pretty profitable line in small contracting jobs.

Marty was never happy with Tudwal. He became more and more confused and torpid as the months went by and he found a diminishing peace with Ursula, who no longer tried to hide the dismay and impatience he caused in her. And when Ursula no longer wanted to hide something she made it plainer than the surrounding hills. Short of an explosion there was nothing we could think of less subtle than Ursula when she was trying to make a point. With Tudwal on one side and her on the other, Marty was like a bull in the last stages of its anguish, getting it in the neck with the lance, dart or sword whichever way he turned.

Willie Silcox, who was the best psychologist in our group and was for this reason called Silcox the Psyche, said that Tudwal, a quiet man though he was doing so well, had been in love with Ursula at the time when Marty married her, but Willie was always weaving this backcloth of dramatic situations to enrich the content of some current dilemma. Most of us felt that Tudwal had poured every drop of his small, creative sap into becoming a contractor. Whatever the truth of it, there was no doubt that Tudwal got a lot of happiness from denouncing Marty as hare-brained and oafish, and threatening him constantly with the poke.

One evening, returning home late from a house-repairing job, Marty found Ursula with a man. He took one look and left the house. He came down the hill to Tasso's. He sat among us, white as chalk, shaking his great curly head, his teeth chattering on the tea-cup we offered him.

"It was Peveril Pearce," he said, and then added matter-of-factly, as if for a few blessed seconds he had been able to stand away from the crude, hurtful impact of his discovery, "Peveril. He won the Darwin Drew Tango Cup at the Damascus last year. A very nice stepper, Peveril. He was there."

"What did you do?"

"Oh, nothing. Peveril is very small, very dapper. I didn't dare start on Peveril. I'd have killed him . . . him or Ursula . . .".

"Look, Marty, why don't you come back to the Aeolians?

We'll get Lucknow Lewis to let us sing nothing but old tunes. They'll take you back to when you were a kid. They'll give you a nice secure feeling, the sort you had when you could look forward to seeing Peveril Pearce doing nothing but the tango. Come back, boy."

"What for?"

"Because your mind is coming apart and that's a thing that's better kept in one piece."

"What are you talking about?"

"You, Marty. Why don't you come back to the Aeolians?"

"One of these days I will. Really I will. So long."

He left us, and our sad, pitying silence was broken by Willie Silcox opening a kind of book on the direction in which Marty's fury, blind now and ripe, a rate-payer at Gaza, a poor area, would explode. Many of us felt that Marty would wait outside the Damascus one night, get hold of Ursula and Peveril, and beat their brains out to the rhythm of some fast Latin-American item which Marty, in his gentle way, would recognise was the last thing Peveril would wish to hear on his outward trip.

But the storm broke in quite another direction. Four days after our talk at Tasso's, Tudwal and Marty both disappeared. Everybody could see the point of Marty's vanishing but Tudwal's case seemed more mysterious and sinister because he had always appeared satisfied with the little world of work and steady rewards he had made for himself in Windy Way.

The police examined the empty house in which Tudwal and Marty had just been finishing a long repair job and found nothing. Shortly afterwards the owner of the property sent in the Windy Way sweep, a swarthy little voter called Handel Hughes, and Handel went fairer than he had ever been before when he found that the obstruction against which his brushes kept colliding in the chimney was a pair of boots, Tudwal's, and Tudwal was still wearing them. After a bit more prodding by Handel Hughes, down came Tudwal, changed, dark and terrifying.

The police, and especially Leyshon the Law, gave a lot of thought to this. It was felt that Tudwal could hardly have got up the chimney himself. He was a man who had always liked a sombre, inhibited view of life, but not even Tudwal would have taken it as far as that. It was clear that he had been thrust up with great force.

Windy Way had been waiting for something like this to break the monotony which was dense in the area most of the year round. Posses of people poured into the hills to look for Marty. He was as well searched for as coal had been in the same territory over the last century. The general theory was that he had done away with himself after killing Tudwal, and there were several searchers who came within an ace of breaking their necks peering into the fissures that cracked their way across the dome of the mountains.

During this period we had some very interesting sessions at Tasso's. Handel Hughes the Flues, his hair greyed by shock and laundered by a rest from work, and shaking like an aspen, came to sit among us and we kept feeding him with so much free meat-extract to get his story from him in full he almost turned into a little column of beef before our eyes.

Towards the end of each evening, when we had lulled his nerves to rest and we had brought him to within about three twitches of normality, he would give demonstrations, speaking technically as a sweep, of the posture which had probably been adopted by the slayer when pushing Tudwal into his terrible tomb.

Ursula reacted excitedly to this. We felt that for the first time she was finding a rich significance in Marty. She took out the money from their joint account in the Post Office and did herself up in a mourning outfit of chiffon velvet which was the smoothest thing we had ever seen outside the more expensive marbles in the Black Meadow, our graveyard.

She walked about importantly in a veil, sighing on as loud a key as we ever used to sing on in the Aeolians. She also invited her mother, still a notorious element morally, to come and share her house with her.

We decided that we should make some formal recognition of Marty's non-appearance. We called in on Ursula to express our deep regret at the tragedy: Tudwal's death and, by implication, Marty's. Ursula greeted us in the house's middle room. She was dressed in her chiffon velvet, and each of us fingered it respectfully as we mumbled our condolences, for such bits of calculated loveliness are rarely encountered in Windy Way. Peveril Pearce was there, wearing a discreet pin-stripe suit and his sideburns an inch shorter to show decorum. He acted blandly as host, handing out sandwiches of cold meat and pickles and generally carrying on as if he thought a problem had been solved. Ursula's mother, a woman who always stood ready to nourish every situation with a greater willingness, had laid in a stock of beer and sherry-type wine and as the time went by she delivered her greetings to us all in turn on a conveyor-belt of welcoming winks.

Peveril put some dance records on the gramophone and as Ursula did not feel equal to going round with him, with us putting on choruses of compassion in every corner, he moved about the room on his own, his face brooding, amorous, his arms around an imaginary partner and making the late Valentino look, in this department, like a lout.

It was just as the record of 'Jealousy' was coming to an end that we heard a furious knocking at the back door. Ursula's mother opened it and in rushed Marty, his clothes torn and filthy with mud, his face wild and seamed with pain, his eyes streaming with tears.

He pitched into the food like an animal, trying to tell us, in a voice that whined in its agony, the story of his last quarrel with Tudwal, the hammer that seemed to fly from nowhere into his fingers, the magic that had brought Tudwal's head in front of him, and his crimson rebellion against every fence that had cut his legs on his walk across this earth.

The irruption was too sudden for Ursula. For a whole minute she kept hanging on to Marty and saying, "I'll stand by you, boy. I'll shield you, Marty. Why didn't you come to me in your trouble, Marty, boy?" Then her mother pulled at her and dug her knuckles into her. The sherry drained away, the lights on Ursula's inward stage were doused. She rushed from the house with Peveril at her heels to get in touch with Lavernock Leyshon the Law and have Marty removed to the County Keep.

Ursula finished the case off for Marty. Answering the suggestion that he had suffered from brain-lapses during which he had known very little of what he was doing, she said pertly that he had always been a bit daft, but he had always known what he was about. He had always given his brain plenty of time to catch up. Peveril smiled at us, as if he might have had something to do with the working out of these bright sayings that came out of Ursula, but at the sight of our faces he ceased to smile.

At the end of the trial's second day Marty was found guilty and the Judge ordered him, by way of the hangman, to be banished from this earth, which struck us as funny, for Windy Way was as much of the earth as Marty had ever known, and that is not much.

Two days before he was due to die there was a big night at the Damascus dance-hall. Ursula and Peveril were there and they grew fiercely, exultantly drunk. Ursula talked without pity of Marty, and as the other dancers realised that there was no dread or even sympathetic astonishment in her at what was going to happen to Marty, they drifted in muttering pairs out of the hall, leaving her alone with Peveril. If there were any anguish in her at all, it must have seamed in a desperate craziness, for she began to laugh in high, hysterically fluent phrases with every fresh reference by Peveril to her impending widowhood, the swift dissolution of her partnership with the quiet, puzzled Marty. Even Peveril was shocked. He sneaked away, leaving her alone, jigging round the empty hall to the rhythm of her own cracked merriment, with Darwin Drew, the owner, in his office, scribbling messages to be taken down by fast courier to Leyshon the Law, telling him to expect another coup.

The next day we had news of Marty's reprieve. The medical evidence had been re-examined and he was sentenced to detention in an asylum. And there he might have stayed if it had not been for his aunt, Matilda Mee. This Matilda was virtually a widow. Her husband was Melias Mee, a man of such unflagging insignificance he had once been brought to the attention of the government for putting the whole issue of human identity in peril. Matilda was so pious she kept snow fresh on her right into May. We often met her at Tasso's where she called in to buy a very strong brand of mint sweet, which she took for a state of growing dyspepsia.

Matilda had become angry when Marty's house did not come to her. She lived in a small, flimsy bungalow on the fringes of Windy Way, and the only winds that did not blow right through the house were the ones that had scratched Windy Way off the circuit. She put a lot of her husband's dumb aloofness down to this crisscross of cutting draughts. She began to watch Marty's house with bitter zeal, and she noticed that a large number of men were going in and out.

This worried her and she asked us for footnotes. Tasso's is the home of footnotes and Matilda got a variety. To prevent mischief we told her that these men were probably members of some new sect operating under the baton of Ursula's mother, a well-known conductor. This was likely because Windy Way is full of little organisations set up to air some new interpretation of our troubles. For ourselves, we did not fancy these voters who were in and out of Ursula's as interpreters. If they were, it was of the simplest, most fundamental sort.

When Matilda stumbled on the truth she fell flat on her face and the truth ached even more than usual. Whenever she visited Marty after that she gave him a full account of the horrors that had now taken the place of the sweet old pieties which had filled the kitchen in the days of his father. She always gave us long descriptions of her visits to Marty, but never once did we have the feeling that she was genuinely glad he had survived. Basically she took too Mosaic a view of trespass to be pleased by a drama with so bathetic a finish. "It would be better if the poor boy had gone, had paid the supreme penalty, had settled the final account with his Maker, had eaten that last breakfast they speak of, had been swung into eternity."

"Oh, my God," said Willie Silcox, holding his hair on after Matilda had left the shop. "One of these days Marty is going to break out of that asylum, and it won't be to shake the teeth out of Ursula. It'll be so he won't have to be there and listen when Matilda calls. If you boys haven't before seen a stalactite with an apron on, look again when Matilda comes in. You can see her last mental drop turning into stone in front of you. Yes, I can see Marty changing his billet just to have a bit of peace from that Calvinistic cough-drop."

And so it happened. One night in late autumn Marty escaped from the Home. With his great strength and skill at odd jobs he had managed to leave without too much fuss. He began a slow drift towards the west and Windy Way. Pictures and verbal descriptions of him were printed in all the newspapers, and as there was no nationally recognised war going on at the time, the papers put Marty and Windy Way right in the middle of the map.

Chaos broke loose throughout the territory between us and the Home. Anyone with very broad shoulders and an anti-social look was denounced as Marty and the police would close in on the town where he had been spotted. All over our zone there were these inclosing pools of policemen, and when the circle contracted to the spot in the centre, all they had to look at was themselves. Marty, in an unhindered, undramatic way, was sauntering through traps that had been designed for a man who was imagined to be as raptly conscious as the trappers.

One of the papers, listing marks of identification, said that since he had been in the Home, Marty had contracted a habit of fairly loud humming. Matilda confirmed that this was true, and it seemed that the songs Marty hummed were items from the repertoire of the Aeolians.

"It shows," said Willie Silcox, "that he remembers us, that he felt when he was among us the kind of warmth and security which he now misses."

This humming almost landed Marty back in the Home before he reached Windy Way. He was giving out the baritone line of that fine marching song 'Bonnets Over the Border' in a very unmusical part of the country, where any singing attracts attention. He was challenged by two men who had been given a great edge of weariness by years in the Air Raid Warden service. Marty listened to these two elements for half a minute, realised they were not going to join in the chorus, then threw them away, one into each of the two fields that flanked the path.

There was a tension which most people enjoyed in Windy Way as the bulletins announced Marty's approach. The police offered protection to Ursula, for it was the common opinion that Marty had broken out of the Home to treat her as he had done Tudwal. She kept up a front of screeching defiance. At the top of her voice and at every corner she declared that she had never been afraid to face Marty and prove him a coward and a dolt, and never would be. Peveril went about thin, cold and pale as an ice-cream wafer, and if it had not been for Ursula calling on him to prove his manhood by staying his ground we felt that he would have bolted immediately out of Marty's range.

It was on a Thursday evening that Marty arrived. He had travelled by the hill-paths and dropped down unseen from Merlin's Brow. He went straight to his house. Ursula and Peveril were not there. They had gone to the first-house performance at the Meadow Prospect cinema, the Coliseum. Ursula's mother was there in the kitchen, sharing an immense dish of toasted cheese topped with a jar of grated onion, a leading tasty in our division, with a friend, and there they were at the table, radiant with cheese-grease and pleasure in each other's company. When Marty walked in through the back door Mrs Thowley's man-friend did the quickest retreat from love and toasted cheese Windy Way has ever known. Mrs Thowley tried to follow him, but her greedy desire to scoop up one last forkful of melting cheese before fleeing slowed her down on the way to the door and Marty, without bitterness or fuss, caught hold of her and made her sit down. He took a chair at her side and between them they tackled what was left of the rarebit.

He asked where Ursula was, and there was such a powerful penetration in his eye that even Ursula's mother found the thought of a lie impossible. She told him, thinking that if there was to be a climax it would be best to have it out at once like a splinter. Marty chuckled when he heard that Ursula was in the Coliseum. He said he would take great pleasure in going right into the Col. He knew to an inch where Ursula would be, because she had always insisted on that particular seat during the months of their courtship. He said he did not know exactly what he would do with Ursula, but he thought he might throw Peveril over the balcony into the cheaper seats below, just to create trouble for Luther Cann, the manager, who had swindled Marty on a deal for decorating the interior of the cinema years before.

Marty also recalled his grudge against the man who collected the tickets at the door of the Col, Charlie Lush the Usher, because Charlie had once flashed his torch at Marty when he was busy making love to Ursula and caused him embarrassment. He said that if he could coax Lush into the right position downstairs he would throw Peveril right at him. As he unfolded this programme, Ursula's mother kept fainting into the roasted cheese and Marty had to keep lifting her head to get his fork into the dish.

Just as Marty was finishing his food, into the kitchen came Willie Silcox on an errand to persuade Peveril to be the MC at a dance to be run for the Old Age Pensioners. Another man would have taken one look and made for the hills, but Willie had been fed on such a seam of horrors in those manuals of pathology and studies of the criminal impulse down in the Institute, he just sat right down at Marty's side, patted him on the shoulder and helped him to more tea. His mind was working harder than those kids before they brought in the twelve-hour day. He took some little bits of curled onion out of Mrs Thowley's hair to make the scene look more homely and ordinary.

Willie was on his way to a rehearsal of the Aeolians, and he suggested to Marty that before going on to the Col he might drop in at the little vestry where we practised. He took Marty's arm and led him out of the house, leaving Ursula's mother sinking sal volatile by the pint.

We were all assembled and waiting for the down beat of Lucknow Lewis when they came in. Marty was blinking hard in the light, uncertain of where we or he stood. He was wearing a tight, borrowed raincoat that gave him a maimed, clownish look. If Willie had not been there to stage-manage the meeting, I do not know what Marty's reception might have been, for in the Aeolians there were several voters who were naive, vindictive or timidly panicky. They may well have wished to beat him off, to denounce him as outcast and untouchable and to drive him into the night. But Willie gave us our cue, putting on an intense grin as the gesture to imitate.

We crowded around Marty, asking how it had been with him, saying how good it was to see him again. Even Lucknow, who had been a bit frigid with us since our big quarrel over his attempt to break us out of our loyalty to the sol-fa and hurry us back to the old notation, beat his way through the press with his baton and shook Marty by the hand. For a few minutes the ice around Marty's mind stayed firm and he glared at us as if he suspected each of us in turn of having behind his back the manacle, the noose, the pill of cold contempt that would make foolery of our words of esteem and brotherliness.

95

Willie meanwhile whispered the situation to us. He told us that Marty was on his way down to the Coliseum, that practically all the police had been rushed to the other side of town in answer to some false alarm about Marty that had been raised earlier on, and that Marty was undoubtedly sincere in his intention to do his worst to Ursula and Peveril. He gave us an urgent directive. "Start the singing. And sing all the slowest, tenderest numbers we know. The songs of memory and tears, and let them drip."

We marshalled ourselves. We put Marty to stand right in the middle of the first row of baritones. For the first two songs he was silent, his face sad and moved. We took turns at touching him on the shoulder to encourage him out of his solitude. He began to look pleased as can be to find himself so noticed, so prominent. He opened his mouth and slid into a harmony.

The singing was magical, and we practised a cunning, voluntary diminuendo to allow the great, golden bass of Marty to emerge more strongly. When we got to the hymns and the songs of mourning, Marty was crying like a child and Willie was standing by his side, speaking the elegiac words plainly to allow Marty's grief no respite. We could feel the shadows of fear and resentment being flooded out of his mind.

Willie directed me by gesture to slip out and fetch Leyshon the Law. I found him with a cloud of assistants trying to throw a thin cordon about Marty's house. Luther Cann the Col and Charlie Lush were there, having heard that Marty intended slipping down to their cinema and doing some mischief. They were calling on Leyshon to provide tremendous searchlights to play upon the house as they had seen done in the thousands of films in which this very kind of crisis had featured, and they were loping like greyhounds on the flanks of the crowd shouting out such slogans as, "Come out, Marty, you haven't got a chance. You're caught like a rat in a trap, Moore. Come out with your hands up, boy. Get the tear-gas, Leyshon, for God's sake, and stop dawdling."

Leyshon told these two elements that this display was bringing the whole concept of social vengeance into disrepute. Any more of it and he would be drawing his baton down the partings of Cann and Lush's hair.

When Leyshon walked ahead of me into the little vestry,

Marty and the boys were finishing Lucknow Lewis's special arrangement of 'Lead, Kindly Light', which had caused more pneumonia in Windy Way than draughts because it keeps the mourners hanging about the Black Meadow going over and over the last verse. Marty smiled through his tears at Leyshon and took the handcuffs as if they were a friendly embrace. We followed them out of the vestry and began the walk down Windy Way. In the patch of light from a shop window we saw Ursula and Peveril. Ursula, for once, was silent as a stone, and Peveril was trembling. All Marty did was smile and wave his arms at them, as friendly and resigned as any human being we have ever seen. Then, as we continued our march down the street, the only sounds we heard were a loud, satisfied humming from Marty and a wild, bitter weeping from Ursula, whose nerves, up with the eagles and ready to strike for days past, had been shot to earth by the sudden, senseless intrusion of gentleness and acceptance.

As we walked home we watched the stars over Merlin's Brow. "It's funny," said Teilo Dew. "He comes all that way to hurt Ursula. And all he does is join in the singing."

"Perhaps that is what he came for," said Willie Silcox. "A man wants to feel at ease, at rest. Sometimes he does it by killing. Sometimes he shares a little ice-floe of beauty." Willie looked up at the great, consoling ring of lights around the mountain's top. "Malice has no stars in its night. It is eyeless. It has no fixed constellation of purpose. It awaits the sound or hand that will speak to it of love. Then it cries the aching grit out of its old and grieving sockets."

We came to Tasso's Coffee Tavern and walked in, feeling the need for a little silence and hot cordial.

The Leaf that Hurts the Hand

Last night, Nathan Durbin, the president of the Ferncleft Gardeners' Union, and a nuisance if ever there was one, pinned a medal to my lapel. Nathan is as fond of irony as he is of growing monstrous marrows, and the medal was small and cheap, the gesture impish. The award was not made for my having kept the best garden in Ferncleft during the past year, but for having arrived at the end of the summer with a garden that was not such a disgrace as to cause Nathan to faint in his tracks at the sight of it. Everybody in the long room at the Ferncleft Arms where the presentation was made laughed out loud, flattering Durbin with the notion that he is a wit. But I stayed solemn as a cow, and I will tell you why.

My house, into which we moved ten years ago, had the longest and stoniest garden in the row. The day after we moved in, Nathan Durbin was around telling me how pleased he was to see me with so large a plot and saying that he was looking forward to a record crop of flowers and vegetables from this desolate acre. My wife, Deborah, daughter of sturdy farming stock, joined in with Nathan and said this garden would be my first real chance to stop being a bemused loafer and provide her with cheap greens. Deborah also muttered that she had a craving for beauty which had not been wholly satisfied by her married life with me, and a fine flowering of blooms outside the back window would help to make her less bitter, and heal the ravaged patches of her ageing self. I thought this a good point because, most of the time, there was a very vinegary quality about Deborah.

I made no headway with that patch. The tools I used were not good. They had belonged to Deborah's grandfather, a sardonic old subject who had probably weakened the implements the day before he handed them over to me or rented them out to woodworms just for the pleasure of seeing me break my neck when I dug them hard into the ground. Besides, there was something peculiar about my relationship with the earth itself. I had been brought up among machines and had been spoiled for the simple peasant raptures that did such steady business in the skull of Nathan Durbin.

I really saw nothing wrong in the tall, magnificent weeds that soon reached a climax of health and strength in my garden. They had a sap, a variety, a confidence, a singing mastery in the face of neglect and contempt which I, a timid man, envied. The earth, I thought, is a badgered thing, persecuted enough by boys like Nathan and the wickeder tyrants of the prairie lands with their swifter methods of spoliation. Whenever I stuck in my spade, driven to make a gesture of compliant zeal by the sharp-bladed tongue of Deborah and the malicious, inquisitorial face of Nathan, the smell of opened, outraged earth would make me weak with a sense of guilt. I seemed to hear the torn clods saying, "You, too, Willie Palmer?" My nerves would go into a giddy whirl and I would go flying over the handle of the spade and lie there penitent and prostrate among the weeds, with Deborah standing over me, denouncing me as the biggest domestic misfit since Rip Van Winkle. No question of helping me up, soothing me with a sip or a sniff of sal volatile or offering me a new set of glands. She stood over me as I lay prostrate, I pink with shame like a severed rhubarb, she pouring over me a rich, thick custard of malediction.

Then Rufus Clapham came to lodge with us. I think Deborah took him in, in the first place, because she had often heard Rufus boasting, in the choir to which they both belonged, of his love for the soil and his great wish for a garden of his own. Rufus came to stay with us one January, and night after night he would tell Deborah and me what a landscape of fertility and joy he was going to make of the patch in the back when spring came. Deborah listened, fascinated, for there was a sinister influence about Rufus and a jet-black gloss on his hair that would have predisposed most women towards him even if he had not been fond of gardening. Among my other troubles I have thin hair and a slow style of address.

I waited for the spring, hoping that when it came the weeds

and stones of the patch would break either the neck or the heart of Rufus. I had grown tired of hearing him describe the talks he had had with Nathan Durbin about the load that would be taken off the street's mind when my garden was again under cultivation. Sometimes I tried to put in shyly that this world-wide interference with weeds was going, one day, to do some damage to the rhythms of the earth's physical life in the same way as certain kinds of moral interference had plagued and hurt man's inward life. This brand of thinking was a mile too deep for Rufus, whose mind was simple and tiny and his only answer was that I was not only a sluggard but an infidel. That pleased Deborah and at supper she gave Rufus an extra cup of malted milk to encourage him to scald me some more with his censure.

I knew she liked him, but it shocked me all the same when I woke up one morning towards the end of February and found that they had both left the house. They took with them no more than two small suitcases, and I had no idea of where they had decided to settle. Nor did I try to find out, having a respect for the wishes of others. People were disgusted to see me so torpid and complacent in the face of this disaster. But I found the house pleasantly quiet without Deborah and Rufus. I knew her well enough to realise that Rufus would in his turn grow tired of her urgent and domineering ways and would leave her. Then she would come back to me, and I had decided that my forgiveness of her when she turned up at the front door would be the great masterpiece of compassionate conduct towards which my quiet, kindly but flatly uncreative life had been heading. I worked out for her a fine speech full of mellow tenderness, and often, thinking out some new detail for that speech at the cinema during some sentimental scene, I would cry.

Also, their flight helped with Nathan. I told him that Rufus' departure, coming shortly before he had been due to put the prong of his fork in my garden, was a sign from above that my weeds were under some kind of special protection and were not to be disturbed. Nathan, still reviling my patch as the richest source of weed-pollen this side of hell, and half killing himself standing on his wall trying to blow back the darnel seed that floated in waves from my patch when the wind blew down the hillside, instituted a search for the runaways but there was no trace of them.

People began to admire the brave, resigned look on my face and even tended to forget that the poor quality of my gardening was giving Nathan ulcers. Things would have continued in this good cosy groove if it had not been for Waldo Flint. You probably remember the case of Waldo. He was a leading sensualist in this area and was keeping about six homes going and becoming confused, bankrupt and desperate in the process. So he tossed a coin to decide which of his six lovers he liked best and, being a bit simple and ferocious in his concepts, decided to get rid of the other five. He managed it with two and buried their bodies in different parts of Ferncleft, where they were soon discovered by the nosing tactics of dogs, birds and kids who were helped by Waldo's poor spade work. He had given so much love he was as poor a digger as I. The police asked Waldo if he had killed more than two, and Waldo, never precise in his replies and not eager to save the police work, said he was not sure. This was a year after Deborah's departure.

These discoveries started a panic in the county. Every woman who had vanished from sight for years past was explained as having been killed and buried by Waldo. When confronted by this name or face, Waldo, wishing to reduce life to the same state of perplexity as he was in, just nodded his head. Then Felix Studley, a small alarmist who lived at the bottom of our row, told the police he was sure he had seen Waldo with a bundle over his shoulder and a spade in his hand at the bottom of his garden during the hour of dusk. The police hastened to Felix's garden and dug it up thoroughly but found nothing.

Then there was a flood of people reporting that they had seen Waldo with bundle and spade hanging about their gardens at twilight and into the gardens of these people came the police digging and double-digging for dear life. This was at the beginning of the gardening season, and it tried the temper of the policemen to see the householders following them down the gardens as they went digging, slipping in the early potatoes, and Nathan Durbin standing guard over these rites, crying out that there was nothing like double-digging to send earlies off to a flying start.

Then a tremendous idea struck Nathan. He came into my

house one night and told me that he had informed the police that Waldo had been seen by at least half a dozen people disposing of something in my garden. Nathan sat there chuckling like a madman, happy that he was at last going to get my soil turned over. I begged Nathan to revoke this report, told him that it would put my nerves in the ash-bucket to see a corps of policemen ruining the peace of my patch and as a last resort I told him that I had now decided to cut the weeds with a scythe and cover the whole garden with a fine, sterile rockery.

But it was too late. An extra large body of policemen, all looking waspish and hot from the extra work they were doing on account of Waldo, marched into my garden and started to dig. The sight of their strong arms and new tools cutting into the ground upset me totally, and I went down to the club for a gill and a game of crib.

Coming home I was met at the door by a policeman who said something to me in a solemn voice. There was a high wind blowing and I did not hear distinctly what he said. The war was on at the time, and I knew that it had become an offence to neglect a cultivable patch of ground. So I thought that this policeman, having seen my collection of weeds, was now going to take me along and teach me how to be more socially responsible. But the hand that the policemen laid on my shoulder was remarkably heavy for so trivial an offence.

Fifteen minutes later the charge was repeated and, as there was no wind in the police station, I heard it. The policemen had at last discovered the body of another woman in my garden and the woman was my wife Deborah, and the man who put her there could not have been Waldo Flint because Waldo had been in prison for back payments on three affiliation writs at the time Deborah had vanished.

Nathan became very busy, as if he had taken on in person the job of knitting my noose. He told the police of how I had pleaded with him not to let them dig my garden, of how I had planned to plant a huge rockery over the secret of my guilt. He knew the motive too. I had been murderous at the thought of the way Rufus Clapham was going to turn my desert into a paradise. Nathan was sure that I had killed and buried Rufus too, and at his suggestion the police dug my garden again, and a visitor to the gaol told me that the soil of my garden was now looking black and lovely, waiting for the seed.

There was little I could say except "No, no," and that word in itself has little meaning. It was a rainy spring and rain depresses me to a point where I would not even argue that my name is Willie Palmer. They found me guilty of killing Deborah and there was a vague suggestion that when I was hanging for that act the unfound body of Rufus Clapham would be avenged and pleased.

The very look of the law from the inside is more terrifying than anything it does in a strictly objective way. I was so impressed by the gravity of all the people who were intent on hanging me it would have seemed frivolous to oppose them in any way. They had the height, the well-nourished force and assurance of my weeds and they fascinated me in the same way. I found myself switching from "No, no" to "Yes, yes", thinking that there must be something basically and eternally sensible in keeping in well with such elements even though they hanged me in the meantime. And if it had not been for Rufus Clapham and the way the human brain sometimes has of turning itself inside out to release the fumes I would most surely have been turned off.

Being in gaol, I had to get the facts second hand. I found them hard to believe, for I was mentally kippered from the strain of the trial and then awaiting execution, wetting a pencil to write a completely false account of my life as a felon for a Sunday paper which had offered me a nice sum. I wanted the money to help my club start a library to wipe out some of the effects among the members of thirty years of ale, crib, and pigeon flying.

Then suddenly, the gaolers smiled, threw open the doors, and this is what they told me when they led me out to freedom. The man living in the next house to mine in Ferncleft had, at three one morning, heard a loud peal of laughter from the garden of my home. This startled the neighbour, for there is little to laugh at in that row even before midnight. At first he had refused to budge, thinking that this racket came from my spirit, already dead and happy in my crimes. Then he looked at the calendar which his wife keeps above the bed and he found that I still had a week to go. The laughter started all over again and he and his wife went out to complain. There in the middle of my garden, sobbing, writhing and plunging his hands frenziedly into a hole which he had just dug was Rufus Clapham. He was shrieking: "Where are the tall weeds? Where is Deborah?" He kept repeating these questions as he was being led away by the police. He was quite gentle, unresisting, and clearly as mad as a hare.

Rufus told his story to the police. He and Deborah had arranged to run away. They were standing in the kitchen at two in the morning packing the suitcases and Deborah, a fanatic for neatness, had insisted on tidying up before she left. She even wanted to give the stove, about whose brilliance she had a phobia, a quick rub-down. Rufus followed her from task to task telling her there was a time and a place for tidiness and he had never seen an elopement mentioned in this connection.

His nerves were on the grater, thinking the sounds of cleaning would awaken me. Then he had a fit of conscience. These had been the best lodgings he had ever had and he realized he would be foolish to lose them. Just at the moment when Deborah was flicking her last speck of dust and saying that she would not leave the place anything but spick and span, even for adultery's sake, he was frank enough to tell her that he did not think he loved her enough to leave such a soft berth and anyway, he really was keen to get to grips with the garden. Deborah must have been riding the high acrid tide of some special desperation and she lunged murderously at him. He struck her; she fell and hit her head against the stove. He had carried her out to the garden to a point where the weeds were highest, dug furiously for an hour and made her a grave, not likely to be disturbed by anyone else, least of all by me.

Then he had fled. They asked him if he had seen the news of my arrest and sentence. No, he said. If he had, he would have come back sooner. He had found a job as a grave-digger in a small town seventy miles away. He had no friends, read no papers, lived in a tiny cottage in a corner of the Black Meadow where he worked. His life was brooding and digging, too much brooding. One day he found his thoughts repeating themselves endlessly and all were edged with the purple fringe that comes to the thoughts of those who find that they can no longer keep up the high rent on sanity. He thought of all the people to whom each day he was giving decent, secure burial, in excellent sites, beneath the branches of specially chosen and well tended trees of mourning. And then he would think of Deborah, dead by his hand, outlawed from heaven and earth in the worst weed-patch in Ferncleft. So he had come back. He also said he had been haunted by my face, hurt, bewildered, wondering through what hole in the bottom of my life all love and grace had bolted. But I think Rufus just put in that bit about me to round off a paragraph.

I often go and see Rufus in the place where they have put him, for they could not possibly have hanged so candid and guileless a man. What pleases him more even than the books and chocolates I take him is the fact that when I was released, in the sheer absent-minded happiness of being free, I bought a dozen packets of seeds and poured them over the black expectant soil of my patch which had been dug so well by hands other than mine. I give Rufus a month-by-month account of the harvest and he is glad about it, sincerely glad, not in the sly malicious way of Nathan Durbin who winks at me over the wall and says, "It's the double-digging that does it. You can't beat it, boy."

The Pot of Gold at Fear's End

To provide coal for us during the period that saw the pits closed down, my brothers Dan and Emrys drove a hole into the mountainside. From this hole they dug barrow-loads of coal. To poke about there and watch them at their work was our delight. We liked entering the rough jagged tunnel, cautiously feeling our scalps grow cold at the stink of wet earth and coal gas. On occasions my father would come up as well to see how the boys were progressing. On these trips he was accompanied by his good friend from next door, Waldo Treharne. My father never failed to reach a peak of passive melancholy when he came in sight of the hole. Dan's Delusion, he called it. He would sit chewing grass a yard or so from the entrance gazing at Dan's operations either with the stupefaction of one regarding a total mystery or with disgust. If there was a strike on, my father believed, there was a strike on, and this tomfoolery of digging up the mountains was a betrayal of principle. It showed there were some men to whom digging was some kind of drug. They had to have it to keep their brains numb, for there were men who denied growth and freedom to their minds with the same insistence as the rich denied parity to the poor. For my father the strike was a sacred affirmation of his most profound personal rights, going deeper than any matter of wages or hours, a passionate gesture of withdrawal, Buddha-like, levelled at all the strong ones, selfish ones and cunning ones who lived by demanding the right to damn their fellows by the millions to lives of digging, hauling and black bewilderment. My father laid his kiss on every moment of sunlit stillness that hung its beauty on the idle valley. He was happy to be inert. The pit ponies, which he tended underground when he worked and which seemed to kick him all around the auction, were now free on the mountaintops until the strike should end, and they, too, were happy. Only boys like Dan kept re-stitching the pall of our ancient misery with this digging antic.

Between my father and Dan there was little contact, so no conflict. Dan sometimes looked at him as he sat there on the hillside, talking, dreaming, chewing his strands of grass, proving something or other to Waldo, and Dan's expression would be curious, as if he was wondering whence such a man as my father could ever have come, to where such a man could be making. Dan was strong. The burden of my father's passivity was a light one on his shoulders. If he sometimes felt like shutting up my father's musings by dragging him into the hole and putting him to work, he never said so. In our family, even in the most precarious phases of our relationship, an obstinate tolerance was a first rule of life. But when my father became more insistent than usual on warning Dan that he was murdering his brain with toil too gross for bearing, Dan would round on him with a belt of blasphemies that rocked the hillside and sent the sheep for cover.

"Murdering what, do you say?" Dan would ask.

"Your mind. Your brain. No mind can stand up to all the digging you do. Honest, Danny, life's got a rhythm. Some kind of rhythm, sense. That I honestly believe. And I believe, too, that you and such elements as the coalowners are hellish out of step. Keep it up and you'll find yourself being led to the front room of Josephs the Registrar pleading to be born again or to be sworn in as an idiot."

"So I'm murdering my mind, am I? About time. The thing is a nuisance. Look what it's done for you."

"That's a terrible thought, Danny. Terrible."

"You're glad enough to warm yourself with this coal that we dig in the evening. I haven't seen you backing away and rushing out at the sight of a fire in the nights."

"That's no way to judge a man, Dan. When a man's cold it's like when a man's drunk. His philosophy slips downwards and he doesn't know where the hell it's going to land next."

At this point Waldo always put in that he did not see eye to eye with my father on this question of toil, and that he would be in the hole toiling like a beaver if it were not for his complaint, a hernia, which would have him in pretty much the same shape as a beaver if he did such a thing.

"Just sit there, Mr Treharne," Dan would say, "keep on sitting there. The old man's got to have somebody to sit out here and listen to him. If he didn't he'd be in here bothering me. So you are a big help."

That would set Waldo arguing patiently with my father that his whole attitude was reactionary and anti-social, and that with such a fine son as Dan he should feel honoured to be there in the hole with him, digging like a beaver and widening it with all his might and main. Either my father would get annoyed and tell Waldo to go the whole hog, renounce mankind, and sign up for good and all with those beavers from whom he seemed to have sprung, or he would be weakened and moved by Waldo's protests.

"Waldo," he would say then, "I wish sometimes I had that complaint of yours, this what you call...hernia."

"This damned thing? It's no cop, Eli. Why do you want it boy?"

"Because if I had one nobody'd bother me. Is there any way you could lend it to me for a spell? It seems to work like a charm."

"I could give you a sharp kick. Then we'd have one each."

"No. Just a lend, please."

Then my father would tense himself for an approach to the mouth of the working. Nine times out of ten, still tense, he would sit down again.

"I can't do it, Waldo. Study the principle, boy. Twenty-five years now I've been grinding my life into dust being closeted with those horses underground, getting no friendlier with them as the years went by and being kicked from every direction except the roof. And after this spell up on the mountain they'll master the way of working from the roof with my skull as the new target and, their aim unfailing after this long rest, they'll be able to finish off the job they began so well during the Boer War when they flattened me for the first time. But so far I've survived. It's been a great feat, Waldo. Greater than you think, boy, because I'm a man who attracts disaster. Every breath I breathe is a hymn of pride in that fact. I didn't survive it to be buried or choked in a hole in a mountain working for nothing at a time when I'm not even supposed to be working. Are you trying to make a farce out of my life and this strike, Waldo? You ought to be ashamed of yourself. I thought I had made my ideals clearer. Your beaver blood is probably making you very blind to my ideals. That hole those boys are working in is full of gas. By right they should be paying rent on it to the gasworks. I can feel the stuff bubbling under me even as I sit here, asking for a light. One day it'll go off. When that happens, Dan and Emrys are going to come shooting out of that hole like a pair of torpedoes, so fast people with ordinary eyesight like you and me won't notice them. Luckily, there's a high mountain right across the valley from here and they are bound to come to a stop when they run into that. So we'll at least know where to go and look for them. Wouldn't surprise me though if they just went right on in and then they'd have two tunnels to be getting on with, and I expect you'd want me to go labouring my life away in both. I can't understand your viewpoint at all, unless you think the sight of just two people being shot out into space isn't enough. You want three, me being the third. I never expected that sort of thing from you, Waldo. That complaint is doing something to you, boy, giving you an appetite for toil and horror."

But there would come moments when my father, as if driven forward by some ironical imp in the very spirit of his frustration, would come quite close to the mouth of the Delusion and study it in a most workmanlike way, as if wondering if the place was really of the right size and character to suit a man of his own type of experience. He would even hold his thumb up and squint at it to give a more skilled look to his study. It was a day in early August when he decided to come in with Dan on a basis of full co-operation. He heralded this with a lot of advance propaganda taking up a whole afternoon and evening explaining to Waldo, and when we were near, to Lloyd and myself, that for a man like himself, destined from birth to a life of labour, the role of stander-by was bound, soon or late, to become tedious. Toil, he said with a sadness that seemed to come right out from the ground on which he sat, was a thing he had to have. He had tried to keep this knowledge from Waldo and us but out it had to come. He could not be without the feel of the old pick. A hell of a thing, this having a craving for such activities as digging and hauling and getting filthy and grinding your brain into mud in a mill of muscles driven by a stream of sweat. But there we were. That was what came of living in a society organised like an ant-heap. If you were born the wrong sort of ant you could not even sit down without having the other ants crawling up and down your leg and making you itch with the mood to be moving on or, if the target happened to be a hole like this death-trap of Dan's, in. As he made these remarks he was stretched out on the grass, a very prince of passivity.

"Eli," said Waldo, "what you say surprises me. Judging from the gift you've shown for sitting smack on your butts, even though the dew be falling thick around you, or even slates, I would have said that nature had cut you out to be a coalowner."

"Not I. Just watch me tomorrow. There'll be an astonished look on your face. Dan's methods are untidy. 'Coal,' he says, and tears at it and loads it in a barrow. Nothing like that with me. The way I understand nature, I sometimes think I must have married the damned thing. I've got a natural nose for seams. I feel just like the stuff there in the ground that's been pressed black and shiny for God knows how long. I can guess the way it'll run and curve because most likely I'd want to run the same way myself, being like it, with a heart that's been pressed black and shiny. When I go in there tomorrow, you won't find me taking up the first tool that comes along and digging. I shall study the look of the earth closely and I'll ask myself, Eli, if you were coal and you were cooped up in this bloody hole, what direction would you travel in? The first answer would be 'Outside' because I've got to be true to myself. Then I'll remember that coal can't go outside because it's more tied to the place it's born in even than we are. So I'll poke about a bit and direct the tools of Dan and Emrys in accordance with my findings and prophecies, and before you know it they'll be uncovering tons of the stuff. Wouldn't surprise me if the whole lot of us were not beyond the need for any further work after a week or so."

The next morning we accompanied my father on his trip up the mountain. He was full, at first, of an analytical keenness that left Lloyd and myself with the impression that if it had not been for the depth of personal kinship he had felt with mountains and the minerals within, only a few of Glamorgan's major seams would have been uncovered. As he approached the hole his keenness diminished again and gave way to a look that was half worry, half speculation. "Dan picked the wrong place altogether," he said, and would have sat down there and then if Waldo had not been at his side to paint a picture of Dan wasting his manhood shovelling tons of dirt in vain for lack of proper guidance from the coal-diviner. My father relented at this and shouted to Dan that he was now ready.

"Ready for what?" asked Dan.

"To come in. To put things right for you."

"God help us."

My father advanced, followed by Waldo and ourselves. He paused at the entrance and glanced at the rickety, rotting timbers which were the only things Dan had been able to provide as supports for the damp, crumbling roof.

"I think I'll do my sizing up from out here," said my father. "I'm used to making quick impressions."

"But what can you see from here, Eli?"

"Enough, boy, enough." He raised his voice to talk to Dan and Emrys, who were yards inside. "What kind of faith keeps you boys at work in a place like this? There's no security here. Look at these timbers. Even a rat would refuse to work in a place like this."

"Rats are smaller than we are," said Dan. "They can get about more than we can to choose the places they're going to work. They also live less time than we do and need less to eat and wear. So stop bothering and come in or stay out."

My father entered, like the weakest Christian towards the hungriest lion. Soon we heard the sound of a boot being kicked against wood.

"Who the hell is doing that?" we heard Dan shouting.

"Me," said my father.

"What are you up to?"

"Testing the timber. That's the first step of all."

"There's no need to test it. It's rotten to the sap. It'll last as long as we need it and no longer. Stop fooling about with it."

"Don't you think you're a bit high on the mountain to come across any decent seams, Dan?"

"Of course. We're not looking for seams. We are just trying to make the mountain a bit lower so we can have a better start and less to dig in the next strike."

"This is no laughing matter."

"Who's laughing? One laugh in this place and the whole mountain comes down on you."

"Good God! Honest, Dan, listen. I'm speaking as a father. This is a terrible place to pick to come and die in. Just think of that, Dan. Death, alone, in a place like this."

"Don't bother. You've got company. Dig. What have you got to live for anyway that makes you so fussy one way or the other about dying?"

"Nothing. Nothing." My father served up that judgment on the toast of a wingless laugh that had the same heavy ochre quality as the earth around him. And as if he were taking himself at his own word, my father resumed his kicking at another rotten prop, further in this time.

"The first thing we do," we heard him say in a soft, meditative voice that carried clearly to where we stood, "is to test these things. A stitch in time . . ." Halfway through the proverb we heard the prop on which he was working crack like the report of a gun. There followed a great rattle of stones and a slither of damp earth. My father came shooting out, his arms outstretched as if looking for something to hang on to. Behind him came Dan, his arms also outstretched as if looking for nothing more to hang on to than a length of my father's windpipe.

"Of all the potchers . . ." bawled Dan, his brows right down and tiger-wild.

"Emrys," said Waldo, "where's Emrys?"

Dan forgot my father and bounded back into the tunnel. We stared at the tunnel's mouth, fear thick and slow as grease around our minds. We heard Emrys's voice. He was only partially entombed. Dan helped drag him over the rubble. They came out, yellow-streaked and pale. Emrys was a quiet boy, thinner than Dan, with much less to say. He smiled at us and sat down. We smiled back at him, our leg muscles curiously rigid and without the wish to bend and be at ease. My father lay down flat, his arm over his forehead and muttering, "It's worse than the horses. God, what a place to die! Worse than the horses. Worse, much worse."

"Look," said Dan, standing over him and pointing at my father's head with his forefinger as if wanting to make something very clear: "Until you came messing about in there, it was very quiet. Quiet and pleasant. Then, you come in. Do you dig? Do you shovel? No. You kick away a prop. It takes a lot of talent even to think of that. What have you got against us? God knows what goes on in that head of yours, but whatever it is the Angel of Death is behind it and her target is me and Emrys. So keep away. Do you want to be the first man to boast he brought a mountain down on two of his kids? If you want to do that, go to the very top of the mountain where it's fresher and keep on stamping. You're bound to manage it sooner or later. But keep out of that hole and we'll give you a private prop to pull from under yourself out here every time you get tired of feeling just alive and safe."

My father made no reply. He looked at Dan with a tragic dignity and gave a glance at Waldo which said clearly that for him, whichever road was taken, at the end of it waited some cruel, thoughtless rebuff of the sort that he has just received from his own son. He tore up a stem of grass, bit softly upon it and walked away. He returned an hour later and told Dan with quiet pride that he had just been taken on as an auxiliary at the working of Naboth Kinsey, a little down the mountainside.

"Good," said Dan. "I'll call in at Naboth's on the way down and tell Naboth's wife how sorry I am."

"Why?"

"Because Naboth Kinsey with you on his flank is doomed. He'll be safe for a bit because you won't be able to decide how exactly you're going to do it. By the time you finish you'll have found as many ways of breaking them as there are necks. But once you've done your sizing up down at Naboth's and you've made your mind up, all we'll have to do is pick Naboth's bearers. You may bump Naboth into the roof or the roof into Naboth. I leave it to you. Naboth is welcome."

Most of the outcrops driven into the mountainside by the men in their search for free coal were level workings, driven straight in. Not so the working of Naboth Kinsey. Naboth's enterprise was in a narrow cleft of the hillside and not much noticed. This suited Naboth for he was an obstinate, secretive man, not given to the long idle arguments about method that were loved by most of the outcrop workers, especially my father, who was a noted theorist. So it was with great interest we heard that my father had been taken on as an auxiliary at the working of Naboth Kinsey. Everyone said my father and Naboth would get on very well, as well as a busy flame in a deep petroleum well.

Naboth had scorned the level working adopted by most of his comrades. He believed in going down as perpendicularly as he could to contact the seams worked in the pits themselves. When it was suggested to Naboth that this might take a long time, he would take off his cap, play with his fingers on the top of his bald head and say he did not feel rushed. He had lived for long enough in the neighbourhood of mountains to know that it saves a lot of burns on the inside of the skull to dim the light of immediate thoughts by dipping them into some shadowed apprehension of the everlasting. If you were going to do a job said Naboth, be thorough. So he went on with his perpendicular digging. Some said he would reach coal about fifty years after the coming of the New Jerusalem and by then he would have got so far down he would not be able to hear what the voters were saying who were telling him that there was no longer any need for so much digging. Others said he would probably strike a layer of salt and end up talking about vinegar with Lot's wife. But the majority simply held that one day Naboth and his companions would go down and find it too much trouble to haul themselves back up again. So, when it was announced that my father was teaming up with Naboth, there were quite as many people to feel sorry for my father as felt sorry for Naboth. In the latter camp, my brother Dan was a kind of president.

During his first few days with Naboth my father was full of enthusiasm.

"You're like me, boy," he told Naboth. "You've got a feeling for where the seams are. Me too. To us it's simple. The coal is somewhere underneath us, so down we go, straight as a plummet. That's a fine deep hole you've got there, Naboth. It's straight, boy, and it's deep. You didn't waste your plummet there. Perhaps it's a little too deep from one point of view but there we are. The seams are down there and we are the boys who go straight at them. No messing. When do you think you'll hit the main seam, Nabe?"

"There's no hurry, Eli. We'll take it nice and steady."

"That's the right spirit. That's the talk I like to hear. There are chaps working on this mountain who'd spit their hearts up with grief if they couldn't have a certain amount of coal in their hands every day. The romance of this antic doesn't seem to appeal to them at all. There's a lot of beauty that they don't see in just making a hole. God knows where we'll get to before we finish going straight down like this. They say the inside of the earth is just like the pan in a chip shop. You know those pans, Naboth, bubbling all the time. It would be a good idea if we got to that heat before we get to the seam, to take some potatoes down and do our own chips and cook them on the lava or whatever it is that does this bubbling."

"We'll take it steady," said Naboth. "There's no hurry." Not even the thought of chips which was the favourite food of the valley could stir this Naboth from his calm. It struck us that this man was a digger strictly for the sake of digging. Ends seemed to matter to him not at all and he would probably have started digging this hole in the bedroom if he did not have a wife and a bed that needed holding up.

To us, Naboth's little pit was every bit as dangerous as the level working of my brother Dan and if my father, with his quick eye for danger of all sorts, had not noticed this, we were sure it was only because he was still keen to show Dan what a way he had with him in this matter of tracking down seams; either that, or the swift, passionate flight of his own desires found something to detain and fascinate them in the serene, objectless methods of Naboth. Naboth's companions, Windsor Ellis and Elias Thompson, were like Naboth, quiet, sad-looking men who went about their work without any zest or relish as if glad that at least they were in no doubt that one day soon the whole issue would cave in around the whole pack of them ridding them, without fuss or expense, of air and trouble. The gear they had rigged up to get the diggers in and out of the hole looked most insecure. A bucket on a rope was let down from a cross bar. The digger got into the bucket and his two colleagues, three counting my father, took the strain on the rope. The earth was loaded into the bucket, hauled up by one man and emptied by the third. Windsor, whose moods, cradled in as mossy a nest of life-long mishaps as the valley could show, often took a bitter turn, regarded my father as frivolous and treated him with caution, especially if my father was anywhere near the rope and it was his, Windsor's, turn to go down into the diggings. But with Elias Thompson my father had much better luck. Elias was a man who had spent his whole life dominated by a woman of narrow religious tendency who had converted their bedroom into a centre meet only for prayer and bleak decency, numb with deep solitude and fitting texts. From this chaste cranny Elias peeped out at my father and found him to be, by his standards, a king of the goats and he looked upon his most harmless remark as a sin-soaked novelty to be stored away in some mental cupboard where not even his wife's probing life-hatred could pry. Later, it would be taken out to warm the frozen fragment of some thoughtful night.

My father's close friend Waldo Treharne was depressed by the venture. Every time he looked at Naboth's pit-head gear with its rope and bucket we could see his mind painting a frame of doom around them as the shadow fell across his thoughts. It was clear that in terms of calamity he viewed Naboth's whole outfit as a fitting pendant to the bodily trouble, a hernia, which kept him idle.

"It was a bad step teaming up with Naboth," he told my father. "After one week of this, Eli, you will be praying to be back with the ponies. It wouldn't surprise me," went on Waldo, "to find that Naboth is in league with Richards the Undertaker. I bet Richards calls on Naboth nightly to ask him when he can expect the big coup. Come to think of it, I saw Richards last night lurking by the door of the Library and Institute keeping an eye on you. Taking a rough measurement, no doubt. It would be more honest by a mile if Naboth threw aside all such dishonest tomfoolery as that bucket and tied the rope direct around your necks."

"Waldo," said my father very gently, "your view is darkened by that trouble of yours, the hernia. It's pulled all your hope and joy clean out of shape. Naboth is a man to watch."

"I'll do that, Eli. He won't be around to watch for very long. Nor you."

Naboth kept my father out of the hole for several days and put him on the rope with Elias. This labour half killed my father who had done little in the past more strenuous than warding off the ponies and picking himself up when he couldn't. But he began to ache furiously from the strain of pulling the rope tight when Naboth or Windsor went down and his face went red as a sunset when it came time to haul them back up again. After his first day on the rope his body seemed to become fixed in the posture of rope-tugging and he walked as if he were being carried on a chair, his legs bent forward and his spine bent backward almost parallel with the ground. We followed him and Waldo home and it was very interesting to see my father performing this Chinese bend and Waldo leaning as far forward as my father leaned back. They had to keep adjusting their step to be able to talk to each other at all.

Later that same evening, my father did what he always did when he found that life had once again put its foot upon his neck. He went to the Workmen's Library in search of a book that would provide him with an answer to this animal labour he was called upon to do at Naboth's hole. He found it. It was called *Through Breathing, Strength*. He brought it home excitedly, still followed by Waldo with a look of even deeper wonder in his eye. He stayed up reading it far into the night. Our bedroom was directly above the kitchen where he read. Off and on, we could hear a sound like that of a man drawing his shoe sharply across rough matting. That was my father filling up with breath. Then there would be ten minutes of coughing, choking, stumbling and swearing. That would be my father trying to rid himself quickly of breath that had got into parts of his body where breath had no right to be and where breath had never been before.

But the next morning he seemed cheerful and confident and we heard him tell Waldo on the way up to the outcrops that he had taken in enough of this breath doctrine to make a trial trip and that, in confidence, he now thought that most of Naboth's troubles were over.

"There are two ways of taking that, Eli," said Waldo.

At the first opportunity my father took Elias aside and explained to him the advantages of this new system of taking the load off the muscles and putting it on the lungs. It took my father a long time and a few rough drawings to show Elias that this meant something more than simply tying the rope tightly around his chest. But Elias had faith in my father. He took it all in but owned up that he had no head for book work, had gone through life in a one-style sort of way, like a horse, and would stand little chance of making his own labour less by means of the new system.

"Once a horse, always a horse," said Elias forlornly, and he said it so often, my father, the most bruised and aimed-at stableman of his age and weight, stood clear, as if expecting Elias to fall in with the other ponies and throw a hoof at him.

"When I'm on that rope, Eli, pulling," said Elias, "I find it difficult enough breathing in the ordinary way without trying anything different."

"You'll get into it, Elias. Patience and practice!"

"All right then. But don't say anything about this to Windsor or he'll stop us breathing altogether. When he's in the bucket he likes a steady hand on the rope. And he doesn't think so much of you as it is."

"Windsor's a savage. He'll die toiling."

It was when they were hauling Windsor up that morning that my father made his first experiment. We watched him closely. His eyes were closed. He scarcely seemed to be breathing at all and he wore around his lips a soft but masterful smile which he was copying from the man, a dark, wise-looking voter, whose photograph had appeared in the front of the book on breathing. The grasp of his hand on the rope was light and it seemed to pass through his fingers smoothly and without effort. At first we thought my father had got on the right track and the system was working. Then we heard a terrible gasping from Elias. His face was purple with overstrain and he was almost collapsing under the burden of pulling the whole load himself. When Windsor was safely delivered and out of earshot my father bent over the collapsed Elias. "It works, Elias. It's a marvel, boy. Your mind seems to settle down into quiet sleep and you seem strong as a lion though you don't seem to be making any effort. And look at you. You stick to the old ways. You stick to muscle and brute strength. And look at you. You can hardly talk. You're a greater wreck than my friend Waldo who is also wedded to ancient ways. Now when Windsor goes back again, you try my way. Just control your breathing and put your mind on something that makes your mind feel good, anything but the rope."

Windsor re-entered the bucket. He smiled, a brief, rare smile, at Waldo who was staring at him with eyes that were full of the most startling interest and pity. To Waldo, who had heard my father's words to the helpless and enchanted Elias, Windsor was now little more than a fly winging directly to its doom in the dark web of my father's dreams. As soon as Windsor's head sank out of sight, my father turned to Elias and said, "Now, Elias. The breath. Hold it, boy." Elias did that. He did it deliberately. His glottis jerked up like an arm, as if his breath were a fleeing dog that had to be caught before it could be held.

"Watch them now," said Waldo tensely. A pattern of agony began to pull at the browskin of Elias. His mind was obviously seeking that something that would make it feel good and in all the gutted wilderness within his skull there was nothing that did not shrink away from his questing thought, weeping its still tininess midway between great good, great evil. Then his face began to change colour and he pointed at his mouth to tell us that he no longer seemed able to breathe at all. He looked terrified. He started to writhe and let go the rope. My father was taken by surprise. He himself, as senior breather and mentor in the team, had been leaving it all to Elias. He was jerked forward at tremendous speed by the descending mass of Windsor who was now hurtling out of control through the last few feet that separated him from the bottom of the shaft. The bottom was soft mud. It did no harm if you fell clear of the bucket. My father had some of the skin knocked off his chin when it smacked with shocking squareness against the crossbar of the hauling gear and Windsor, on reascending, swore himself hoarse. Beyond that, no harm was done.

That afternoon, Windsor, in general discussion with Naboth, insisted that the one place where my father could not put the whole enterprise in danger was at the very bottom of the shaft, doing some digging. My father protested that this was foolishly wasting a high talent, now that he was well on his way to becoming a specialist on the rope. He hinted that if Windsor would stop being a clod and feel an urge to experiment they would soon see perfected a method of human haulage which would give Naboth's winding gear, now no more nor less than an organized pain in the bowels to all concerned, the force and efficiency of the steam-driven units that lined the bed of the valley. Windsor, in no mood for dickering, stood over my father, snarled and said he would have none of this. And into the bucket my father had to go. As he cocked his leg to enter he wore a look which from one side recalled Colombus and from the other an old, worn gnome who knows that he is definitely on his way to his last frolic. Even as he descended, he kept on orating until the mumble of his voice vanished into the thick sucking clay of the walls.

We gathered around the top of the hole to see how he was getting along. We had been invited to do this by Naboth who was wanting to know why it was that after so many minutes no bucketful of earth had yet been sent aloft by my father and Windsor had shouted down to him to know what in hell's name he thought he was supposed to be doing down there. We peered down. After we had got him sorted out from the clay we could see him clearly enough. He was sitting at the side of the excavation, doing nothing but looking petrified and staring up, apparently at the sky.

"He's gone jingles," said Windsor, putting his hand to his temple and beginning to wind, to leave us in no doubt as to where he thought my father had gone.

"He's frightened," said Waldo, "Eli has funny nerves."

"Good God," said Elias. "Is that what it is? Look at his eyes. They are filling the hole. He must be holding his breath again. Tell him to breathe, Waldo. He looks horrible."

Then my father started to shout. He shouted with a piercing suddenness that sent Elias bounding back from the shaft like a ball. "It's coming in," roared my father. "Waldo! Elias! It's coming in. Get me up! I'm trapped! Get me up!"

They told him to get into the bucket. He fell silent instantly and hopped in. They hauled him to the surface. He spent the rest of his day explaining what had happened. As soon as he got down there, he had looked up. And what did he see? Nothing. He said it again. Nothing. We looked as if we did not believe him. Not a damned thing, he repeated. Blank. Nothing. The sides of the hole had seemed to slope inward until they met and he thought he was trapped and shortly to be entombed and choked, the sides crumbling in upon him, with Windsor, still vindictive, shovelling a bit of extra stuff down from above to make sure. There was a name for the panic he had felt, he said. He had seen it in a book which had described this thing driving people mad by the thousand. But no book could really tell you what a hell of a feeling it was. It was written on his heart and unless we wanted to wriggle down his throat and have a look there the horror of it would have to remain unread. "This is another worry I've got to face," he said, after he had rested a while. "Now I know I'm not to be trusted in any hole where I'm supposed to be able to see the opening and can't." He grew bitter about this. "Afraid. We're all afraid of something always. Life is black and lousy with fear. Night is only the stuff that rises from all the fear we sweat out of us through the day. It shouldn't be. I'm going back down there. I've been afraid of too many things. Bailiffs, bosses, dreams, neighbours, now holes. But I'll conquer this fear if it's the last thing I do."

"It will be," said Waldo, sombrely.

The next day Naboth decided to give my father one last try. He prepared to descend. Naboth, Elias and Windsor manned the rope. Before entering the bucket my father rested his arm on the cross-bar of the winding gear. Windsor began to mutter. My father put on that soft but masterful smile again that he had picked up from the dark-faced breath-controller in the book, as if to say that Windsor, victim of toil, knew not what he did. He told us that he could not let this moment pass without a few words of explanation from himself. He then gave us a long survey of fear through the ages and the manner in which it had nibbled upon the fibre of the poorer voters like a rat upon cheese. He described himself as a bit of cheese so nibbled he would have to bribe the average rat with a bonus if he wanted to shed a few more crumbs. He told us of the deadly effects fear had had upon the lives of his listeners, blaming upon it such diverse complaints as Waldo's hernia, Naboth's baldness, and Elias' wife. They all became very interested and by grunts, shrugs and nods agreed that this fear was a lowering thing to be having about the place, a thing ripe to be shown the culvert. It was clear that my father was treating himself to a course of intense auto-propaganda to get his courage to the peak and when he arrived at the passage where he passed his own fears under review and he marked himself down as being descended from a long line of shudders, his self-pity welled up to a rising rhythm. It welled up so far he failed to see that Naboth, Elias and Windsor, thinking that this address would see them safe for at least another fifteen minutes, had dropped the rope and were following his argument with a dour mournfulness, as if it were a hearse. My father, thinking to make his exit dramatically, with the spotlight of his audience's sympathy still upon him, stepped quickly into the bucket and hurtled to the bottom at about a hundred miles an hour.

Windsor clambered down the rope after him. We all manned the rope to bring him, with my father on his shoulder, to the surface. My father had fallen nimbly and after a minute's hard slapping by Windsor, he opened his eyes. Naboth, who was a first-aid man, said there was nothing broken and went pulling at my father's every limb as if he were disappointed about this and wanted to put it right. But nothing, not even Naboth trying to get everything out of the socket, could persuade my father to rise. He had had the wits scared out of him.

"I'm finished," he kept saying. "My doom was coal. But there's nowhere I'd have wanted it to happen better than here on my native hills." We could see him sucking the pleasure from those words.

Then we called Dan and on to Dan's barrow we loaded him. We wheeled him home, watching the look of total, stricken bemusement on his face. Waldo explained to Dan how my father had taken up with the breathing caper.

"He learned it from an Indian in a book."

"Old fakir!" bawled Dan as we came into the main street. "Old fakir, one and four a sack. Cheap, cheap, buy now, buy now!"

My father waved the barrow to a halt. He stared piteously at Dan, got out and walked, offended to the very root of his strange, wondering self.

The Cavers

"What we four need," said my brother Dan, "is change, change and adventure."

The four to whom he referred were himself, my brothers Barth and Milo and myself. Milo was a shop assistant and at that point he was very badly frayed. He moved so fast from one section of trade to another the Meadow Prospect Chamber of Commerce had raised the possibility of his being a spy.

At that moment he was working in a curious sort of shop that sold seeds and a wide range of poisons to be used against roaches, slugs, mice and rats. Some of the advertising posters which announced what the poisons could do were horrific, and kept Milo so persistently on the blink, he made many mistakes on the seed flank, and created so much confusion in gardens that some of the customers fingered the poison advertisements and looked straight at Milo.

The shop was known as Searle's Seed and Health Store. The Health part referred to a herb section that Searle had never been able to develop. Since he had taken up with the poison line Searle had been asked, for charity's sake, to drop the word, Health, from his heading. Searle, smiling ambiguously, said he knew his business.

We lifted our heads when Dan mentioned adventure. We had little of it. A whole fence of policemen, landowners and moralists had kept us on a straight, dry road in things like trespassing and sex.

"I came across a valley of caves in the hills north of here a few days ago," said Dan. "We are going to explore those caves. I am going to give you boys such a dose of danger and darkness as we crawl about those secret chambers, life will never again have the power to make you feel alarmed or depressed. Have you heard of potholing?''

We hadn't. Pot-heating, pot-making; we had heard hints of these things.

"We'll take a tent to sleep in," said Dan. "A week Monday we'll go." He turned to Milo. "Tell Searle to double up for a couple of days. You want a change from those seeds and venoms. And tell Searle, too, that he should aim at a shop where death is not so cheek by jowl with life."

Milo was not able to get the whole of this message over to Searle. Just as he was getting ready to tell Searle that he badly needed a rest from those posters, Searle told him that the customers badly needed a rest from Milo. He told Milo never to come back unless he wanted help with the roaches.

"You're better out of it," said Dan. "That Searle has cracked under the strain of contradictions. Promoting harvests with one hand; knocking off everything that creeps or crawls with the other. One of these days he'd have been slipping a few deadly pellets into your salad as part of his general campaign against slugs. He has soured your spirit. This caving will be a sweetener for you. Your outlook will emerge from the sack created for you by Searle. And there'll be no expense. This holiday will be the only economic miracle of this decade. There won't even be bus or train fares. This valley of caves is a proper paradise. In between our jaunts to the underground Kingdom your eyes will have a treat."

Dan was as good as his word. At first he proposed that we should walk to the caves.

"Do you realise that a dewy lane can wash the spirit clean?"

We didn't and said so. In any case our spirits felt spotless.

"Walk?" said Barth. and went on to say that a whole term of walking up and down his bedroom memorising formulas had given him some trouble with his pedal arches that now made him a poor marcher. Milo and I also tried to look as flat-footed as possible.

We had also been thinking of those caves. We were going to remind Dan of a family tendency to go insane when exposed to too much darkness. But we didn't want to seem to be making too many difficulties.

"All right. I'll get Richie Rudd to run us down there in his van."

This gave us no joy. Rudd was a neighbour who was organising a rudimentary sort of removal business. If he ever got a second van, people were keener on shifting about than we had ever imagined.

Rudd's van turned up on the Monday. It was a large van but it looked most unstable. Barth said that the thing was kept together only by the rush of air on longer journeys, and would, through the same agency, one day fall apart.

Barth went around, rattling bits of the fabric, frowning and saying that it might be easier to try out Dan's theory about dewy lanes. Dan kept nudging Barth and telling him to shut up, thrusting back into place bits of the van that came off in Barth's fingers. Then he would rush over to Rudd, a cheerful, calm man and tell him, it was only a matter of time before he was telling such agencies as Wells Fargo and Pickford to fall out or move up.

Then Dan went off and came back with the friend who was lending us the tent. The friend had spent one short, stormy summer in the scouting movement. He had been asked to hand in his pole but had managed to hang on to the tent. As we loaded it into the van, he told us that in this very tent had been the heart and pride of many top-rate jamborees.

It was a big tent, large enough, by the look of it, to house one of the eisteddfodic capers popular in the area. It could, as well, have been a main mast wrapped around with a fair sample of rigging. By the time we had got it erect and habitable, we would be too tuckered out for the sort of groping exploration that Dan had in mind.

"Where we are going," said Dan, "is hard country. We'll need a hard tent."

As we felt the weight of it, we knew we had one. It said a lot for the depth of Rudd's van that we got the tent into it at all. But there was still enough of the pole sticking out over the flap to be a nuisance to traffic.

The van was already crammed with furniture, and Rudd invited us to fit ourselves in among the sofas and beds.

The journey began. It did no good for Milo. The van's engine, as soon as it tackled the gentlest of slopes, seemed to explode, weary itself and stop dead. We also seemed to be running into a series of violent collisions as if Rudd was going through hedges and walls, instead of around them.

The furniture itself was also a problem. Rudd had clearly not been in the business long enough to know how properly to stack and rope his load. Whenever Milo, to lighten his dread, would shift his position, there would be a jolt and some article would land on his head.

And in every town we passed through there would be a band of youths who looked as if they had been waiting for us for years. They would jump on to the protruding part of the tent pole, hooting and laughing, and almost persuading Milo to clamber out and join the swingers.

We stopped half-way to the caves at a country inn. We all had half a pint of cider, except Rudd, who was well known at the inn and drank from a quart pot. We discussed the van. We mentioned the shocks and bangs and suggested that the van was not manoeuvrable, and the steering and the wheels were not even nodding at each other.

"I'll show you," said Rudd, and when he spoke his voice had more bravado and challenge than it had before.

The cider he had been drinking was not only in a much larger pot, but it seemed rougher and stronger than the stuff we had been drinking.

"I'll show you," he said again.

I leaned over to Dan.

"What does he mean? What's Rudd going to show us?"

Dan explained that Rudd's steering was first-rate and that the wheels responded to Rudd's every breath. Barth said that either Rudd was blowing too hard on the wheel or was not breathing at all.

"The engine's really warm now," said Rudd. "And between here and the caves there are some terrible bends. The van will show its true quality then."

Rudd smiled and from the inflamed state of his face it was hard to see what he really meant.

We boarded the van again. The three of us pressed into any fissure that seemed habitable. We were in a brooding mood. We thought about the caves and wondered what we had that Dan wanted to inherit. We thought about Rudd and those bends. It would have taken just one decisive phrase to have us clambering out and walking home.

Dan shouted through to us that we were approaching one of the hairpin bends which would allow Rudd to show his mastery. Milo, to lessen the number of things which had been falling on his head, had now squeezed himself between a mattress and the side of the van. I was talking to him without being able to see him. I was saying things about caves and edging towards the suggestion that we should take hold of the flag-pole and thrust it through to the driving cab, wounding and immobilising Rudd. To all these remarks he gave low, worried replies, speaking directly through the mattress.

Then Rudd swung the van as if he were rounding the earth, and there was a triumphant shout from him and Dan, as if they had just sighted the lights of Woomera. I told Milo that this had made up my mind and asked him and Barth to help me with the pole. Milo made no reply this time. I peeped behind the mattress. One section of the van's side had fallen away. And Milo had gone with it.

I banged on the van's floor to give Dan notice that Milo had left us. But the engine was now going off like massed cannon, and it took me a minute to get my message through.

The van stopped. Rudd did not seem upset.

"I guessed that there might have been a weakness on that side of the van. Now we know. We'll go back to find him. It'll be better really. We are at the bottom of the last hill before the valley of the caves. And we'll need a good run up."

Rudd swung the van recklessly around and I had the impression of someone jumping out of a car to get out of Rudd's way. But by this time I was so anxious about Milo I might have been seeing scenes of this kind as part of a fixed nervous blink.

When Milo came into view he was being helped along by a man in very rural costume who was propping up Milo with one arm and swinging some type of bill-hook with the other. Over the next few stammering months Milo filled in the context of this tableau.

The man was a County Council workman called Warlow, paid to keep the hedges trim. For weeks past he had been becoming neurotic. Nature in those parts was lush and apt to make a monkey out of the quickest hedger, especially when you were a very slow perfectionist like Warlow.

Also, the local foreman of the hedging squad had taken a dislike to Warlow, and would hide in nearby clumps and thickets peering out to check on his methods of pruning and lopping, and occasionally shouting out that he was still waiting to see Warlow make any sort of an impression on a hedge.

So when Milo left the van and landed on Warlow, Warlow thought this must be the foreman, now taking the most direct action by landing on Warlow from the sky. If Milo had not let out an instant scream of terror at the sight of Warlow's vengeful face, Warlow would have let him have one with the bill-hook.

We thanked Warlow and helped Milo into the van. Milo sat well away from the sides, watching the whole van with a crazed caution. Every few seconds he let out a little sob and told us we could now do with him as we pleased. We thought about that and shouted through to Rudd to take it easy, to go along at the kind of amble that would keep Milo in the land of the lucid.

Rudd's answer was to increase the speed of the van from ten miles an hour to forty. We told Dan to tear the wheel away from Rudd and come back to reason. Dan said that the great speed was necessary to take the long, steep hill ahead in one smooth rush.

A porcelain statuette, the one representing a boy with cherries, fell between Milo and me. Milo took a furtive look and thanked the boy and even tried to take a cherry. I put a cushion over Milo's head and told him not to look or listen.

The van began to heave and cry with strain. There was a hissing sound from the engine. Dan shouted that the water in the radiator had boiled away, and we wished that we could have that sort of luck. The hill at that point was sheer. The furniture started to slip, and it was only a matter of seconds before we were crushed against the back-flap.

We leaped out and after a short attempt at definite flight, we were called back by Dan to help Rudd push the van on to the side of the road. Rudd went off for water. We helped Milo on with his rucksack, a high-pitched article that seemed to come further above the head than any sack of this type had done before. He looked like the first and most desperate Martian to come our way.

"What are we doing out here?" he said. "Why did we leave the house? What did we set out to do?"

We stared at Dan with faces of black hostility, daring him to tell Milo the truth. He didn't. We started walking the mile to the nearest bus stop that would take us home.

Hastings

A man is leaning against a rock. His bits of mediaeval costume suggest a minstrel, warrior, thief. His face is as sad as the stone which touches his shoulder. He gives the impression of having been harassed twice around the earth and to have enjoyed, in a sombre sort of way, certain phases of the trip.

The man is Alcwyn, and these are his reflections:

I

Their days are come, the days of the hawk, the falcon, the kestrel and the kite. All the way along the path I've trod, and a heavier treader never lived, at every turning of every lane, a brilliant beak has appeared, a bird of burning eyes that chooses only the softer, nicer bodies.

Do I follow the butcher birds? Do they follow me? We are united in ignorance and rapacity, the sky-scavengers and I. The birds loot for food, I loot to give a sense of purpose to mutilated days, a sense of consolation to intolerable nights. I have plucked crowns from dying princes. From the hands of expiring lovers I have torn the trinkets of their troth. I am loath to steal from the fully dead. I love to inflict upon the half slain the last obscene jest of palpable deprivation. It is nice to tickle the final wrath of the brave, beautiful boys who come from the far forests and distant seas, hastening, hurrying, like the swallows on the autumn wind, to the jest of their bloody liquidation.

Listen now, listen to the sounds of this October night. It is full of a loud, mounting rustle. The lovely and passionate lads are emerging like armoured bats from the multiple caves of their folly to knock at the doors of their long, implacable graves. I will spur them all on, whatever their land or language. To the men I will proffer the prod of flattery and the lullaby prayer. To their ladies I will volunteer the consolation of a verse.

Among a small circle of word-fanciers I, Alcwyn, have gained some little fame for poetry of plangent mourning. Among the graveyards of the slain I am as firm a fixture as mead at a wedding feast and just about as helpful to the mind. I have sold the war-secrets of my masters as nimbly as I have rifled the bodies of the fallen. As an artist I have a vested interest in disaster and degradation. Life is loud to me. Even as I stand here, a mere hour's march from the bay where the Norman Duke has landed with his horse-riders and bowmen to take this kingdom from the English, I hear its ticking heart of wrath and greed. I watch the skies. As the light comes fully on I will give warning to the hawk, the falcon, the kestrel and the kite to be ready to gather, to exult, for Kings have come together to fight, to add another round to the ancient game of thrones and bones.

I shall present that rhyme, with no charge, to my master if and when he makes his exit from this life some little time from now, just down the road from here.

I have come a long way. I began at a place called Dinas Lludw, the fortress of ash just across the Saxon border into Wales. Three times in my youth it was sacked and burned. Three times I wrote funeral odes over its ruins that won me the commendations of the Prince's bards. Then, one evening, I interfered with the strict rules of Welsh versification and the chief bard's daughter and I was banished.

That's when I met Harold the Englishman. With him I marched far and saw a whole variety of seas: the endless oceans to the east and west, the smaller seas of Siluria. I saw Tostig die and sold his jewelled belt for ale. I saw the Norwegian wolf Hardrada die, but on his body there was nothing worth the filching. A stark fighter, Hardrada. Deaths were the only gems he wished to wear. Harold God-wine I love. But tomorrow, and the light is spreading already, but tomorrow . . .

In my left arm I have that numb feeling which it always has when someone I esteem is shortly to leave the fight. He will embrace me. I will weep his passing, make a song which I will sell for honey-juice. Then I will rob his grave and fix a wondering eye upon William the Norman lout.

Now my other arm is going numb. Bad for my craft, numbness. So Norman Will too may be plucked away. But Harold God-wine is gentler, more sensitive to doom. And he has dodged ruin too often before. His luck has run well but I hear it panting now, weary. And I'm ripe for a change of master and direction. Two kings dead upon a single field? By tomorrow's end this part of the world could be very, very quiet.

Listen . . .

They are ready to march.

II

Once more, as before, alone. On the road downwards to the sea there were trumpets, there were torches. The lips that blew the trumpets are dead. The lighted torches have gone with their bearers to the grave. William the Lout tramples the fields on his way to the north and the city where he will find his throne.

Men move, birds move and we are changed. I am changed. Seven days ago, six nights ago it were better to say, I was in the banqueting hall of the great abbey in the great city. It was as brilliantly lit as the sun. The smell of meat and bodies was strong. I drank and sang with Gyrth and Leofwine, brothers of the King. Our bones ached from the long march south, from the place where we left Tostig and the Norwegian bear, Hardrada. We could have slept forever, but William the Wolf had landed. We drank and sang ourselves into a frenzy of lustful wishing.

Harold the King stood aloof. His light green eyes were sad and as near to dread as they had ever come. Weariness, of course, and lack of food, for whenever events had him by the throat, Harold was loath to eat.

I joked about his quietness to Gyrth. "Gyrth," I said, "you have more the spirit of a king than he. If he dies, in all this realm there is no fitter head for a crown than yours."

The thegns and housecarls sang and drank and whored their way to stupor. Little wonder that they rallied so slowly to the banners when the march to the sea began.

I had never before been in the middle of a fight. Those

horsemen came at us like the wind. I had a battleaxe and wielded it like a feeble fool. Not a bruise on my body inflicted by anybody but myself.

My own man, independent to the last, I could have sworn that the death of Harold, Gyrth, Leofwine, would affect me not at all. But dead they are and in my heart are three gaping, weeping holes, full of the remembered sound of three of the most golden men who will ever breathe in my sight.

It was all the marching. So many fields and hills beneath our feet. And the trumpets and the torches and the deaths. These things make bonds with other men's minds and bodies.

And I am become a fool, once more, as before, alone.

I will walk forward now with Gyrth and Leofwine glowing at me from the grave. And in front of us walks Harold, the sad-eyed man whose soul had made its peace with death long before the arrow found its mark.

III

It is cold. But not as cold as it was out there in the fields.

They tried to hunt me down, caught me, too. Good huntsmen, these horsemen of the Lout. It will be a crafty Saxon rabbit that finds a safe warren in this land. One of them said he had seen me next to Harold in the battle. But I put on an idiot look and sang a quick little tribute to the Lout.

I am in the great city now. The smoke of fires and a moving multitude have coaxed some of the aches from my bones. Yesterday was Christmas Day. They gave William his crown. In the morning, in the very banqueting hall where I revelled with Gyrth and Leofwine, the new conquerors set up a feast for a mob of us, to sweeten us into an ecstasy of love for the newest King. The meat was as hot, the drink as strong as on the night before the battle. The same woman who had then offered Gyrth her favours, she was there at that Coronation revel. When Gyrth spurned her, she muttered of a dark, impending doom. She had broken teeth which made her curse sound worse. A harlot and a soothsayer, the worst sort. I promised to write her a melody to go along with her street cries, for she says her business is slack.

Twenty years ago, she said, this sort of political confusion would have increased her profits a hundredfold. But age, split teeth, and a tendency to prophesy have taken the bloom off her charm. She breathes and moves . . . And Harold and Gyrth, whose teeth and souls were white . . . No matter.

We have done well by the kestrel and the kite. And will do better.

Yesterday morning, the day of Christ's birth and William's power, we drank ourselves into a mood of adoration for the Great Trampler. We saw him walk through the banqueting hall on his way to the throning chamber. A thick, heavy man, not as given to dreams or gentleness as Harold, not as given to laughter as Gyrth. He passed through our ranks in a cloud of bishops, priests, incense, prayer. We raised a huge shout of acclamation. The guards outside thought it was insurrection. They rushed in and slaughtered half of us.

On the day of his ascension, within a breath of the birthday of Christ the Lord, William had his third baptism. The first was from a priest. The second was from the blood of the only friends I ever knew in the only battle I ever fought in. The third was this.

The last to leave the hall of butchery were the harlot with the teeth as broken, dark and jagged as fate, and myself. They spared us. The minstrel and the whore, the necessary buffoons, camp-followers at the burial of solemnity.

IV

I am old now. My memories are shuffled and scuffed. My duplicities have played so long a game of incest one with the other that my original self, if I ever had one, is now like melted snow.

Sometimes, at night, my memories stir and rise like birds. Not the birds I once laughed with, the falcon and the hawk, but sweet birds with soft voices. I see Harold, the man of long silences, a prime killer of his kind but given to longings for a more peaceful earth. Gyrth, for whom life, death, kingship, love were jests of infallible richness. Leofwine, the brutish and impassive boy. Once only I saw him weep and cry out. When Gyrth's body took the whole sword of the Lout.

A month ago, in the great city sleeping in the shadow of the abbey where Harold and William first felt the crown upon their heads, I thought of these things. And being old and cold and tender now in ways I never was before, I resolved to do a great and memorable thing. A new wreath for the graves of Harold, Gyrth and Leofwine: the death of William.

I followed him across the sea to his Norman land. I travelled in one of the very ships that William used so many worlds ago to come and stuff the English earth with splendid dead.

For William's death I stole a dagger and chose for the deed the very day of the week on which his horsemen ripped us to pieces at that place by the sea.

I found the town where William was. He had just reached it. The place was aflame. I discovered the name of the inn where he was to take meat and wine. I resolved that there he would die.

He died, but through no act of mine. His horse trod on an ember from a house William had burned down. The fall hurt him mortally. I was summoned to his deathbed. A minstrel can assuage the fear and delirium of the dying. I sang him into death. And before he left, he paid me with one smile and a golden coin.

The smile I will cherish. The coin I will lay on a group of graves on the southern edge of England where men I knew hastened to a strange ragged battle which they did not win. Because I could not fight? A bad thought, that, a destructive thought . . .

I shall return that single smile to that silent Lout. And I shall retrieve from that group of graves within the sea's old sound my golden coin. I wish to leave no trace.

What can I buy with my golden coin? Has it the brightness to illumine my scarred prodigious path through my bit of time? Has it the pity to assuage the phantoms of me and the men whom chance laid low and banished to the earth . . . When . . .? Yesterday . . .

Will it ever be further away than yesterday?

The Teacher

Mrs Monroe had taken the history teaching post after the departure of her husband, Mr Glen Monroe. The cool wisdom and gentleness of that man still haunted our minds and the rooms of the school. He was the only person we had met who had thought himself into a state of serenity on this earth, and in his presence we marvelled and gave thanks.

Often when we had been in the lower school, badgered into a lethal rawness by some teacher who had long since ceased to regard teaching as anything but a squalid trap for himself and the taught, Mr Monroe would come in with his smile and his quiet voice and we would, in seconds, be soothed back into tolerance, then a contentment. His was the sort of humanity which, laid like a kiss upon any phase of the far past, would make death and folly apologize for their crass obstructiveness, bow and make way for the healed and resurrected death.

Then he himself had vanished into the gullet of time and change. We could still remember him and Mrs Monroe from the days before the war, addressing meetings in this vestry, that hall, on behalf of peace, collecting signatures for the Peace Pledge, convinced that no man, however mad for his own power and the pain of others, would want war again.

War came, and we watched the sad, stricken face of the man as he walked through the school, masking the outraged fury of his heart with a quiet melancholy. In lessons he would fall oddly silent at places where before he would have attempted a defence, an apology for some bit of vile destructive violence on the part of the world's strange ring-masters.

"Life has been and still is," he would say, "in a state of fever. The germs of fear, greed, frustration still burn in its blood. The fever will pass. The body will grow cool. The mind will become normal and will address itself to the task of living with the affectionate brotherly humility, which we in this room expect from ourselves. Always think of mankind as one body, with limbs that move jerkily, ridiculously now, but to be treated with the same love and patience as you would give to a cripple of your near acquaintance."

In 1942 he was called up. His wife, Mrs Monroe, came to take his place in school. With her we had the same mental experience as we had with him, the same attempt to lay a soothing unguent of tolerance and understanding on the raw hot places of our past. In 1943, in the autumn, he came under heavy shell fire in a tank in Italy. His chest and face were shattered. In 1944 he was brought back to a military hospital which had wards for the unseeable, the virtually dead, the survivors by miracle and irony. It was about seven miles from Mynydd Coch, a lovely village called Tremscott. We had often walked there by way of a path that led through the sea of ferns on the plateau above the town. In 1945, on an October day, Mrs Monroe called us, our group in the fifth form, Wilfie, Spencer, Bosworth, Sam, Leo and the rest of us to her side.

"I've been to see Mr Monroe today."

"How is he, Mrs Monroe? When will he be back?"

"He's just the same. He won't be back for some time."

"We'd like to go and see him, Mrs Monroe."

"That's what I wanted to talk to you about. He kept talking about that outing he did with you to Caerphilly Castle."

We remembered Mr Monroe had promised to take us on that trip when we first began the study of Norman castles in the second form. But something had always cropped up to prevent it. When Mr Monroe had gone into the army we thought we would never make the pilgrimage, for Mrs Monroe, out of school, was always busy with her mother who was ailing. And then quite suddenly, one summer afternoon, Mr Monroe, in uniform and on his embarkation leave before going to Africa, came into the classroom where we were sitting. He asked the headmaster if he could take the boys who had originally put their names down for the trip to the castle.

We travelled by bus, through the valleys and over the moorland. He pointed out the huge defensive details of the ruin, somewhat impatiently, for the whole apparatus of violence bored him and made him ill at ease. He looked at the great circle of the surrounding hills and described how Owen Glyndwr and his men had poured forth from their fastnesses to break their hearts and bodies upon this fist of stone.

"The clenched fist of fear," he said. "Look at it. The defensive stranger in a strange, hating land. For such there is no victory. Owen in his grave is a prettier sight than this mausoleum. Man will ache, man will bleed, for as long as even one member of his tribe knows he has some power, some wealth that is not rightly his and keeps his finger for ever on the gun. If the rapacious lout were only rapacious and willing to go when his crop is full, all would be well. But he is stupid also, and proud, and will not withdraw."

Then he took us to a café and treated us to a meal that took us an hour to eat, spam, chips, ten sorts of cake and four sorts of cordial as well as tea. As he raised his last cup of tea to his lips he stared at his khaki sleeve, smiled and said:

"Each age hugs to its heart its own brand of Black Death. We are not happy without a pestilence. I wonder what my germ will be."

He urged us to clear the cakes, especially Sam who had hardly eaten a mouthful. Since he started in the school, Sam had hung on Mr Monroe's every word.

"But never mind," said Mr Monroe, "remember what I told you. Mankind, one body. Even if it stumbles and mortally crushes you, remember that its limbs are still strange to one another, its brains in fragments, kept in fragments for aeons longer than has been strictly necessary. If it bleeds, clean the wound, let no dirt remain in it to rankle. If it falls, never snarl at it for clumsiness. Smile at it, lift it to its feet, tell it its legs are getting stronger, its direction surer."

Then we walked briefly once again in silence and failing light around the ruin, across the rough neglected ground close to the walls, allowing our senses to be touched by the hazards and outrages of dead time. At my side Leo Warburton was full of pouting reservations, for he had always believed in the placing of a cold authoritarian fist on the hot fuss of our kind. No one was in a mood to argue and Leo said nothing.

On our way home from the castle the hilltop road along which we travelled was upheld in the great golden glow of an all-out sunset. We sang in snatches. For a while Mr Monroe listened to our singing and smiled at us. Then he looked at the red sunset and his smile vanished in a thoughtful silence. We said good night to him on Mynydd Coch square and we had not seen him since.

"He would like to have you visit him," said Mrs Monroe to us, "you boys who went with him to the castle."

"Yes, Mrs Monroe, we'd like to very much."

"Shall we wear our best suits, our dark ones?" asked Bosworth Bowen.

"He won't be able to see you."

Bosworth looked stricken and turned away.

We made the journey to Tremscott by bus, covering in part the same hill road we had taken on our way to the castle, driving through the serene fern-sea that had movements of light trembling over it in the fitful sunlight of the afternoon.

In the hospital, approached through a thick and lovely wood, we walked through long corridors, bringing an unnatural noisiness and jollity with us. Mr Monroe was in a small room, alone. Of his face we could see nothing through the helmet of bandage. His arms were in sight. He said nothing. We looked in a pain of wonder at him, at Mrs Monroe, at each other.

"Just talk," she said. "About yourselves, about the school."

We were silent. We could feel our stupidity bore its way right through to the end of time.

"He wanted to hear your voices, all together," said Mrs Monroe. "He finds it hard to talk today."

All the silence on earth was around us and it had the unmoving white helmet on the pillow for its core. I heard Leo begin a slow stiff formal declaration of gratitude to Mr Monroe for all he had done for us. Leo had heard his father, a councillor, pass these votes of thanks so often he was a master of them. There was hardly a sector of life in Mynydd Coch that Mr Warburton had not covered with his thanks at one time and another, and we had been told that even at table when he thanked Mrs Warburton for a meal he got Leo to second the vote. Leo droned on coldly. The rest of us fidgeted, marvelling that amidst the pelting tears of things Leo should so invariably be the boy with the blotter.

A nurse peeped in at the door, stared and nodded at the bed with a look of unhappy preoccupation and went away again. For myself I was remembering the afternoon in our first year at the school when we had been taken by Mr Wilkins, the small, trembling man who had taught us chemistry.

We had been at the school long enough to realise that most teachers have a wound, some special ineluctable bit of rawness, and ever since we made the discovery we were to be seen wheeling sacks of salt up the school drive to speed on the work of mortal aggravation. Mr Wilkins' mania was a conviction that humanity was covertly muttering about his lack of natural strength and dignity, the failure of his voice to penetrate to the rooms' corners and to ours, his inability to make plain the magic which he knew to lie at the heart of his subject, to have it take wing before us and lift us out of the pool of shabby mischief and malice.

Then there were his tremors, hesitancies and minutes of downright, abject silence in which he seemed to go below surface and stare his defeat and sickness in the eye. To torment him, we would, whenever his eye fell on us, engage in a bit of prison-style, side-of-the-mouth whispering with a neighbour. That afternoon we had driven him into an evangelical frenzy. He appealed to our honour, our pity, our friendship. He explained to us how ill he became if ever he was vexed or ill-tempered. His gestures were big and intense. They struck us as comic, and our laughter was loud and savage.

"Boys, boys, boys!" It was not so much an appeal as a note on the nature of hell.

Then he became silent and greenly pale. His jaw dropped and his eyes bulged. His hands pawed helplessly in front of him as if he were trying to jostle away the evil that was plainly smothering him. He slipped out of sight behind the desk in a faint. As he fell he gave out a moan that shocked us. At that moment Mr Monroe came into the room. He rushed down the aisle calling for some water. It was brought. He leaned over Mr Wilkins, helped him to revive and half carried him to the staff-room.

We waited for Mr Monroe's return, speechless and dismayed, our eyes full of prophecies of blood upon the moon, of heads banged together with such force there would be a quick exchange of teeth. But when Mr Monroe re-entered the room, he merely looked around with his usual grave mildness.

"The march out of barbarism," he said, "is the widening and deepening of the power to be kind. Accept no definition more complicated than that. I will now select an incident from history that will help you, though still utterly barbarian, a little more swiftly along the road."

Then, in the tiny ward, Spencer's voice cut across Leo's. "You know what a boy Sam is for sweet stuff. When he gets his pay from Turner the greengrocer on Saturday night he goes into Jacko Galeazzi's shop and puts down six of those chocolate biscuits that are off points."

"You're a bright one to talk," said Sam. "The way I've seen you shovel it away in that dining hall in school. If you spent Saturday lugging a loaded bike up and down hills you'd bite a bit off Jacko's arm as well."

"No doubt," said Spencer. "Well, there was Sam, the day Mr Monroe took us to the castle. He was thinking over what Mr Monroe had said about the way the hill people had shattered their lives against those bastions and he was very broody. Mr Monroe had got him a plateful of those cream slices that are very special in that café. Mr Monroe had said: 'We have known so much of things like castles, brutal mindless things, that there is a defensive castellated zone of dread in every heart, barring the way to the perils and glories of a full comradeship.' Do you remember that, Mr Monroe?"

I thought I saw a movement of the head, but it may have been an illusion due to having stared for so long at the whiteness of the bed.

"Well, Sam," went on Spencer, "was struck quiet as a mouse by this notion, and he was busy working out what it meant and drawing up a list of elements in Mynydd Coch who might well be called Offa for the dykes they carried around in this connection. He asked Leo if he ever felt a strong sense of mortar in his emotions. Then Sam noticed the cream slices and his eyes lit up. But Bosworth and me kept asking him leading questions about this thesis, and every time Sam got worked up over a fresh point Bosworth or me would nip in and whip a slice."

There was some more talk. Wilfie gave an account of his dealings with Mr Rawlins, the second senior assistant master, in the matter of Bible readings in the hall for the morning assembly, and Wilfie wondered why Mr Rawlins always kept picking passages of intense fury from the Old Testament denouncing adultery when this was not yet an important activity in the school. Leo explained some new suggestions made by Mr Rawlins for bringing greater dignity and uniformity into the dress of the prefects.

"He says it's about time somebody struck a note of pomp in Mynydd Coch. The place is so deficient in a sense of hierarchy it's no wonder it suffers from a sort of social rickets."

"He said its feeling for the ceremonial was bandier than any corgi."

Then Sam related the tale of a persecution maniac called Elmo Allen living in Minerva Meadows, his street, who had chased his entire household around the western side of Mynydd Coch, shouting that he would rather see the world perish by conscious personal malignity than by the impersonal idiocies of war and hunger. Elmo grew tired, for his family was fast and the hatchet a great weight, and he called in at the Library and Institute to listen to a debate on the mechanics of love and pity before handing himself over to the constable.

"He had a point," said Mrs Monroe. "But I am disappointed to hear of him trying to enforce it, in just that way."

"About Minerva Meadows," said Bosworth Bowen, "they are nearly all jingles, with Sam giving out the beat mostly."

A nurse came in and said we should go. A slight convulsion shook the figure on the bed. He raised his arms. We shook his hand in pairs. Then we left.

On the way back a night full of rain clouds fell rapidly. We spoke little. Mrs Monroe, staring out at the plateau which stretched towards the tall rounded hills that stood between us and the west, said nothing.

As we began the downhill road into Upper Mynydd, the rain began to beat around the bus in a temper. We got a sense of dangerous desolation, exposedness, from the thorough ferocity of the large plastered drops against the panes. We were alone in the bus except for its conductor, Galway Davies, who had been at school with us, a few years ahead.

Then Mrs Monroe threw her head against the back of the seat before her, loudly, hurtingly. She broke into a storm of weeping as wild and without curb as the downpour outside. We signalled to Galway Davies to stop the bus. We filed out leaving Mrs Monroe to herself.

The bus resumed its way and soon disappeared into the hissing shadows. For a few seconds we saw the face of Galway Davies looking out at us from the back window of the bus darkened and bewildered. We continued our journey down into Mynydd Coch, soaked. Our thoughts gave out the same strong dank smell as the ferns dripping on either side of us.

Two days later Mr Monroe died. They held a special service in the assembly hall. Mr Rawlins had all the prefects lined up in the front of the whole assembly. Leo, Bosworth, and Pendennis Vaughan all stood rigidly to attention as the Head, in a voice that moved with the jerky anguish of an arthritic limb, read that passage about a new heaven, a new earth, and no more pain, no more death, a truce to pain and an end to tears. But Sam, Spencer and myself, our bodies seemingly relaxed by a sorrow that struck us in some way as familiar, well worn, stooped slightly forward.

Sam's face was ashen, inconsolable in a basic and terrible way. Our voices, when we came to the hymn, were low, uncertain and full of dark-tipped reservations as we came to the lines urging a shroud of acceptance for the outrage of goodness betrayed, the pushing away of lives still creative into the darkness of death and waste.

O Brother Man

"You will know," said Mr Rawlins at the beginning of his civic morality talk to the assembled prefects on Friday morning, "that no one has done more to tackle the practical assessment of juvenile delinquency than myself. Theorizing about the thing is easy enough. Colleagues of mine in this very school are good at it. They talk glibly about the wartime blackout, broken homes, unbalanced curricula, ill-functioning hormones, and the rest, but do they ever venture into the front line in this battle? They do not."

Mr Rawlins paused. His normally restless face was whipped into stillness by bitter thoughts.

"You will remember a boy of this school, Chaplin Everest. I can speak freely about him now because I have arranged to have this boy placed on a farm many miles from here and if he has not, by now, rustled all the livestock, burned the cornfields, and poisoned the farmer, he will stay there and keep the hair of myself and his neighbours on this side of total greyness for another year or so.

"Everest started off at a brisk rate at the age of ten. Department stores were his meat. He one day looted the outfitting department of one such store. Just loaded the clothes on to his person and then asked the manager for a drink to refresh him when he was nearly fainting from the heat of this enormous cocoon of raincoats he had on. On another occasion Everest stole a gramophone record and took it back because there was a scratch on one side and a ruse by the tenor to dodge a top note on the other. He would lift a pen and then create an uproar demanding a finer or thicker nib whatever his fancy might be. Since Everest was never known to do any writing this gesture can be taken as a piece of sheer virtuosity. A queerly vocal and, in

144

a sense, responsible kleptomaniac, that was Everest.

"You know the value I set on music as a means of diverting criminal impulses. I thought this would work with Everest. I offered him a place as a violinist in the small orchestra that plays in the Junior Assembly. While there he made some of the sharpest moves in the history of any musical group. He undid the strap of and removed the watch of that very sensitive and self-absorbed flautist, Walter Fawcett, when Fawcett was half-way through the descant of 'Angels of Jesus, Angels of Light', a first-rate hymn whose libretto I had urged Everest to read beforehand so that he could get the full flavour. And within three weeks of Everest rubbing in his first bit of resin the music stands of the entire band were found in a second-hand shop, and a chemist informed that Everest had slipped into his shop and taken some first-aid material to apply to his legs which had been abraded by the stolen metal on his way down to the town. At that period Everest was working part-time with a draper and when the draper found things getting a little bare around the walls he made a search of Everest's home. Everest's bedroom was found to have a stock of haberdashery that ran Austin Reed a hot second. The draper did not know whether to take Everest to court or trundle his counter to Everest's bedroom and start afresh from there.

"I was on the point of giving up hope and breaking Everest's violin over his head when we found him one morning sitting in a corner of the orchestra almost out of sight behind a wall of brass. He had found a euphonium and in the course of that morning's hymn, a simple one admittedly, he managed to strike a series of tremendous and relevant notes on this instrument. Some of these notes were of excessive volume and sea captains in the roads off Cardiff wired in to ask what we could see that they couldn't. Everest assured me that he had come quite fairly by the euphonium. His father, he said, had bought it out of the product of an insurance policy on an uncle, a chapel-goer, who had been worried into the grave by Everest's conduct.

"Everest seemed reformed. Looking back at it now, I am prepared to explain this by the heaviness of the instrument. Anything that hinders movement makes for virtue.

"Now you may think the thing could have ended there. The

town well rid of a delinquent and Everest blowing himself into a torpor of righteous conformity." Mr Rawlins sighed and stared at a far corner of the sports field, where boys dressed in white were jumping over each other. "Life will at times wear a look of idiot tranquillity. Be sure that at just such moments the monstrous ironies which are shortly going to batter you flat are dusting each other's truncheons and urging each other courteously to take the first whack.

"In the second month of Everest's serving as euphonium player this town was made a borough. The prospective mayor, having made the switch from a short chain to a long chain and rattling both with what I thought a certain ostentation, made his first mayoral procession through the town. He considered that the parade had a quiet, sour look and matters were made worse having groups of Dissenters on the flank, fanatical lovers of a drab, civilian status who went up and down the procession making crude, flatfooted remarks about the mayor's chain. The mayor demanded more colour, body, tone, a blare and a blaze of municipal pomp that would shame or silence the critics.

"The word went out that the two military bands the town had once had were to be revived. They were called the Institute band and the Legion band. The Legion band got restarted promptly because they had a licensed club and that could feed them with funds for new instruments and uniforms. But things were more laggard with the Institute band and no move was made to reopen their old band club-house on that waste patch near the gasworks.

"While the old members of the Institute band were being encouraged to limber up for a march back into history Everest came up to me one morning and said: 'Please, sir, you know my uncle? He's not dead.'

"The statement meant nothing to me. That was the way with Everest. He would state something and you would have to tramp through a thousand feet of tangential facts and fictions to reach the point from which he was actually speaking. Besides, that morning I was confused, not at my quickest. I had found a whole row of boys in the hall fitting grossly secular words to that splendid hymn 'Bread of Heaven'. I was in no mood for Everest and at the back of my mind I felt that there were drunken, un-Welsh overtones about some of the notes produced by Everest on that euphonium which had encouraged the tap-room humour of those interpolations. 'In general terms, Everest,' I said, 'I am glad your uncle is not dead. But what is this to me? I do not wish to appear callous, but do I know him?' 'You remember, sir,' Everest said very earnestly as if reproving me for the shortness of my tone, 'you remember the uncle who died and left the insurance and my father bought my euphonium?' 'Oh yes, Everest, of course. The insured chapel-goer. Let his life and the fruit of his prudence be a lesson to you. What about him now, Everest?' 'Well, sir, he isn't dead.' 'You mean . . .?' 'Yes, sir. There was no insurance. My father didn't buy the euphonium. I stole it.'

"This was too much for me. To hear 'Bread of Heaven' and that tortuous confession from Everest on one morning was going too far. Two nights before, I had seen a film at the Y.M.C.A, specially screened for youth-leaders, in which the priest in charge of a camp for delinquent boys had shaken one of the less regenerate boys like a rat. The priest himself had made that point. 'I am shaking you,' he shouted in his rage, 'like a rat because you are a rat.' That, I thought, was the line with Everest. I grabbed him by the tie and started to shake, trying rather foolishly as I see now to explain to him that I had seen a priest do this in the Y.M.C.A. Everest's movements were quick and hardly perceptible. I found myself shaking the tie like a kind of lasso, but Everest himself was now standing, patient and cool, about six feet away. The Headmaster came in that moment. Try explaining to anyone why you should be waving a noosed tie at a boy who just stands there looking tolerantly at you.

"I visited the home of Everest that evening. A broken and demoralized home. The father, a peering and thoughtful man, had a long record of dishonesty and had been to gaol. His life and personality were of the most shuffling and indeterminate sort. The mother had vanished, perplexed and tired, years before. As soon as I stepped through the door father and son got down to it and made me a meal of excellent fish and chips. It was good to see them fend so well for themselves. On his second chip Everest owned up to having broken into the bandhouse near the gasworks and taken the euphonium. 'The back window of that bandhouse is very easy,' he said in the sort of slow cold voice that should be reserved for science. The father cried a little as if this sort of roguery had never come within his experience, but it might, too, have been the very strong vinegar of which the father had poured a good half-bottle over his chips.

"I consoled the father and said: 'It'll be all right. The boy will take it back and all will be forgotten. Any day now the Institute band will be returning to the old bandhouse to dust off their instruments and it is important that the euphonium be there waiting for them.' I turned around to repeat this to Everest but he had slipped out of the kitchen. I went outside the kitchen door and shouted around for him. No trace.

"I told Mr Everest that he himself would have to take the euphonium back. He lifted up his wet face from his chips, then hobbled around the table and put his hand on my shoulder. I had not noticed the hobble before. When frying the fish he had seemed pretty spry when moving out of the range of flying fat but now he had one of the most pronounced limps I had seen. I felt the night filling up with vast deceptions. Everest had probably left the kitchen in that covert way at some signal from his father. I tried to make my face as hard as I could.

"Then Mr Everest started to talk. He explained that if he had only been in a fair state of health he would have been down to the bandhouse to replace the instrument while the chips had been on so that we could have had our meal without any taint of fear or guilt in the air. But he told some tale of having fallen over a fellow-prisoner who had dropped in a faint in the exercise yard of the prison while some brutal overseer had been making them run at top speed. Mr Everest had been in a condition since then which made it impossible for him to get into any building through the window, however much he would like to do so and once or twice he had so liked. 'Anyhow, not with a euphonium,' he said. 'That's a very hampering article, the euphonium.' Then he put his face very close to mine. He said: 'Mr Rawlins, two things will keep me out of gaol in the future. The first is the terrible pain I get whenever I cock my leg, which is bad for burgling because it makes me give out a terrible groan.' He cocked his leg suddenly and scared the wits out of me with the groan he gave. 'And the second thing is the wonderful friendship you've shown my son.'

"And I knew at once that he wanted me to set the seal on that friendship by transporting that piece of brass tack to the bandhouse. Normally I would have told Everest to get back on the hinge and start finding his son or carrying the thing himself. But I had been touched by the fine meal that had been prepared for me by those two lonely and desperate beings, even though I wondered who in that neighbourhood might still be looking for the three thick cutlets we had enjoyed. Besides, I felt like some scratch of dangerous action to ease the itch of embarrassment I had felt when the Headmaster had come into the hall that morning and found me apparently trying to snare Everest back into his own tie. 'You're a scholar,' said Mr Everest. 'You can do it. And remember what my boy said about that window in the back of the bandhouse.' I listened and as my fingers drummed on the table I realized more clearly than ever that morally that family could not have been better named. High, remote, and glacial.

"He handed me the euphonium. 'After this,' he said, 'the boy will be able to consider himself as much your son as my son.' And the way we smiled at each other we must both have been made a little drunk by all that vinegar and emotional excitement. Then he added that I had better leave by the back way. By now I was entering into the spirit of the thing and I asked Mr Everest whether it wouldn't be better to have some cover for the euphonium like a shawl or a mac. My panic made the thing seem larger as Mr Everest stood ready to clip it to me. I thought we should be lucky to get it through the kitchen door to start with. Mr Everest was against any covering. He said that kind of camouflage would only make it worse. 'Draws attention,' he said. He gave a bang on the metal. 'Best be brazen,' he said and laughed.

"He wished me luck and I started up the garden path. I was nervous as a kitten, stealthy as a cat, using only the tips of my toes and holding the euphonium lightly in my arms ready to toss it instantly into a bush if challenged. As I fumbled with the latch of the door that led into the back-lane I swore I saw the face of the boy Chaplin staring at me from behind a rose bush. The face was grave, quite unselfish, and I had the feeling that if it were really Everest he was wishing me well.

"I reached the bandhouse in the shadow of the high wall that surrounds the gasworks. There is a greasiness in the shadows in that part of town and the smell of gas which is perpetual near that wall did not take long to skim away all the resolve and high spirits that had come so oddly upon me in the Everests' kitchen. For a very small fee I would have returned to the safety of my sitting-room and thrown the euphonium over the gasworks wall, there to puzzle the people who run this undertaking. But I thought of Everest, of how much more likeable and stable the boy had been since playing at the morning services. I owed it to him now to see that he would not be saddled with another stretch under the probation officer or in a reform school for an offence which was not, in a fundamental sense, immoral. How, I asked myself, and no question has ever rung out with such sonority at such a small distance from a gasworks, how does the law stand on thefts committed to procure the means of salvation?

"I found the window mentioned by Everest. The window was shaky to the touch but awkwardly far from the ground. The same man had designed the Institute bandhouse as had designed the Institute and he was far gone in Gothic. Even without the euphonium the entry would have taken a lot of deftness. The only thing was to get the window open, balance on the sill and lift the euphonium in after me.

"I got the window up and hoisted myself on to the sill. I found myself sitting squarely on one of the longest and most penetrating fitments ever used in the building of a window frame. That and the feeling of terror which had come upon me from the moment I had set my hand upon the sill had done something to shrink my legs, and the euphonium on the ground outside looked as far away as if it were at the bottom of a cliff.

"Then I heard a good deal of noise from a public house about three hundred yards away. It was a place called The White Rock because it was traditionally the place where the legendary harpist Dafydd took his last careful look at Mynydd Coch and gave up the ghost and harping with one angry kick at the strings. A considerable group of men were leaving The White Rock and they sounded happy about something. They were happy, as I found when their voices grew nearer and the gist of their talk grew plain. They had not only taken drink but had, just a few minutes before, in a long room of The White Rock, decided to reform the Institute band without delay and were at that very moment on their way to the bandhouse to lubricate and polish their instruments. I could hear the louder of them declare that they would soon be shaming and outblowing the Legion band. 'That lot!' I heard one of them say. It was the voice of their euphonium player, Nathaniel Roscoe, a man barbarous in his devotion to noise. 'They've never risen a cultural notch above Sousa and that selection from Chu Chin Chow where my cousin Reynold Roscoe makes a special effect in the Cobbler's Song by tramping up and down the stage looking pensive, humming very low and using a hammer.'

"I heard them rattle the door in front of me as they inserted the key. For all my patiently laboured gentleness I could at that moment have killed Everest and I could also have spared a side-blow for Nathaniel Roscoe but I instantly prayed to God to forgive me that thought and to help hoist me off that prong or catch on which I was impaled. One day I will ask the boys in the bandhouse about the shape and function of it. No doubt it is connected with the strange inner lore of bandmanship.

"By an act of sweating fury I lifted my body off the sill and fell to the ground outside. I pulled the window down just as the front door was thrown open. I heard the roaring voice of Roscoe say a second before the window closed to: 'Hullo, these Legion boys have been here.'

"I gathered the euphonium into my arms and bolted. I am not sure why I did that. Probably some foolish fear of fingerprints planted in me by my recent traffic with the Everests. It would have taken an hour to wipe that instrument clean at all thoroughly. I ran at full speed through the lane that ran parallel to the main street of the town that debouches into the square.

"My movements were crouched and erratic with panic and strain and every ten seconds or so I heard the metal of the euphonium strike hard against the asphalt as if trying to brake me. I heard the sound of a brass band playing but my time sense had been disordered by shortness of breath and I supposed that the Institute band, in the few seconds since I had started my run with the euphonium, had grouped around their conductor and launched into a tune. I tried to check my run to think more carefully about this point but my fears were making fools of all my limbs and before I knew it I was in the main street at the very moment when the Legion band, in their civilian suits and making a rehearsal march, swung past the opening of the lane through which I had been making my way from the bandhouse. Few people had spotted me. Thoughts fell like bolts in my mind. With a brass band coming up the street, what is the public to think of a euphonium player who darts away from them at right angles? I pulled my hat as low as I could over my eyes and fell in as a kind of extra in one of the band's back rows where the instruments seemed roughly of the size and shape of the one I was carrying. I put the mouthpiece of the instrument to my mouth, imitating the angle most general among my neighbours, but fortunately produced no note that might have proved my lack of right to be there. My posture must have overdone because I was told sullenly by one of the drummers to go back to the orthodox hold and keep in step.

"As we approached a zone of clear light I saw the Headmaster of the school come out of one of the local vestries. I held the euphonium up high enough to hide my face and just as I was doing this and trying at the same time to pull my hat down even lower, that brusque drummer who had cautioned me before, that ex-wrestler Noah Finney, banged at my euphonium with his drumstick and said that he was beginning to suspect that I had been sent by the Institute band to break up the harmony and the order of march. He also leaned forward and pulled at my hat, saying that any sort of pressure on the brow was the worst thing out for a euphonium player. I fled up the very next opening. I heard the kettle-drummer, that timid semi-invalid Benjamin Boon, say to Noah Finney that if he had known that things were going to be so jumpy on the march he would never have joined except for sit-down performances.

"I found my way back to the Everest home. Father and son were in the kitchen prepared to start on another considerable meal. Not one of them asked why I was back or what had happened. The boy took the euphonium from me and played what I took to be some sort of rogue's grace over the food. He said the instrument did not seem to have taken any harm from its jaunt. The father invited me to help them in putting away the very oily dish of cheese and onion. I said nothing. I shook their hands to compliment them on being on point duty at what was without question one of the busiest and brassiest sections of the life force. I put my fingers briefly into the hot cheese to get some warmth and confidence back into my body. Then I left.

"The next day I was busy. I bought a new euphonium and caused it to be delivered anonymously to the door of the Institute bandhouse. The boy Everest joined the band the next day and he and Nathaniel Roscoe made a good pair, but I think there is an essential nihilism in Roscoe, a baritone in light opera as well as a euphonium player, which did not help Everest solve any of his later moral equations.

"And there was another thing. I was pretty certain that the Headmaster had spotted me as I walked on the flank of the Legion band despite that last desperate tug at my hat, which had left little more than an inch of my face in view. My flannel trousers had been freshly washed and were excessively light and easily recognised, and the Headmaster had a naturally downcast glance which made him good at trousers. I remembered that his father, years before, had written a history of all the chapels between Cross Hands and Seven Sisters. These had been issued in a de luxe leather-bound edition at a high price and at a time when the market for leather-bound books about chapels anywhere had dropped down dead. I paid the full price for this work and asked the Headmaster to accept the collection on behalf of the school. He did that and I do not think his opinion of me improved much even then.

"All that expenditure was not without its bitter little echoes in my private chambers. At the time I was becoming friendly with a charming and dignified lady of this town. I had the intention of subsidizing a trip to the National Museum for about twenty members of the Sunday School in which she was interested. These were children from a rough quarter and had maximum need of some cooling thoughts about the past. I had made the promise to my friend. Then Everest, the great gutter of hopes, had come along and that was that.

"Behind every piece of virtue on this earth there is a legion of aching hearts and empty pockets. Somebody has paid. I know."

That Vanished Canaan

"There is still a vicious vacuum in the lives of the young." That was the first thing that Mr Rawlins told us when he had assembled us all together in the Sixth Form Room. "I was at a meeting of the Juvenile Delinquency Committee last evening. We were discussing the case of a boy of eleven. Utterly Americanised in his speech and ways. Walked about with a peculiar strut which caused his parents and the workers of the clinic to think he had some deformity. But it turned out that he was imitating an actor on the screen who takes the part of gangsters. This boy confesses to going four or five times a week to the pictures. At first he used to steal in without a ticket, but later this struck him as being a little naïve, well below the standard of skullduggery set by his idols and guides in the films. So he took to breaking into chapels and rifling collection boxes. You see the progressive and terrible line? The flight from any coherent tradition we ever had, like piety absorbed at the knee of one's father and mother, instruction in a fundamental morality at the Sunday School and the provision by the members themselves of their own wholesome entertainments in such cultural foci as the Band of Hope and penny readings. The first result is a mere oafishness, a repellent lack of thought for others, a failure to respond to beauty. From there it goes on not merely to felony but felony in terms of blasphemy."

Mr Rawlins' face had grown quite pale, his voice quite shrill.

"I'll be blunt with you. For a rifler of collection boxes in a holy place I would regard no punishment as too severe. The offender in a case like that forfeits any claim to decent treatment. This little fiend had opened out a nice little road for himself. If there was money in a box he would smash it and empty it. If the box

154

were empty he would scribble an obscene message to the congregation telling them in terms I could not repeat to look sharp and have a thought for the young.

"On one note which I saw he even quoted a bit of Scripture in which charity to the young is praised as a great virtue. It was lucky that he had this streak of literary bravado. One of the notes was written on the back of a court demand for maintenance served by his mother on his father who ran away leaving the woman with four children to fend for. There you have the whole ghastly process of disintegration spotlit."

"But don't you ever go, sir?" asked Benny Turner. Benny belonged to a very advanced dance band called the Mynydd Coch Mixers, an empirical covey of jivers who were trying to achieve a rhythm which would perfectly reflect the effect on the human nerves of Marx and New Orleans.

"For myself and the cinema," said Mr Rawlins, ignoring Benny, "I will say this. I did not go until I was fourteen. The last film I saw was de Mille's 'Ten Commandments', a film with a strong enlightening theme but marred for me by the excessive carnality introduced into the scene of Miriam and the Golden Calf. I have seen Mynydd Coch on nights of national celebration turning a leering and drunken face to the world, but that Miriam and those goaded Israelites around that idol carved their own deep repulsive niche in the prison wall of the libido.

"A man sitting by me, a man whom I had long known as utterly clean living, a doyen of organ pumps-men and the painter in rough oils of some of the most moving missionary studies I have ever seen drawn on the back of linoleum, Philo Wren his name was, he kept groaning as this Miriam kept putting her limbs more and more deliberately before the public. I remonstrated with Wren because he was setting a whole belt of groaning going in our part of the cinema.

"At first he said he was doing this only out of sympathy with Aaron, who now had lust on the agenda of nuisances to deal with as well as weariness after all that time in the wilderness. But then Philo Wren leaped to his feet and went clearly berserk. He had to be led out. Then he was taken home to his mother. I have not been to the cinema since, but the case of this boy, the ravisher of collection boxes, makes me think that the screen has now entered into an even more sinister phase than the one in which it was spinning towards climax in the writhings of that Miriam. I haven't been since." Mr Rawlins dropped his arm from its predicatory stiffness. "But I intend going again."

"Good show this week, sir," said Bosworth Bowen pleasantly.

"What's that you say?"

"At the Alcazar in Anniversary Row. An exposure of marijuana."

"Of what?" Mr Rawlins read no Sunday papers. The only drugs he had ever heard of cured people.

"It's a drug. A happy herb, as they say. Scenes in this film that will thrill and revolt you." Bosworth passed all three of our cinemas on his way to school. He studied their advertisements carefully. Get him on the subject of films and he could talk exactly like a billboard. Mr Rawlins was looking cautiously at Bosworth.

"Men turned into beasts and women driven mad with desire," said Bosworth. "The flesh made clay and the soul made dross. There are pictures showing these antics plain as day in the porch of the Alcazar. Can't get near them. Like that Miriam, I would say, but the elements down at the Alcazar in this picture don't even have the excuse of wandering through deserts. They just take a few drags at these fags and they're aflame."

Mr Rawlins blinked again but said nothing. His head dropped, his face painfully pensive. His mind was away, in a tiny cinema in the border country, beating its head in a tattoo of fierce protest on the seat in front against the activities of Miriam and the self-betrayal of Philo Wren.

"You can plant it in the garden," said Bosworth very genially, smiling at Mr Rawlins as if thinking that Mr Rawlins, who was always on about the world's dwindling resources, would be glad to hear about this.

"A nice change from leeks," said Benny Turner, and Benny's voice brought Mr Rawlins back to the challenge, his head up, his nostrils wide and sniffing evil on every wind, and his arm up stiff for the assault.

"For most of you," said Mr Rawlins savagely, "the cinema has been a subversive scourge, an ugly rash of flippancy upon the golden earnestness of yester-year. The cinema and the urge to do paid work out of school, holiday work and the mania on the part of the young to forsake the ancient ideal of dedication to study and to lope like hounds after coin and more coin for every imbecile craze and opiate indulgence that comes upon us, these are the things that are making whole cemeteries jump with astonished and rotating grandfathers. I have known boys in this school who spend so much of their time in the cinema they could not find their way from the back of the class to the blackboard without an usher's torch behind them. I knew a boy whose consumption of ice lollies, bought from his earnings as a balloon blower-up at the local fairground, was such that he would pause in the middle of a sentence wondering whether to develop diabetes or frost bite. This mood of hesitation, together with the permanently pursed, flute playing type of pucker on his lips brought on by weeks of balloon blowing, put one and all on edge. I worked it out that his private expenditure on lollies was equal to what my dear old dad spent on his front-room suite when he married. True, the suite was meagre and the front-room small but there is no doubt that this boy put the equivalent of a sugared glacier under his belt. Moreover, his experience with the balloons was such that his mania to be blowing into anything that looked a little deflated landed him more than once on the psychiatrist's couch."

Mr Rawlins dropped his chin on his chest and thought about depravity. When he got into this mood he would usually, after a minute or so of darkening reflection, grunt and leave the room. But what he did that morning was fling his head up and stare at the ceiling with a terrible disgust.

"I wonder," he said, "how many of you have ever thought of becoming monks."

Some of us closed our eyes, some nodded, some slid along the treacherous, splintering benches of the Sixth Form Room to show that even for Mr Rawlins this struck us as a novel bit of speculation. We had come across some strange elements in Mynydd Coch but we had not yet caught up with monks.

"A pity," said Mr Rawlins. "It would mutually be of enormous advantage to us all if we could arrange for massive withdrawls from the common contract." He examined some selected faces of boys right at the back of the room who shared their time between Mr Rawlins and a study of the life that shuffled along the road that flanked the north side of the school. "Enormous benefit," he said. "There are some of you who could be improved no end by enlarged cowls on your duffel coats and a rigid discipline of the flesh."

He paused for a moment to give us a chance to ponder on why he had brought up this subject of monks. We realised he did not mean it as a serious contribution to his weekly talks on 'Career Patterns'. Geo-physics was his latest career craze and he had shepherded so many boys into this new field we could see the earth's strata taking as bad a beating in the next few decades from professional meddlers as it had from all the earthquakes we have had to date.

"I was speaking to an old boy of this school last night and what he had to tell me made me very thoughtful. His name is Jethro Sugden. The name Jethro strikes me as having had this boy in a kind of truss from the very start. It is a name with patriarchal overtones and sounds as if it had just been spoken through a thick beard. I have often told parents who have discussed this matter with me that there are certain Christian names that lie on the heads of the infants to whom they are given like helmets of lead. And Jethro, I think, is well up among the helmets. Sugden proves it. He is now doing research in Semantics at one of our better universities, and I feel myself that if Sugden had been steered into geo-physics and a fine open-air life with an oil company his present mood would be very different. Semantics is the study of how emotional weather has twisted the shape and significance of words and in my view it has led Sugden to the very porch of the clinic. A few months ago he told me: 'There is no sin, there is simply an ignorance or distortion of words. If man wore his skin as thin as he wears his vocabulary his blood could not be contained. Believe me, Mr Rawlins,' Sugden told me, and there was a terrifying earnestness in him as he spoke, 'if a man is not making himself clear he is sure to generate a huge darkness either to avenge himself on the lucid minority or simply to hide his own embarrassment.'

"I told Sugden that these ideas struck me, a scientist, a manualist, a man of simple traditional faith, as being slightly manic. I told him to take up walking or bowls.

"But last night there was no assurance in Sugden. He said that the disorder among men struck him as being irreparably squalid and he was now thinking of leading a purely meditative life with all words safely dumped in the bin outside. I pressed him for reasons. He explained that with a tribe of yelling traumas encamped in the very midst of us and asking Crazy Horse's permission to go out scalping, any active contribution to the social stock would only deepen the current idiocy. He asked me if I knew of any good monasteries. I was proud to tell him that I had been brought up in a part of the Nonconformist body that most virulently rejected the kind of recessive defeatism that finds virtue in a ritual aloofness.

"Let me explain more fully about Sugden. He is a boy who is too easily set alight. Any new enthusiasm kindles him into a blaze. And when that happens, be sure that it is with your own tears you have to supplement the efforts of the Fire Brigade. When he was in the middle school he urged me to make the obstacle race in the school sports more and more difficult because he said his spirit felt purged after grappling with a really good obstacle. It was he who suggested such innovations as the cream puff suspended above a bucket of water on a piece of swinging string. See four boys snapping at these confections without using their hands and you have a grotesque parody of man. It was three ministers of religion, no less, who came personally to me and asked me to banish the cream-puff test from the obstacle race. Hideously Babylonian they called it and I had to agree. Sugden also introduced the ladder between the rungs of which the racers had to squeeze themselves. He himself was much larger than the average competitor in this race but he insisted on competing. He had gone around every other boy in school big beyond his years and still young enough to enter for the race and whipped them in as competitors. The ladder was used only in the final round and Sugden and his friends were all qualifiers. They approached the ladder at the same time. They got stuck half-way through. It was a terrible sight. There was Sugden urging his companions to compress their muscles for a final effort and the companions cursing Sugden and threatening to kill him as soon as they got free.

"I approached Sugden and asked him the position because

disci and javelins would shortly be landing on the very spot where Sugden and his friends were trapped. He asked me if the sports committee would allow the bodies of himself and his fellow racers to be well greased with a view to helping them through the ladder. At that moment I was being stared at by the three ministers of religion who had just been carrying on about the cream puffs, and I had to tell Sugden that I thought this grease motif would be introducing too overt a note of sensual pleasure into a day that was supposed to be strictly Spartan. I got hold of the groundsman and a few prefects and they lifted the ladder bodily and took it, with Sugden and his friends still inside, to a corner of the field where the groundsman sawed them free. After an experience like that you only need something like semantics to finish you off.

"Sugden carried this disproportionate zeal into the odd jobs he took up to supplement his pocket money. He covered a unique range of out-of-school work. When he was still a pupil here he had the biggest newspaper round in Mynydd Coch. To get the papers distributed he had to get up well before dawn. His father was a kind of insomniac who would spend hours of the night reading and meditating, probably about Sugden, in the kitchen. He and Sugden would often meet on the stairs, one on his way up and the other on his way down, both in a fair stupor and they would nod a greeting. Sugden would sort out his papers at the station with great haste and he would then, moving quickly as a ferret through the shadows, distribute the wrong papers to a record number of houses. Conservatives, Liberals and Socialists found themselves receiving the sheets of the opposite party and Sugden carries more responsibility than the cost of living for some of the baffling results at recent elections. The three political agents had to bring pressure to bear to have Sugden's round cut down and the lighting at the station improved. His papers delivered, he would crawl into school just for the warmth and a nap. He is the only boy I have heard reciting the Vitamin Tables who has started on a genuine singing note and ended on a snore.

"While still at school he went to work with that well known Mynydd Coch dairyman, Coronwen Cridland the Cream. At this stage of his life Sugden seemed to be on a kind of perpetual dawn patrol. I warned Cridland about Sugden and the hazards to which he stood exposed with Sugden on his flank. But Cridland, himself made torpid by milk and early rising, was indifferent to my warnings. Cridland had one of those electrically driven floats that purr at one through the dawn. Sugden was keen to take the wheel of this float but he had no licence for this. Sugden at this time was not licensed for anything at all. Cridland warned him off. Cridland had been touchy about keeping on the right side of the law since 1929 when he was accused by that malicious rival of his, Iolo Chard the Churn, of putting so much water into his milk he was sued by the Water Board for aggravating a drought and abusing his taps, and lowed at by complaining cows who thought Cridland was getting them a bad name.

"Cridland made the mistake of fitting Sugden out with a long snowy-white coat which gave the boy a priestly and powerful look. This coat deepened Sugden's urge to be at the controls of the float. One morning Cridland had reason to dally at some house and Sugden stepped aboard. He was at the top of that slope which runs down Mynydd Coch's west end. Sugden told me later that he intended nothing more than a trial canter of about ten feet, a little purring spurt to show Cridland his mastery. He started belting down that slope like a plummet and Sugden was quite unable to find the lever, knob or button that would bring the contraption to a halt. He even tried, half-way down the hill, pouring three or four bottles of milk over the engine but all this did was to produce a kind of meringue or souffle, which, thinking he might as well go well-fed into eternity, he scooped up and ate. It was still dark and the streets unlit and early morning workers were sent scattering like chaff by this scarcely audible chariot with what seemed to be a crouching ghost at the wheel. Things were not made happier by having Sugden lean far out of the float bawling warnings at these elements. There are still some of the latter who are convinced that there was nothing human about the apparition at all. The float came to a sharp rise and stopped of its own accord. Cridland had followed on foot at a good speed and also in a white coat and finishing off those few who still had a little serenity left after their brush with Sugden. There is no doubt that they would still be trying to separate Cridland's toe cap from Sugden if Cridland had not tripped heavily over the white coat that Sugden had slipped off as a token of defeat and withdrawal.

"My next encounter with Sugden was near a fairground on the beach at Ferncove. He was at University by this time and was earning some vacation money. He was in charge of a stall that was vending a type of sandwich called, repellently, Hot Dogs. Sugden was wearing the sort of tall linen hat associated with chefs and I have seen yachts proceeding under a smaller swell of white cloth than Sugden had on his head at that moment. He was introducing a note of intolerable buffoonery into his showmanship, shouting 'Dogs, Dogs,' and then rattling off a little catalogue of canine breeds such as Sealyham, Corgi and so on. There was quite a lot of laughter from the less thoughtful but Sugden soon fell to stammering when he caught sight of me. His hand as he slapped mustard on what he was now calling 'the bangers' was less confident. But he soon regained something of his old effrontery. He offered me a Hot Dog. As he had already focused the attention of the crowd on me by referring to me as a distinguished judge at dog shows I could not refuse. I then found it difficult to get the sandwich out of Sugden's hand. I saw that in his confusion he had laid two of his own fingers alongside the two sausages and in my haste to get hold of the thing and have done with the whole embarrassing business I almost jerked Sugden over the counter. I told him that this introduced a very unwholesome note into catering."

Mr Rawlins went to one of the windows and started tapping at a pane, as he always did when his thoughts had reached some kind of bend in moral space.

"Last night," he said, "I spoke sharply to Sugden about monasteries and the folly of his wishing to become a monk. As these memories fall into place I am beginning to change my mind."

Land! Land!

U sually the annual trip of the Debating Club at the Library and Institute was an austere thing, a sombre drag through the adjoining vale with such boys as Edwin Pugh and Nestor Harris taking the members down long lanes to see a cromlech or a mansion where Henry Morgan, the pirate once lived. We were interested in Morgan because he was one of the few Welshmen to fulfil himself without ripping up a coal seam or conducting a choir, but if Pugh was right about the number of mansions in which Morgan had at one time lived he could not have had much time left over for piracy.

Then Edwin and even Nestor ran out of facts and we ran out of patience. The members decided to organise a trip of frankly pagan bent. Theo Morgan the Monologue summed up our desires: "Let us give the dialectic a rest and let debauchery take the floor. We shall go forward through a gateway of chips and ale."

Moelwyn Cox, the tenor, wanted a trip to Glyndebourne to hear an opera, but this was turned down by Willie Silcox who said that many of our most thoughtful members had been made tone deaf and averse to opera by falls of heavy concepts inside the skull and also, that Glyndebourne did not favour the charabanc trade. That commission agent, Kitchener Bowen the Book, wanted a trip to Ascot but Silcox said that horses running at speed would be in too vivid a contrast with very static things such as gorsedd stones and cromlechs that Edwin Pugh had been showing us for years.

So we decided on a trip over the water to Weston and then inland by bus. Moelwyn Cox hummed a little Mozart and Bowen recited a few tempting odds but there was no real protest.

The trip was on a Sunday because as Celts we wanted to get

away from our licensing laws and the sight of a pub open on a Sunday struck a note of miracle, but Edwin Pugh told us not to overdo this note of wassail.

"If I see any sign of jocosity ripening into swinishness, the Debating Club will see me handing in my larynx and the draft of next year's programme as a mark of protest and withdrawal."

The bus was to go around Meadow Prospect picking us up in time to be in Cardiff by ten for the boat. A fairly heavy rain was falling as the bus started out and our chairman, Gomer Gough the Gavel, asked for a formal motion on whether the rain would stop. Most of the members were in their Sabbath dark, very tidy. Edwin Pugh got right out of his seat and said formally that he thought that the weather, far from improving, would probably get worse. Nobody disagreed.

Gomer Gough made the count of members.

"One short," he said. "Who's not been picked up?"

"Dewi Dando."

"Where was he supposed to wait?"

"Corner of Harmony Crescent," said Teilo Dew. "I told him it was there he was to wait. But there was a high wind blowing at the time and also Dando was singing at the top of his voice. So he might be mistaken."

"Try his home," Gomer shouted to the driver. "And that reminds me," he said turning to the rest of the outing. "I am glad that Dando has started this Pimpernel antic so early in the morning. It touches on an issue I'd like to air here and now. On a trip like this the party disperses from time to time and it is vital that we reassemble on the dot to get on with the next stage of the tour. Dando is a terror for straying off and I remember a disastrous trip before the war when we got back two days late due entirely to Dando slipping his urges off the leash and becoming involved with women and so on."

The bus stopped outside Dewi Dando's house. His wife told us flatly he was waiting outside the Library and Institute.

"See?" said Gomer, "as vagrant as a grain of sand, this Dando."

We got to the Institute. An old voter, who had helped to build the place in 1905 and seemed to have been resting on the steps ever since, told us that Dando had been there, had grown weary of waiting and had now gone back home.

We moved on through the quiet streets.

"There he is," shouted Bleddyn Bibey the Blast, the euphonium player, who on all trips made a point of hanging out of the bus and acting as a scout.

Way down the road was a stooped sad figure in a long top coat. We were all silent when the bus stopped because there had been something tragic about the look of Dando from the back. He climbed into the bus, as if reluctantly. He was very wet. He had his cap pulled down almost to the middle of his nose, but some of us thought he had done this to deepen the doomed look he wished to put on at that moment. He let his eyes wander around the bus and at last they fell like a bag of iron on Gomer.

"You lot," he said. "You bright beauties. Wanted to leave me behind, did you? I suppose that Gough there has been poisoning your minds against me with tales of how I was forty minutes late for that bus twelve years ago in Tewkesbury. And all I wanted was another little look at those very old graves."

Gomer was fanning himself with the typed itinerary and looking detached.

"He saw the graves all right. And when he came out of the hallowed precincts, as the pious call them, he was lugging the statue of an angel and had a posse of vergers just behind him demanding bolts of vengeance. In some phases, Dando, you're a bit of a vandal."

"Now don't quibble, Dewi," said Edwin Pugh. "Sit down here and get dry."

The boat was packed and as we marched on to it from the bus Dewi Dando stuck like glue to Gomer, glaring at him and as if defying him to say that he was not there to be counted. The sun had come out strongly now but Dewi would not take off his top coat because it gave him a suffering look.

As soon as the ship moved out of the harbour we went down to the bar and a multitude of other trippers flooded down behind us.

"Two centuries of religious intensity have given the Welsh thirst an unnatural edge," said Edwin Pugh but I noticed that he went down the stairs as briskly as anyone. "The collective suction of these voters when they start serious drinking will slow the boat."

The boat was rocking noticeably. People holding their drinks with landlubberly stiffness found a lot of their beer being shaken out of the glass.

"Let your bodies swing with the motion of the boat," said Teilo Dew, who had spent a short time in the navy. "The motion of the boat."

We did as he said and found the whole drink being whirled out of the glass, and we had some sharp words from the people around. We cursed Teilo and told him to forget his years at sea.

An accordion struck up. There was a large group of middle-aged women in the bar, women, we were told, working in a button factory at Birchtown. Their basic weariness was gaily painted over and they were out to enjoy themselves. We did not blame them for we have heard that making buttons on a large scale can be demoralising. The women tried to dance in the tiny bar, lifting their skirts and singing a song called 'Knees up, Mother Brown', an inscrutable item. They were led by a woman in a chintzy skirt who looked as if she were going to wring from that day the stored juices of forty years waiting.

Edwin Pugh stared at them fascinated, and said he was just staying down in the bar as an anthropologist. Sitting in a corner was an ancient voter who rarely had the bottle away from his lips. He was also pitching into a pile of sandwiches. He winked at me.

"It's a hard old life, isn't it?" he said and laughed in a key that made Willie Silcox say that a holiday steamer was no place to come and go off the hinge.

Dewi turned to the accordionist.

"Tell me, Waldo, do you know 'The Wreck of the Birkenhead'?"

"No, thank God. I fancy something frisky myself."

"Take a rest then."

Dewi sang 'The Wreck of the Birkenhead' and dragooned a group to stand around him when he got to the last stanza to suggest the lining of doomed men. The ancient voter in the corner chuckled and said again that it was a hard life, but there was an edge of malice in his eye which said that he would not be sad if Dando were really going down for the third time. Other people pretended to be hanging on to their bottles. Some looked

pensively at the waves dashing against the porthole and asked if
Dando had been sent along by the Rechabites to spoil the trip.
Dando roared to a finish to a glugging of ale.

We arrived at Weston. Edwin got Dewi by his side and I could
hear him pelting Dewi with a round of cautionary axioms, like
how awkward it would be to drop down dead in sin thirty miles
from home and in the middle of a jaunt that the lads had been so
long saving for. Gomer Gough, waiting for the crowd at the
gangplank to thin, had sat down on a bench where the spray had
formed a deep puddle. He was now walking with a duck-like fold
of the frame that increased his look of gravity a hundred times.
The accordionist had started again and a girl in a yellow jumper
was singing 'At the Parting of the Ways' with no tone and
gestures that were as upsetting as the roll of the boat.

We shuffled up the long grey pier. Teilo Dew was holding his
Sunday paper at full stretch above his head. He said the gulls in
this section of the coast were mean and anti-tripper and out to
humiliate the Celts at every turn of the wing.

We had a brush with the man collecting tolls.

"You boys take up where the Vikings left off," said Edwin,
and then we began marching across the long pier, our eyes fixed
alternately on the hostile sea beneath and Dewi Dando, who was
roving up and down the flank of our platoon like a demented
sheepdog.

Gomer Gough marshalled us outside the bus at Weston for the
second stage of our outing, the tour through North Somerset.
Stragglers and strayers had been brought back sharply to the bus
by a shrewd manoeuvre on Gomer's part. He had our friend,
Bleddyn Bibey the Blast, to stand outside the bus with his
euphonium at the ready and at a sign from Gomer he blew a
major note. This sent a lot of dignified looking people, who were
walking in and out of hotels, running for shelter, and a
policeman came on and touched Bibey on the shoulder. Bleddyn
just kept on because when he is firmly on the job with his
euphonium he is numb. I have seen the most amazing things
happen to Bibey when he has been blowing into this contraption,
and not a ripple of reaction out of him. It is a kind of death.
Gomer explained to the policeman about the great trouble we
had the year before with members who had to be sought out and

chased up every whipstitch.

"That's all right." said the policeman. He jerked his finger at Bleddyn Bibey. "Just flag this boy to a halt. This is a very dignified place. He's lowering the tone."

We went for lunch to a roadhouse not far from Weston. The place was so large, cool and elegant that Jehoidah Knight the Light, a prophetic radical, said its high windows, soundless floors and shaved lawns could well be used as a rough guide to the New Jerusalem. There was a softly lit bar into which we tramped as genteelly as we could and we tried to forget how sullen the barman looked when we revealed no interest in the expensive liqueurs he showed us.

"Our tastes are ignorant and simple," said Willie Silcox and the barman looked as if he believed him.

I shared a table with that very mean voter, Caradoc Shanklyn. It was Shanklyn who, in the most lightless days of the '30s, uttered the phrase that was later used on the more sombre type of Christmas card: "There's only one trouble with a threepenny bit; once you break it it goes drib-drab." He had also tried to save on cigarettes by making a crude sort of cigar from a cabbage-like herb which must have contained some stimulant drug because after three or four drags there was Shanklyn racing up and down the street shouting "God is not mocked" and demanding death for Gomer Gough, Edwin Pugh and Willie Silcox, three implacable rationalists at the Institute.

For years Shanklyn had come into our club taking this member and that for a cigarette or a drink and boasting that the catch of his purse had rusted. But that day the boat trip had relaxed his tight frowning fibres. The sight of our happiness, and the lush trappings of the roadhouse moved him to a mood of joyful affirmation. He asked the four people at our table what they wanted. At first we thought he wanted to know what we expected from life in general terms but he said he was referring to drink and here and now. We told him, asking if we could go higher than a weak beef-extract. He told us that the sky was the limit. He went to a bar with two of us just behind him in case he fainted or fled. He came back with a tray full of drinks. His legs were bowed with shock and his face was like old paper. He just planked the tray down and told us in a voice that had gone twice around the tomb to help ourselves. We did so. He had no drink himself and all he did was stare at us and gulp in unison. We just thought he was leaving himself free to enjoy the sight of liquid bought by him being put away. His lips and hands were trembling, which was strange, for Shanklyn was normally kept very cool and still by avarice.

"What's up, Caradoc?" I said. "You bad after the boat or what?"

"Do you think," he said, "do you think they'd cheat me on the change in a place as posh as this?"

I looked at the sullen barman who was now apologising to a group of women for our presence in an accent that went with amateur drama.

"Almost certainly," I said. "That voter, the barman, is out to clear club outings from the earth."

"I gave him ten bob," said Shanklyn, "and I get eightpence change." He clutched my arm with a violence that jerked my glass away from my mouth. "Eightpence change from a ten bob note. Just for these few drinks."

"Challenge him," I said. "That barman has an insolent look on him. Go on up there, Caradoc. Make him recount the bill and denounce him as a cheat before all those women."

Caradoc almost ran up to the bar. I saw the barman refer Caradoc to a printed tariff. Then he carefully made the recount, using Caradoc's fingers as well as his own, and roughly, as if he would have liked to present Caradoc's pelt to the women as a souvenir of the day the Silurians came.

When Caradoc came back he was even more bandy-legged with dismay and his lips had gone beyond even trembling. He sat down. "Oh God and Holy Dewi," he said. "And as for you, Ganelon," he told me, "if you want any challenging and denouncing done, do it yourself." He pointed to the barman. "He made the recount. He had cheated himself. He had charged me a shilling too little." He prodded each of us in turn as we lifted our glasses to our mouths. "Enjoy that. Enjoy every sip of it. You've just about left me bare for the day. Now lend me fourpence. I've still got to square up with that rodney."

After the meal Gomer thanked the manager, a suave, bearded man, for this golden glimpse of elegance, urbanity and repose.

The manager was delighted and went into a corner where there was a piano.

"I will send you on your way, my friends, with a caress of sound," he said with a smile.

Very softly and tenderly he played some Chopin preludes. "Damn, if this isn't style, I ask you," murmured Gomer, touched by the moonlit lining of the moment.

But Dewi Dando who had had two pints too many kept tapping his table with his fork and saying to his companions that the bearded pianist was just trying to take a rise out of us with his squirely airs. Half-way through a prelude Dewi approached the piano.

"Now, let's have a bit of life, boy," he said. "Give me the opening bars of 'The Trumpeter'." This was a baritone song about cavalry charges and death, and full of notes that gave Dando every chance to rattle the cups and intimidate adjudicators.

Dando gave out a note that startled everybody except Bleddyn Bibey the Blast. The pianist looked pained and closed the piano. He nodded across at Gomer.

"If you leave now, sir, perhaps a little of the charm of our first encounter will survive."

Dando was in a high rage. He stood in the middle of the dining room, shaping up, rubbing his nose with his thumb, an occupational tic with all the fighters we've produced in Meadow Prospect, and calling on the manager to defend himself. "And spare a couple of pearlers for that barman," said Caradoc Shanklyn malevolently.

From there we went on to the caves of Cheddar and Wookey Hole. Edwin Pugh and Iestyn Clovelly, who were the joint education secretaries of the Excelsior club, had been attending a course of lectures of pre-history and they had managed to work the places into the itinerary. They pooh-poohed extroverts like Dewi Dando who said caves were too gloomy and no improvement on the two-foot nine seam at Meadow Prospect, a cramped sector. "Judging by the number of holes we are being taken to," said Dando, "it wouldn't surprise me if there's somebody in Somerset paying Gough to keep the outing out of sight."

The caves had a poor effect on Caradoc Shanklyn. That

business of the ten shilling note had brought his latent anxieties to a bursting head, and he was followed around the caves by Teilo Dew the Doom who kept telling Caradoc about a cave he had once seen of which the walls and ceiling shone with a type of bat that specialised in dropping right on your head with a view to nesting in your hair. By the time we got to the Witches' Chamber at Wookey, which has a deep pool, we had to hold Caradoc tightly to us and offer him a bagful of rum dainties, a wrapped toffee which was about the only thing except money for which Caradoc had shown anything like love. Had we not done so Caradoc would have gone head-first into the pool and he would have taken Teilo Dew with him, just to get a little peace. Iestyn Clovelly went around saying that in some ways the early cavemen had led gayer and freer lives than many voters who went bald the quick way with a kitchenful of kids and nerves singing misereres in Meadow Prospect. We all agreed except Caradoc Shanklyn who wouldn't have a cave at any price.

Our next call was the Bristol Zoo. The club's thoughtful stood and listened fascinated to the laughter of people as they watched the lonely, humiliated rages of the monkeys and chimpanzees. Edwin Pugh organised a small delegation to approach the curator there and then to complain that the exhibition was anti-human and morally corrosive.

"That is our view, as a covey of worried Darwinians."

We were not allowed to see the curator but a minor official told us that he would load the whole monkey house on to the bus for us if we would leave him Dando.

We lost Caradoc Shanklyn at the zoo. We split up to search for him and scoured the zoo at least half a dozen times. We were anxious, for we would not have put it past Shanklyn to try to steal some rare animal to recoup his losses on the drinks. Then someone remembered that Shanklyn had done service briefly in the Camel Corps as a way of avoiding human company in the Middle East. And it was indeed near the camel pound we found him, fast asleep. We got him awake and he told us with a smile that he had been dreaming of the quietness, the serenity and the cheapness of his days in the desert before his wife had fitted him with his suit of shabby thrift. He went around the pound patting each of the camels before he left.

The sea welcomed us back at Weston. His contact with the camels and some spring of refreshment he had found in his dreams had softened Shanklyn once again and he spent like a rajah, a rajah who has come away from home with about fifteen shillings. Women, who on the trip over that morning had been doing fandangos in the lower deck, were going down in defeat after the day's fatigue and the greasy oppressiveness of the ship. One woman, sitting near me, her eyes wandering about like dogs inside her head, was saying, "Take me, O God" and twice she grasped my arms and asked me quite clearly to take care of her son Harold who was thirty-five but still inept. From above we could hear Bleddyn Bibey and Dewi Dando giving out 'Rocked in the Cradle of the Deep', scored for euphonium and bull, and the captain was forced to use the main hooter to tell them to stop.

Hugo My Friend

That Monday saw the beginning of Meadow Prospect Fair Week. The fair was marshalled in a field just outside the town and there was always a great crowd of people standing around appreciating the colour and the music. The hub of the fair was the boxing booth of Royston Pugh. Royston normally had three boxers, and each evening at seven he would line up this trio of fighters on a bit of a balcony outside the booth and challenge us to fight three rounds with one of his boys. This was usually followed by complete silence. If you came through three rounds Royston gave you five guineas. If you didn't Royston gave you free transport home. And if what we had heard about his fighters was true you wouldn't be bothered about the length or quality of the trip. Royston would let you choose the fighter you wished to take on, provided he had not fought for an hour before.

On the Tuesday night my friend Willie Silcox and I noticed that there were only two boxers, but Royston was there at the side of these bath-robed elements insisting that the total of ferocity was undiminished. We heard that the third fighter, a voter called Leo Long the Lout, had contracted some kind of influenza the night before, and half butchering one of the local challengers had lurched out into the night and stumbled into a meeting being held by a Tolstoyan evangelist called Luther Galley who showed Leo what a hateful thing violence was, and Leo, made very receptive to new ideas by the flu, had just enough strength left to limp back to Royston and hand in his notice. These facts made a great appeal to Willie Silcox, who is one of the most subtle and designing performers in Meadow Prospect.

But Royston was not long waiting for a substitute. This turned out to be Naboth Morse, a cousin of Willie Silcox. We had always known Naboth to be broad and strong as the door of a bank, but we had always considered him to be much too gentle and gullible to be any good in such a trade as boxing. But there he was on the balcony outside Royston's booth in one of the shortest dressing-gowns ever seen in Meadow Prospect and blushing like a girl.

We found our friend, Hugo Finchley, at our side. He was looking sad and shattered after as consistent a series of disasters as can be stabled inside one life. He was totally without interest. One of his eyes lacked lustre and the other focus. After a bit of urging from us he started looking at Naboth's two companions with a desperate melancholy as if sympathising in advance with all the victims who would fall to their fists before the week was done.

"Five guineas is a very handy sum," said Willie.

"Yes," said Hugo dully, not imagining that either he or I could come anywhere near the context of Willie's remark.

"And three rounds isn't long," said Willie.

"That," I said, "depends on whether you want to be on the inside or the outside of a coma."

"True, true," said Hugo, in no doubt as to the side he'd be on.

Then Hugo shuffled off to some tent where horrific sketches were on view. Willie had told him it would do him the world of good to be taken on as an actor in one of those sketches because there was no recipe for the morally defeated as tonic as having a chance to chill the public spine.

"Who," I asked Willie, "who were you thinking of when you made these remarks about guineas and rounds?"

"Hugo. That boy is too supine. He is a chronic victim. He must be taught to face up to life again with a look of challenge in his eye."

"Hugo? Up against one of those gorillas? Have a care, Silcox. He'd be dead of fright before he got into the ring."

"I don't know. I've heard Hugo give some very interesting little talks to the boys in the draughts room at the Institute on the lives of famous fighters."

"He gets those from the Sunday papers and fag cards. That doesn't prove anything except that he reads on Sundays and is in

touch with fags. Some of the weakest voters I know are wo.
perfect in the careers of Dempsey and Greb."

"It shows he's got the interest," said Willie, "the creative
spark that might be fanned into flame. Leave the rest to me."

The next day at work I heard that Willie had talked Hugo into
doing some special training and submitting himself as a victim at
Royston Pugh's booth. I went straight up to Willie.

"Silcox," I said, "have you got some special insurance policy
on Hugo?"

"No. Why?"

"You are proposing to feed him whole and helpless to
Royston's baboons."

"Nothing of the sort. Come up to the old stables tonight."

As soon as I had finished my tea I was up by the old stables.
There was Willie Silcox with a towel over his arm and looking
more masterful even than Royston Pugh. Hugo was there too in a
singlet, his white shorts and a pair of black, very ancient daps on
his feet. The strong sunshine and the stream of vitamin in
Willie's talk had had an effect on Hugo and he was doing a series
of brisk exercises, such as knees bend. His bones crackled with
every movement at such a volume that had the horses inside the
stable neighing with wonder. His shoulders were showing
bruises and Willie whispered to me that he had put Hugo on
some elastic device for developing the back muscles. Hugo had
taken the hand-grips and marches away from the wall with too
much will and too little art. He had been bounced back against
the wall with the force of a bullet.

"With Hugo," said Willie, "we need a quieter approach." He
raised his voice. "Now then, Hugo my boy, go for a bit of road
work." He produced a knapsack which he handled with
difficulty. "I've got some metal weights in here to make it more
of a test of endurance. Go up by the old reservoir and run around
it with the knapsack on."

Hugo looked at me but I was watching the sky, waiting to ask
Silcox what exactly lay behind his determination to shuffle
Hugo off the earth at such pace. Hugo adjusted the knapsack and
set off at a tremendous pace but badly stooped.

"He'll be like a hoop when he gets in the ring," I said.

"It'll give him a natural crouch," said Willie. "Just the thing when you are facing a heavier, fitter opponent."

"If the opponent is willing to get down on the floor with Hugo."

"Don't worry," said Willie. "You know that Naboth Morse is my cousin. He'll be Hugo's opponent. I had Naboth in to tea this afternoon. I told him how distressed we were as a family to see him parading in front of the public in that very short dressing-gown, although privately I think it's the first time such an article, long or short, has found its way into our family. I had a very deep talk with him. You know he's very keen on Tydfil Galley, the daughter of that evangelist, Luther Galley. Luther thinks that boxing is the mark of the devil and Tydfil follows suit. When I put this to Naboth he wanted to cash in his checks with Royston straight away, but I said while you are about it you might as well put this boxing to some use. Then I told him all about the trouble that Hugo Finchley has had from birth onward and I said: 'There is no one, Naboth, who so badly needs a boost for his heart and pocket as Hugo Finchley. And this is your chance of winning a moral crown that will make you shine like a star in the eyes of Tydfil Galley. And we'll explain to her old man that you're only going into the ring to discredit boxing and Royston Pugh with a noble gesture of courtesy and passivity.' "

I stood away from Willie, thinking that all this subtlety must be changing the shape of his head.

"Did Naboth Morse follow all that?" I asked.

"I had to break it down a bit, but he understood at last and agreed."

Then there was a lot of clamour from around the corner. Hugo came into view supported by two friends. He was dripping wet, gasping and groaning and without his knapsack.

"He got giddy on the third time around the reservoir," said one of the friends. "He fell in. If I hadn't shouted to him to undo the straps of that knapsack he'd have drowned for sure."

Willie brushed him aside and got a change of clothing for Hugo.

"Now don't fret, Hugo," he said. "I only sent you around the reservoir to see when exactly you'd get giddy. Now we're going to exploit your natural nimbleness. Evasion and retreat are the tactics. Now shadow-box for a while."

Hugo started weaving about, blowing hard and wiping imaginary blood from his nose to get the atmosphere.

"This boy's footwork will live for ever," said Willie. "It'll become a legend of the roped square. Watch me, Hugo. When I raise my hand jump back as if your life depended on it."

Hugo did this, giving the longest backward jump I had ever seen.

"I thought at first," I told Willie, "that you were going to have trouble keeping Hugo in the ring. After this I see that your problem will be keeping him inside the booth."

On the Friday night Willie did not wait for Royston to begin his spiel. He said dramatically: "Hugo Finchley wishes to share the ring with Naboth Morse."

"Good," said Royston calmly. "Go in there, Finchley, and change."

The crowd entered the booth. I asked Willie if he thought he could still rely on Naboth Morse.

"Absolutely," he said. "But I'm taking no chances. I've persuaded Tydfil Galley to come along and look disgusted at the whole idea of violence. That will keep Naboth steady in his resolve to spare Hugo and betray Royston."

Willie hurried off to apply a sponge to Hugo, although Hugo at that moment was looking as fresh as paint.

Into the booth came Tydfil Galley. She was looking blithe and eager. I went up to her and said how surprised I was to see her in such a place.

"Well, I'm not surprised," she said. "Just had a quarrel with my father about going to the dance tomorrow night. So I told him I was glad to be friendly with a real man's man like Naboth, and I'm going to cheer him to the echo."

The first round showed Hugo at his best. He buzzed around Naboth like a wasp. Once or twice Naboth pushed him away and Hugo went twanging against the ropes feeling for his ears and pushing his eyes back. Willie began raising his arm to caution retreat and Hugo started shooting back even when Naboth was nowhere near him. The referee was worried by this and he came up to Hugo on the blind side to warn him to make his movements a bit more continuous. He did this at the very moment when Silcox was raising his arm for a fresh bout of evasion and the referee was sent flying.

Tydfil now became vocal. She was depressed by the slow, inept show that Naboth was making, and she was crying out quite clearly and in a more savage way than I had ever heard from any daughter of an evangelist: "Show him, Naboth, show him! Put him down, put him right down!"

Naboth heard her and his face became clouded as he reached his stool at the end of the second round. Willie nipped over to his corner and muttered to him that Tydfil was only testing him and to ignore her cries.

The third round started, Hugo was insolent now, dancing around Naboth like a dervish, convinced that he was genuinely the better man. Tydfil's cries became louder, more bitter. Naboth was confused and unhappy. Royston Pugh was watching the whole scene thoughtfully. Then his eye lighted on a dour-looking man in a bowler standing near the entrance of the booth. This was the owner of the ground on which the booth stood, a man from two valleys away, and eager to have his rent paid.

Royston called Naboth angrily to the ropes and while Naboth was pawing Hugo back as he came in for his fierce little attacks, Royston told him that this man in the bowler was a noted promoter from London who had come down at Royston's invitation to examine Royston's claim that in Naboth he had found a new white hope with a right that would split a quarry face. While Royston was talking Tydfil Galley had come close to the ring and was trying to explain to Naboth how she had rejected her father's doctrine of peace at any price, and that she now wished to see a bit of clean-cut action from Naboth. Willie Silcox was standing alongside Tydfil rattling his bucket to drown her message, and he only stopped doing this when the referee bent right out of the ring and told him he'd be removed as a lunatic if he kept it up. "Now," said Royston, "justify my confidence and shatter that shuffling clown."

Naboth did so. There are people in the northern part of our county who claim to have heard the blow. The legend is that Hugo went through the roof of the booth while his white shorts remained on the floor of the ring. The truth is that he and his shorts landed back in the ring together.

Naboth was hugged simultaneously by Royston and Tydfil.

We laid Hugo in a corner of the booth, his legs inside and his head outside to let the cool air get at his brain.

Then Royston bustled up to us looking very malicious. "To discourage irresponsible challengers," he said, "I make a point of charging those who fail to last the distance the full admission price. This also proves their sporting spirit." Royston nodded at Hugo's legs. "One-and-six please."

Willie argued quietly with Royston for ten minutes and then he came over to me looking more triumphant than ever, and said that he had got away with a half-price ticket for Hugo because more than fifty per cent of him was outside the tent.

The Joyful

The mood fell on us like night. We just didn't want any of the established political parties to talk to us any more. We were ready to be taken in by any clownish adventurer who wanted to strike a note of public and witless fuss. We were lucky. Two truly ripe buffoons came forward to answer the call.

The first was Cynolwen Ball. He was a grinning extrovert with a hundred ways of telling truth not to bother and to stand aside. He was a kind of rudimentary auctioneer and estate agent who could bring a genuine sense of love to bear on the properties for which he acted.

He could take a typical mining-valley cottage-type house, one in the full sob of subsidence, and make it sound like Longleat, but nearer and more compact. His ideal in living was a great non-stop guffaw. He deplored penicillin for having failed to do to solemnity what it had done for yaws.

The second was Vincent Hobbs. Hobbs was loosely operative in the fish, fruit and bookmaking lines. He was a snooker player of wizardly grace. "He might," our local paper once said, "have ranked with such masters of the bizarre and fancy shots as W.C. Fields and Joe Davis had it not been for a tendency to become flippant as he saw the last balls vanish into the pockets. This weakness he might have inherited from his father, Llew Hobbs, himself a noted joker who did an impersonation of George Robey that earned Llew a card of congratulation from Robey himself."

In his early years Vincent Hobbs had tried to fashion a comic turn of his own in an amateur way. At any of the outings or street parties that he and Cynolwen Ball were constantly organising, he would stand up and do his act. He would crack jokes of such monstrous indecency that children would be whipped out of earshot and members of the Mothers' Union would walk around the town with armbands of black crêpe and expressions that said that after Hobbs nothing would be quite the same again.

Hobbs had made a big contribution to our political twilight. At political meetings he would wait until the speaker started to lurch through some fit of sweating idealism, then he would point at the speaker with his billiard cue shouting "Snooker" every time the orator found his way blocked by an outsize and impassable cliché.

Ball and Hobbs went in for general promotions. They shared the ownership of a massive marquee in which they had staged some of the most dubious bouts of all boxing time. "The canvas stadium of Messrs Ball and Hobbs," said the local paper, "is the worst-lit venue in the annals of mixing it. It is one of the few arenas where a half of the audience has found itself inside the ring out of simple curiosity. This makes for confused and untidy fighting. Under these conditions, a fighter with normally good sight starts ten points ahead. We can only suggest that the boxers lured into this lair by Messrs Hobbs and Ball should abandon the traditional gum-shield in favour of colliery lamps. Either that or a phosphorescent ref." Hobbs and Ball threatened to sue the local paper for libel but this was now recognised as a kind of nervous tic.

The hub of life for Hobbs and Ball was a club called the Social and Sporting. On the whole world's mental front there was no quieter sector than this. The dialect and the last twitch of Liberal optimism had been raffled off there in the course of one memorably thoughtless Christmas. Any member seen puckering his brow in a way that might have erupted into a political or religious query was hustled out. They had achieved an impassivity that regarded even tombola as a philosophical challenge.

When the traditional parties and the Left were seen entering the tomb of a common reticence Hobbs and Ball came forward as the sponsors of a gayer ethic. They called themselves Independent Progressives and the test they set themselves was a simple one. Whichever of the two got the most laughs, promoted the most obvious delight, would get the all-clear for a parliamentary election. They stated that the lower the total poll the happier they would be at having helped to cleanse the earth of its old plague of sectarian argument and the cult of straight-faced planning. Their ideal, frankly, was to make life an everlasting Bank Holiday Monday.

With Ball and Hobbs bringing to bear every hedonistic flame at their disposal, the town boiled into a froth of the most inscrutable romps. If you can imagine the late Middle Ages with the last moral sanctions of the Catholic Church removed, that was the sort of framework into which Hobbs and Ball were trying to fit Meadow Prospect, and by the continued stupor which lapped the township, the Middle Ages were getting ready to welcome us back and congratulate us on having got shut of the vote and its tedious implications.

Behind their pursuit of the quick guffaw there was an impulse of savage anti-feminism. Ball and Hobbs, nurtured on the notions of the old-fashioned music-hall, viewed women with an all-weather hatred. The gift of women for anxiety and tears had covered the face of life with a moss of misery, and Ball and Hobbs were out to do a brisk job of weeding.

Neither man was married but both had maintained a fairly athletic career in sexual brigandage. In all the antics they promoted in Meadow Prospect there was always some element contrived to make women go blue in the face and black in the heart.

"Given their heads," the local paper said, "Mr Hobbs and Mr Ball will have indignity thriving like convolvulus. If Mr Hobbs and Mr Ball want to sue us for this observation this will be the tenth time they have threatened to do so. We regard this as a high enough score to justify our putting up for the Pulitzer Prize which is awarded in the States for the best journalistic assault on the anti-social."

The first fling at mass gaiety was something that Ball and Hobbs called "a character walking race". About sixty men were to take part in a race around the town dressed as tramps. The route took them past eighteen pubs and at each of these places they were to drink a pint of ale paid for by the promoters. After the tenth call the walkers were having to be winkled out of back lanes, the houses of strangers and even neighbouring towns.

Some of the walkers, glassy-eyed and utterly lost, were lassoed and belaboured by their wives, with Ball and Hobbs holding their sides, wiping their eyes and asking if this didn't beat everything. Just behind them the editor of the local paper sharpened a fistful of pencils.

The next rout was a trip to Paris organised and subsidised by Hobbs and Ball to see an international rugby match. The outing lasted a week and for months afterwards the men who had taken part spoke of it in cracked voices and with rolling eyes. From their accounts they seem to have gone on a safari through half the bistros and bordellos of Paris.

Hobbs and Ball, it was said, had poured out a cascade of francs to break the grip of the gendarmes on their followers. When the rumours grew clear, a flag flew at half-mast over the head-quarters of the Women's Institute.

Our local paper said: "It was not de Gaulle who kept Britain out of the European Community. It was the darkening shadow thrown over Europe by Cynolwen Ball, Vincent Hobbs and the phalanx of satyrs they organised for the Paris trip."

On the betting front Hobbs and Ball moved with skill. They presented bound volumes of *The Breeder's Guide* to the local betting shop, together with six armchairs for the greater comfort of the more literate punters. They also hired the services of a crooked jockey, a local boy called Deiniol Dawes, who had been de-licensed for practising every kind of mounted chicane. Dawes, said Hobbs and Ball, knew all the stables where a corrupt fix was going to be made. Dawes claimed that he had met horses into which so much dope had been pumped they had become addicts and went out looking for the stuff.

"For all the secrets of Newmarket," said Hobbs and Ball, "trust Deiniol Dawes."

"For us," said the local paper, "Newmarket has only one secret. It is not how Deiniol Dawes stopped jockeying. How was he ever allowed to get started?"

We do not know in what kind of moral stroke the activities of Ball and Hobbs might have finished. It was the women who did for them. Every woman's organisation in the town grew loud and militant in their protests. The local paper gave up a whole issue to letters of disgust suggesting various solutions for the problems unleashed, ranging from the deportation of anyone tempting a man away from his family, to an instant disinfestation of the Social and Sporting Club.

Hobbs and Ball found themselves being pursued by posses of furious women and threatened with the nearest a town like ours would allow itself to come to a lynching. Some of the women, excited by the chase, made up to Hobbs and Ball with extreme affection.

Ball and Hobbs were forced to appear before audiences of women to explain and defend their view of life. Hobbs and Ball found the experience of being coherent publicly about their philosophy chastening. The more they spoke the more solemn they became. They even got married to prove social goodwill.

In no time at all they found themselves on the same pebbly beach of well-intentioned platitude as most other political workers. They decided that the best interests of the town would be best served if they joined forces with the traditional political parties.

We persuaded Ball to join the Tories and Hobbs the more cautious flank of the Labour Party. We did not want the two of them to land on one single patch of the national conscience.

Blue Ribbons for a Black Epoch

Dear Myfanwy — A hot, angry and futile day. I was six hours in the House, a deepening torment. I spoke out against that wretched war in South Africa again, and ran into as withering a volley of grapeshot as even I have ever known. Our generals and the Boers, always in politics one seems to have to make a choice of imbeciles. Today a brace of ex-brigadiers on the Tory benches were after my blood. I could hear them muttering. One of them wanted me impeached. The others wanted me privately shot. They were baying after me like one of their fiercer hounds. Strange breed, their two passions shooting birds out of the air and rooting Radicals out of the realm. It's all bound up with the mammoth follies of landlordship. To carry quite solemnly the power and privilege invested in large land ownership a man must be callous to the point of idiocy. So they pursue callous pastimes. Tearing flesh, hounding cottagers, forming a cretinous warrior caste.

I was brought into the world to see the Welsh Church disestablished, the hard core of our poverty softened and finally dispersed, and all our generals humiliated. They are the obverse of the compassion, the mutilating modesty of my kind, your kind. I will never cease to loath these big, booming predators. In the years to come I may experience many vagaries of outlook. I have seen too many men become weathervanes under the pressures of a free and corrupt society.

But in this attitude I will never vary. The hatchet of difference and dislike between us will be buried either in defeat for them or in my neck. At the moment my neck seems to be on the losing end. But I will hurt them before I finish. Their assumption of omnipotence is as firmly rooted as their inherited plantations of oak. But I'll find the chopper for the job.

You should have heard the generals' friends scream at me. You should have seen their manic, mottled faces. You should have heard their applause as the Secretary for War smugly intoned the latest figures of Boer dead. But I told them: "You are a plague of plesiosaurs wallowing in a swamp of your own idiotic-making." A plague of plesiosaurs. (This addiction to alliteration affects the Welsh like a kind of dandruff. I'll have to watch it. Whenever I come out with a fine rattle of matching consonants in the House the Etonians always have a good old snigger, for all the world as if I had come in without a collar.) But when the House broke up I felt ulcerated and faint. Nobody spoke to me. For half an hour I walked along the Embankment staring at the Thames and hating every English drop of it.

I've been thinking of you all day and pondering the wonderful aptness of our meeting. It may never have happened had it not been for that outrageous business at Birmingham when the pro-war lunatics tried to lynch me. I've not recovered yet from the clownish experience of being hustled out of that Town Hall disguised as a policeman: coat down to the floor, the rim of the helmet down to my mouth. I tasted it. It was horrible. It is hard to imagine that the whole of human idiocy has a single vitalising core, but it may well be Birmingham.

I had only one thought in my head. To get back to my warm, Welsh womb. I felt that my first meeting at Bangor would bring my confidence back to the boil. And it was there, of all places, that that pack of drunken jingoes beset me. I didn't tell you about this. That is why, for so many hours during those three glorious days in your village, I was withdrawn, distraught. One of them broke a bottle on my head. They might have killed me had it not been for your brother Tom, a mere lad but a lion in the fray. Lucky for me he was up there that day visiting your uncle. The next morning I set out for Cardiff. Tom was in the same compartment. The train stopped at your village. "I get out here," said Tom. I looked out at the gentle hills around. I felt suddenly sickened at the thought of Cardiff and teeming streets. "I'll get out with you," I said.

We walked down the main street of your village, Gorffwysfa, A Resting Place. And indeed it was. The hillsides were golden with gorse, the sky was flawless. I laid eyes for the first time on your little shop, your post office, your lovely face. And that first meal in your kitchen. The boiled ham, a glutton's dream, and those chips, pale, dry, and perfect. And that session of singing in the little parlour, the calm sunlight of your smile as you looked up from the harmonium as I turned the leaves of the hymnal. Why did I burst into tears as we sang 'Canaf yn y bore'? Exhaustion perhaps; perhaps some memory of the innocence and quietness of my early days which I will never know again. Why did Tom not sing? Some religious doubt, maybe. The sort of thing one uses to spice the embarrassments of early manhood. I will watch out for Tom.

A minute ago I put my pen down to fondle the sprig of gorse you picked for me on our last walk. It's a little dry and withered now but it is still charged with emotion for your sincere friend, D.

July 9, 1904

Dear Myfanwy — Since summer started I've wanted to come down to Gorffwysfa again. I long for the clean peace of the place as other men must yearn for drink. London becomes less and less tolerable. I derived great happiness from the lovely bouquet of laburnum and gorse you sent me in that delicious little box. It was delivered safely to the House and it was brought posthaste by one of the messengers.

I am somebody now. It pays a man sometimes to bring down a massive wrath on his head, because that wrath represents something diseased in his society. When the wrath has been discharged and the victim scourged, the society is purged and becomes more wholesome. I lambasted those vicars and land-owners who denied burial in a graveyard of the Established Church to a Methodist peasant. That fight got me into Parliament as infallibly as my campaign got the Methodist into his consecrated patch. The louts who wanted to hang me in Birmingham and Bangor would now feel more like cheering me as a man of reason and foresight. They know who I am now. They enjoyed their witless outburst, and the shame they felt when peace and sanity returned placed me firmly at the head of the dedicated pilgrimage this nation will now make to the glittering uplands of social justice.

Glittering. The word puts me in mind of the yellow radiance of your little valley in early summer, the emerald lustre of your deep, Welsh eyes. I should have tried harder to come down one week-end this summer, Myfanwy, but I am enmeshed. We've got those indolent snobs on the Government benches on the run, and I am the biggest hammer our party has. I must be on hand for the delivering of every possible new blow at those pampered brats of privilege. But I'll be down soon. I'll watch for a gap in the tumult and nip down. I probably won't have much time to give you much notice. You'll just see me walking down the hill.

I'm glad Tom came up to see me. It's quite scandalous that he should regard the little bit of work he does helping you in the shop as a job. He says he'd like a farm of his own. I told him that I might be able to find something at a reasonable price. I told him that before embarking on the project he should train himself in the basic arts of husbandry — care of horses, techniques of ploughing, crop rotation, hedging and so on. His eyes were very dreamy as I talked and when I told him, rather sharply, to pay attention, he said he had lived in the country all his life and crafts of agriculture were second nature to him. I doubt it. But whatever lies in my power to do to get him a farm, I will do.

I am thinking of the great happiness I have known in the bedroom you let me use, the room that belonged to your father and mother. An exciting privilege. How fascinating are those photographs of them — your father's face, death-marked by the quarry-dust of Llanberis, your mother's face a map of unspeakable privations. But what a golden legacy of goodness and devotion they left in you. On my last visit I wept unashamedly when I picked up the family Bible in which they had inscribed the simple and glorious fact of your birth. I opened the Bible. It was the Book of Isaiah. "He hath sent me to bind up the broken-hearted, to proclaim liberty to the captives, and the opening of the prison to them that are bound." Yes, yes, I wept.

When next you gather gorse from the hillside behind the village send me some. It brings air and light to me.

Sincerely, D.

August 10, 1905

Dear Myfanwy — I was with the leader of the party last night. A long private talk at his house, followed by a banquet. He wants me to concern myself wholly with the financial aspect of the social legislation I have always longed to initiate. I have it clearly mapped in my mind. The era of State-controlled benevolence is nigh. You will find that your little post office will blossom into being the eye of our social conscience, the helping hand of humanity. Your counter will become the first plank of the New Jerusalem. Bless you.

This evening when you play the harmonium sing 'O love that will not let me go'. And get Tom to join in. He needs a bit of inspiration. I heard from him yesterday. His cows have some sort of fever which, apparently, has not affected any of the neighbouring herds. In a sinister way Tom is a man who sets the pace in the calamity stakes. And he told me a long tale of woe about grievances suffered by farmers in general. He says he picks up a lot of information in pubs. I don't like this talk of pubs. In my next letter I will quote you a fine passage from Bishop Latimer about spendthrift and useless malcontents who fritter their lives away in taverns. Read it out to Tom.

About the banquet I went to with the leader. Full of old Etonian twitter and the usual rally of well-upholstered aberrants representing the landlord and 'rentier' factions. One of them told me to my face, "You, sir, are a concentrate of vitriol and vulgarity." I laughed at him.

What a pity the shop keeps you so tied you can't come up to London for a few days to see the sort of life I have to live. And ask Tom either to get in touch with veterinary science or to switch to something simple like sheep.

Keep well, Sincerely, D.

January 9, 1916

Dear Myfanwy — What a villain I am. It seems a lifetime since I wrote to you last. But life is gruesomely hectic. I am the coming man, Myfanwy. I heard a story yesterday. In 1912 a man came out of gaol. He went to the nearest public house. He lifted his pint and said, "Here's to King Edward." The landlord said,

"Edward's dead. George is on the throne now." And the man said, "Good old Lloydie. I knew he'd do it one day." These little jokes are straws in the wind. And I know where the wind is taking me. I wish it were back to those gentle, lovely hours in Gorffwysfa. So often I long to return, pigeonwinged and hot for home, to that fragrant haven, that unforgettably poignant posture of worship around the harmonium.

I was in France a week ago. As you asked me I sought out Tom. He is on the Somme, in one of the most advanced sectors of the line. He is a hero and a fool. If he had managed to hang on to that farm, he would have been outside the orbit of military duties. His health has suffered. As Minister of Munitions I told him that he would no longer suffer from any shortage of shells. He became abusive. He told me what to do with my shells in language that horrified the Commanding Officer, who was escorting me around. A touch of what they call shell-shock, no doubt. I'll have a word with the Commanding Officer. A charming man.

Hastily but always sincerely, D.

June 10, 1926

Dear Myfanwy — I was in Gorffwysfa two days ago. You were not there. They told me you and Tom left the village a year ago, and no one knew your new address. They said you had found the work too much for you, with all the new forms, and Tom, it seems, has not been much good to you since the war. I am sending this letter under cover to the Postmaster-General in the hope that he can trace you. If it reaches you, write to me, Myfanwy. I am getting old and cold. I cannot afford to see the ember of an old friendship, a cherished link with the years of struggle and exaltation slip through the floorboards of my life.

As ever. Sincerely, D.

Off the Beam

Our early winters were snowy and iced with self-improvement. The central fact of this process was the series of lectures, admission by ticket only, staged by the YMCA in the Library and Institute. They were long, wholesome and illustrated with slides. Any family capable of buying a book of tickets covering the whole winter session was regarded with awe, and often burgled.

One of the regular lecturers was Lord Mount. He was a large landowner, very tall and always dressed in a type of tweed so thick and rich he seemed, by our standards of physique and tailoring, a yeti. He was a specialist in the Baroness Orczy approach to the French Revolution; he dealt also with mountaineering and eccentric squires.

The committee of the Institute, anarcho-syndicalists almost to a man, had been sent to hear Lord Mount lecture on these three topics. They listened in astonishment to his lecture on the French Revolution, apologised to Robespierre, and told Lord Mount that he was the only lecturer in this moment in time who made Burke sound like Fox. But they were sure that Meadow Prospect would find a lot of interest in what he had to say about mountains and squires.

So each year we had a visit from Lord Mount, alternating between Nepal and the local landowners and rentiers, whose behaviour had kept them strolling around the porch of the clinic.

In his social thinking Lord Mount was markedly to the right of the Duke of Wellington. He regarded the committee men of the Institute, Gomer Gough, Edwin Pugh and the rest, as seditious savages. He never forgave them for turning down his lecture 'The Echo of the Tumbrils', and in the last few minutes of this address he made it plain that he dreaded the day when

Gough, Pugh and their associated firebrands would be lugging out a few local carts to give Lord Mount and his friends their last bumpy ride.

He had once tried to win Meadow Prospect in a parliamentary contest as an Independent. The official Conservative organisation had disowned him, charging him with having lurched to the right when the dinosaur, by pure accident, turned left. He had invited us to return to a sound, square-bottomed, pre-Chartist outlook. Gomer Gough had threatened to burn the town down if it returned more than ten votes for so wintry an ethic as Lord Mount's.

In the January of 1924 Lord Mount came to give his lecture on 'The Madcaps', the crazy squires who went to bed on horseback and spurred their wives into exile in the attic; who conceived in the cleft of some delirium a fancy for broiled peasant and poured brandy over and ignited some passing menial. Lord Mount's thesis was that the disappearance of those cards from the social scene had reduced life to a squalid bore.

He had been disappointed by our reception, the year before, of his lecture on mountaineering. The slides had shown Lord Mount walking like a fly up perpendicular rock faces. As a rock-climber he had perfected ways of using the most minute holes in the rock. He had been heard to say that when it came time to climb up Gomer Gough he would not falter. But the slides had made little impression. Subsidence was rife among us at the time and there were many voters who had, after a night during which the house had swung out of plumb, negotiated a bedroom floor angled even more acutely than Lord Mount's crags.

Lord Mount arrived an hour before the lecture was due to begin. He seemed raw, displeased and in a mood to bark. Standing at the magic lantern ready to receive the slides was Idwal Osgood. Lord Mount looked at him suspiciously.

"He is not the man who normally manipulates the lantern. Where is the regular man who has served me so well in the past?"

Gomer Gough explained. The man who normally did duty with the lantern was Sylvan Osgood, Idwal's brother. Sylvan was a shy, apolitical man, who had seemed to find in the beam of the magic lantern all the joy that other men find in love and dissent. A fortnight before, Gomer Gough had introduced him to a woman anarchist recently deported from America for some blunt work with the Garment Makers' Union. They had married and were spending their honeymoon at a weekend course, organised by the Council of Labour Colleges. Sylvan had appointed Idwal his deputy. Idwal, like his brother, was shy, inarticulate, but had gone through life in a trance of admiration of the levelling doctrines of Gomer Gough.

"But don't worry, Lord," said Gomer. "Over the years Idwal here has studied his brother's technique like a hawk. You will find him a smooth and intelligent hand with the slides."

The Institute was thronged that night. The stairs were jammed, and Lord Mount was delighted until he was told that a fair proportion of these people were on their way to the regional snooker championship which was being held in a room over the landing from the lecture.

The local challenger for the snooker crown was Theo Morgan, a feckless hedonist, morally fractured but at snooker a magician, only one kiss of the black below Joe Davis. Theo was anti-intellectual to a point that would have puzzled Darwin. He believed that the YMCA lectures should be dumped at the South Pole and Gough at the North. The week before he had been presented with his own private cue by a Sunday paper that believed in keeping the plebs bent over long-drawn-out, scoring games. Opposing Theo was another worldling called Denzil Dando.

"All right," said Lord Mount to Idwal Osgood. "Give me a few sample projections. The timing of the slides is even more important here than in the mountaineering lecture, and I don't want my best efforts butchered by the fumbling of a clown."

Idwal made a start. Between dread and inexperience he seemed pinioned. The lantern itself appeared to be rocking like a horse's head for lack of some screws, which Gough and Pugh produced casually from their waistcoat pockets and handed to Idwal. When Idwal projected his first slides they were as likely to come to life on the floor as the wall behind.

"This," said Lord Mount, "is your supreme coup, Gough. But history will fight back, have no fear."

"Oh, he'll be all right. Idwal is nervous. An artist feels this kind of tension before the big event. If he doesn't improve we'll give the audience permission to shift their chairs to follow the pictures."

Gomer handed Lord Mount a small pointer with which he was to rap on the wall or the screen to request a change of slide. Lord Mount pushed it away.

"I'll want a considerably more substantial article than that to convey my demands to that cretin," he said. "Failing a cannon, get me a longer, heavier type of stick altogether."

Gomer went across the landing and came back with a snooker cue, a handsome and lustrous thing. He handed it to Lord Mount.

A few minutes before the lecture was due to begin, Theo Morgan climbed the stairs of the Institute. He was surrounded by friends and looked like a triumphant bullfighter. I heard Gomer Gough say to him at the door of the snooker room that there was an agent of one of the larger and lusher London billiards saloons present that night to offer a contract either to Theo or Dando.

The lecture began. Idwal Osgood, fed with advice by Gough and Pugh, changed the whole future of the magic lantern. The moon might have been getting his signals, but we were not. Now and then some manic face would appear, swigging negus and paying tribute to the distorting quality either of wealth or Osgood's lantern.

Lord Mount on the platform was beating out a sombre tattoo. He was letting the thick end of the cue fall on the floorboards with a thud that loosened the headbones of the first ten rows.

There was a long pause. Idwal tried to tear a stuck slide out of the lantern. He overdid the tug and there was a tinkle louder than the upper chimes of Aberdovey as a dozen slides landed on the floor.

Lord Mount had had enough. At cavalry pace he came up the aisle towards the lantern. He had the cue raised for one single stroke on Idwal's head.

The cue had started its journey when the door of the lecture room was flung open. It was Theo Morgan, both arms upraised, a fire of accusation in each eye. He roared into the darkness, "Where's my cue, Gough? Who pinched my presentation cue?" Some lights came on. Theo saw Lord Mount poised to crack his cue over Idwal's head. "There he is, the agent. All set to fix the game for Dando. Ready to bend my stick over Osgood's pate so that I'd be potting all my best shots out of the window."

He rushed up to Lord Mount, pushed him back and seized his cue. He glared at Gough and Pugh. "If I had time and this wasn't my presentation cue, I'd go to work on you two until I had passed my own record-break."

Then he rushed back to the tournament. Lord Mount left on the following day for Kilimanjaro, pausing at Paris to promise Danton a return match.

An Ample Wish

Dear Mr Saltzmann, Dear Mr Brocolli,

I hear you are looking for a new James Bond and you suggest a younger man. I think this is a mistake. You need an older man and I think I fill the bill. I am sixty-six. I am still an effective lover and a pretty handy tenor with an extraordinary ear. If ever you should get James Bond to sing, and it's about time he did, for a change, I'm your man. Women singers have always seemed to admire me for the last forty years, and that's a long time in a place like Belmont.

I notice that you want a man who walks well. You say he should move like Robert Mitchum, Gary Cooper, Clark Gable. I haven't actually seen these men. I only went to the cinema when I was on the rota of voluntary ushers at the Welfare Hall. And when I had that job I was too busy sticking tickets on my little wire spear and warning people about canoodling and gambling, and so on.

There was a lot of gambling in that cinema. If the picture was dull, groups of voters would out with torches and cards and start gaming. I don't know whether the darkness did anything to lower their moral standards of honesty, but these gamblers were always fighting and accusing each other of cheating. So I never saw any of the actors you mention, Gable and the others, and I have no idea of what was so special in the way they walked.

I think I walk all right. I live on a hill riddled with ruts and pot-holes. I have grown very agile over the years dodging these traps. Even when I go spinning in the dark I'm up like a flash. I think this would come in useful for me when I have to fling myself flat at the approach of bullets.

I am also a good dancer, although as Bond the agent I would probably have to learn a few new steps. When I was younger I

196

was a good dancer of the slinky type. I was too slinky for some people. Around here they favour a dull, decorous shuffle. In 1925 I came near an award at the Tango Contest at the Arcadia Ballroom in Belmont. Alderman Brinley Beynon still says that he would have tipped me for the premier trophy, a crimson rose bowl, if there had not been so strong a dash of the dago in my style.

I was chauffeur of the mayors of Belmont for five years. I was sacked for driving too fast and putting the mayors on edge, especially Alderman Beynon who was the one who sacked me. I gave Alderman Beynon a rough drive. I had had a mixture of cherry brandy and drambuie in the Liberal Club. I mention this to show that my taste in drinks is not common. I touched eighty miles per hour that afternoon. People on the pavements could hear his teeth and chain rattling.

A few days later he apologised for sacking me and offered me the job back. But I had fixed myself up with a job as chauffeur in the steel works. The mayor was in drink. He confessed to me that he had made love to various women with whom I had associated, and he said that these women still spoke of me with ardour and wanted to see me again.

At sixty-six I am still active on this front, like a well-trained setter on the track of any bit of crumble. That's why I think you need an older man for Bond. It would give people something to live up to. It would encourage them to see a pensioner as lithe and active as a man bulging with youth. Last summer I won the walking race for the over-sixties in the steel-works sports. I'm so thin I had more trouble with the elastic of my shorts than with my competitors.

I think that I should mention that I tend to walk in a rather low-slung sort of way. I asked Alderman Beynon if he thought this would spoil my chances as a successor to Sean Connery. He said no, like a shot. He said there could be advantages in appearing to be sitting down when you are actually standing up. Deceiving people is what secret agents are all about. He says I have a natural gift for duplicity, very double-faced and loose in my traffic with the truth. I'm the man he'd send to tackle any tricky negotiations on behalf of the Council, he says. As soon as I started to talk they'd need flood-lighting to see the point.

So you see my qualities. Ardour, cunning, speed. And you don't need to worry about my speaking voice. I have a strong, clear voice. I can switch from a shout of command to a murmur of love in however short a time you may fancy. I had a lot of brothers and sisters who resented my superior ways and enjoyed being truly vulgar themselves. They tried to shout me down. To counter this I had to develop an amazing volume and flexibility.

In 1919 I gained the Silver Daffodil award given to the best reciter at the Belmont Semi-National Eisteddfod by Councillor Gilbert Beynon, father of the alderman and himself a reciter on whose rounded style I was prone to model my own. The two poems I recited in that victory year of 1919 were 'The Shooting of Dan MacGrew' and 'A Drunkard's Remorse'. The latter was so terrifying in its truth and horror all concert organisers told me to drop it and repeat MacGrew.

In my thirties I had a phase as an open-air evangelist. My missionary area was a corner of the Belmont market square. It did me no harm although it might have foxed a few of the faithful. My home-made pulpit was a large, hollow contraption with an acoustic that made decisions on sound-level tricky. Passages in my appeal meant to cajole and persuade came out like the roar of cannon. People took me for a clown. They laughed at me. A mocking flock and that acoustic did for my mission.

Oh, and there was that chap who had a stall next to my position. It was a canvas stall with two big, smoky naphtha flares. They nearly choked me. A lot of people thought I was peddling a new faith that gave coughing its true place in the human riddle. The stall-holder's name was Glossop. He sold gew-gaws such as painted tea-mugs that leaked and cigarette lighters with fireproof wicks and brittle flints that wore out the thumb.

Glossop had a sharp, knowing face and when it was caught in the glare of those naphtha lamps he had a diabolical look that caused people to buy just to keep on the right side of bad luck. Glossop taught me a lot of quick-fire banter meant to ginger up the slower clients. I also practised his diabolical look and I think those two things would fit very well into the glib cynical things that Bond is always coming out with.

Glossop was a powerful amorist. He paid his women with

those painted tea-mugs and many local kitchens are still full of them because Glossop was busy. He brought me along rapidly in the same field. He lifted me clear over the hurdles of my long-standing chastity and turned me into one of the zone's most persuasive rakes. Alderman Beynon says that Glossop would have been in a position to give the best possible extra-mural course in lechery, and he envies me the experience of having been Glossop's apprentice.

Glossop also gave me recipes for potent restoratives. I never know weariness. Glossop got the secret of these tonics from his grandfather, a herbalist and magician. His mixtures have been known to make old rugs levitate and embrace. Last September, on a mixed works outing to Bourton-on-the-Water, I was still doling out great helpings of affection at a quarter to midnight. It was a field day. Bond would have had his chips by tea-time. If you make me Bond and let me show my true scope he and I will bring a new sunlight into the prospects of the aged.

I'm afraid I've never had much to do with guns. This is a place dead set against anything abrupt, especially bangs. Guns are not liked. I didn't serve in the war. I had a job in security at the steel works. Keeping an eye on things, but unarmed. The Germans would have given their right jackboot to get their hands on a vital industrial unit like that. So I can claim to have been one of the men who, although ununiformed, kept this prize away from the enemy.

But I have a neighbour, Mr Cleghorn, who has a collection of guns. I didn't know about this until a few weeks ago. He always had a bright look about him, as if he had something interesting and important on his mind. I thought it was just greed or a late passion. It was these guns. It is a good collection. It ranges from a frail-looking gun, which, says Cleghorn, belonged to the only highwayman ever to practise around here. The first time I tried it it fell apart. The highwayman probably had the same sort of luck. You can't ask people to stand and deliver in the right threatening tone if you are looking for bits of your gun.

Mr Cleghorn also had a Biretta which Mr Bond has been known to use. Mr Cleghorn was giving me a bit of drill with it last Monday. It was on top of the mountain. If we practised down in the town they'd have whipped us inside before the echoes died away. I saw a woman on our way up to the practice pitch. I fancied her and wished to make her mine.

Mr Cleghorn, a bit of a dry stick, noticed this and told me he did not favour lust. I couldn't explain to him that I had my eye on a role that mingled marksmanship, spying and wooing. His attitude disturbed me. On my first shot my hand shook. Quite without intending to, I shot him. Not much, just a graze, and he's just as patient and gentle as ever. Next Monday, he says, we'll go through the whole collection, starting with the flintlock, and by the time you want to see me I'll be the master of any weapon you want to put in my hand. Knowing that you'll bear me in mind . . .

A Horse Called Meadow Prospect

I t was Kitchener Bowen who made the suggestion. I was there in the Council Chamber when Bowen stood up and put the idea forward.

"I propose," said Bowen, "that Meadow Prospect show a smiling face to the world and buy a racehorse which will be given the name of our fine, old town, Meadow Prospect, carrying the colours of our national emblem, the leek, white and green, colours restful to the punter and stimulating to the horse. I know where I can get you a mount of mixed Arab and Welsh blood for little more than five hundred pounds, which will have the speed and strength to carry the hopes and investments of the voters."

Bowen was our senior bookie and a sporadic politican. He had been on the Council for years but he had never learned to be truly coherent about anything but the turf and odds.

"The horse, Meadow Prospect, after five or six brilliant outings at meetings which I will choose with care, measuring carefully the state of the top soil and the hooves of the horse, will attract the eyes of industrialists to the town of Meadow Prospect. And, by God, fellow members, if there is anything this town needs at the moment it is the interested eye of industrialists."

There were at least a dozen plain motives behind this statement by Bowen. A new mood of solemnity had just struck Meadow Prospect. The post-war hedonism, which had never been more than brittle, had begun to fall apart. A clutch of bettors in a gambling shop run by Bowen had been struck by paralysing intellectual curiosity, had cancelled their bets, had stared at each other in a deepening disgust for half an hour, then sent off to the region's university for the services of an extra-mural tutor to guide them towards heavier themes.

Bowen accused the Free Church Council of having used some

type of nerve gas to subvert these bettors, but the truth was that none of these people ever laid a bet on again, and they sat at least once at the feet of the tutor before they unlaced his shoes and went back to crib, a tepid compromise, by their standards, but, after a long look at Bowen, safer.

At the same time a deputation of local youths had set out to walk around the world on an anti-bomb errand. They planned to pause at every capital and look meaningfully at anyone rich enough to afford this type of weapon, and impulsive enough to use it. Bowen's answer to these pacifists was to demand that they be gaoled before they reached the town's limits. He also assured America that these marchers were loons and that the real heart of Britain was still sound.

Other strokes of gloom had fallen. A small colony of nudists, set up to ridicule the shyness and serge that had driven sex to cover, broke up and the members seemed to be walking about in thicker suits than usual. A mattress factory had run out of orders and was now prone on its last mattress.

So Bowen was out to inject a bubble of gaiety into the bloodstream.

"A horse, is it?" said Geary the Emporium. "You'll buy it out of the rates, will you? And the dope with which you regulate the speed of these animals. I suppose you'll try to milk the ratepayers for that, too."

Bowen, who had an appetite for libel like a cow's for grass, just smiled.

"We'd collect for it," he said.

There were groans. Meadow Prospect was a poor place for collections. During the war when we had set out to buy our own municipal Spitfire the fund yielded resources for no more than a wing-tip, even with Bowen and the Treasurer going around the town explaining about the war and air power. For the horse called Meadow Prospect the pennies would have stopped rolling before we had paid for the first hoof.

But we were never to know. As Bowen sat there, complacent, waiting for the senate to give him an oxygen grant for the new project, Goronwy Franklyn stood up and pointed at Bowen. He did not say anything. He was a poor speaker, but at standing still and pointing you could have taken him hunting; he would have done as well as any dog; Franklyn was the best in the area. He had a shadowed, ravaged face that made him a first-class accuser.

I turned to my neighbour, Hadrian Mills, a newspaper reporter and a leading local archivist.

"What's Franklyn pointing about?"

"He hates horses. And he hates Bowen because Bowen loves horses. Every second he stands there the members will recall anything shady that was ever charged against Bowen and that adds up to a long night. Standing still and pointing also helps Franklyn with the trouble he gets with his back."

The reference to Franklyn's back helped me to fill in his dossier.

In early middle age Franklyn had been a coal merchant, hauling coal about Meadow Prospect in a cart drawn by a huge stallion called Dewi. Franklyn, at that period, was a man of striking good looks and brisk sexual enthusiasm. He did not prosper. Money was scarce and many women, genuinely fond of Franklyn and coal, bartered their affections for a sackful. Exhaustion and guilt made a wreck out of Franklyn. For a short time he would drive about Meadow Prospect saying firmly, but in too weak a voice to be effective, "Coal for money."

His temper shortened by the day and he took to laying his whip on the massive back of Dewi. One day he was caught doing this by Bowen, and Bowen, always eager to win sympathy for horses, threatened to use the whip on Franklyn if he found him doing it again. There was a secondary motive for this. Bowen was a long-distance amorist and he had lost the love of many women to Franklyn.

This finished Franklyn off. He developed some psycho-somatic ailment of the back and he took to a wheelchair which was pushed about by his son. The boy had pushed Franklyn up Meadow Prospect's longest and steepest hill. Franklyn was in a rancorous mood and between that and the heat the boy was edging towards delirium.

At the hill's top he paused. In an effort to drown his father's laments he began to shout over to a passing neighbour an account of a fight he had seen a few nights before between Tommy Farr and some Midlander. The neighbour wanted the boy to render in fuller detail the lightning left and right punches with which Farr had finally floored his opponent. To do this the boy had to take both hands off the chair and before he could drag it back again Franklyn was plummeting down the hill at the speed of sound.

The road was clear except for a cart, the grocery cart of the Co-operative store, drawn by Franklyn's old horse, Dewi, now called Divi. To avoid any possibility of collision, Franklyn, always clear-minded when travelling at top speed, leaned heavily to the right. But when he was about half-way down the hill Divi started to move and with its bulk and the cart's blocked the road.

Some people claimed that Kitchener Bowen had passed at that moment and had given Divi the whispered command that caused it to make a right wheel. Others believed that Divi had sensed Franklyn's plight and had arranged its position to give Franklyn a royal welcome.

Franklyn who had now given up any attempt to guide the chair, was now heading straight for Divi. By an astonishing bit of crouching he passed under the horse with about an inch to spare. He shot over a bridge and up the slope on the other side of the valley. He leaped out of the chair as soon as it slowed down and he began running up the hill he had descended, waving a plaid shawl and shouting that he was going to stifle Divi and his son in that order.

Franklyn went on to do well in his second try at the coal trade. The experience of shooting through Divi's legs had made him Calvinistically uncordial in his dealings with women, and he told me a few days ago that in this career in public office he had known no moment richer than when he had pointed a finger of general denunciation at Kitchener Bowen and buried the prospect of our being saddled with a horse called Meadow Prospect.